D0786413

# THE
# FORBIDDEN

# HEATHER GRAHAM

# THE FORBIDDEN

mira

mira™

ISBN-13: 978-0-7783-1150-8

The Forbidden

Mira
22 Adelaide St. West, 40th Floor
Toronto, Ontario M5H 4E3, Canada
BookClubbish.com

**Printed in U.S.A.**

With love and tremendous admiration for my cousin Dina Watkins, for her husband, Jeff, and sons, Michael and Jeff Jr.

# THE
# FORBIDDEN

# PROLOGUE

*Sunday night*

Men watched women.

Women watched men.

He watched her.

Well, it was Bourbon Street. Most people were out for a good time. They were ready to flirt—perhaps take that flirting a step further. Everyone in a good mood. And if they weren't in a good mood, there was plenty of alcohol available for them to be able to fake it.

He only had eyes for her.

He watched—the way she moved, the way she walked.

There was something dazzling about her eyes when she smiled; her lips were generous in a face created as if sculpted by the most artistic hand.

Her every breath was poetry, creating such thoughts in his head. Eyes like the deepest blue of the sky at the first fall of night, hair as ebony as the wings of a raven, skin as sweet and clear as the finest porcelain made...

He imagined her in his arms. Holding her, touching her. Seeing those amazing electric eyes as they stared into his.

Running his fingers down the exquisite length of her arms.

He thought of her, looking at him, when he was all she could see.

Then a smile touched his face.

She was with friends now, enjoying a beer in a place on Bourbon Street. The band was loud, performing a cover of a Journey song. They were all speaking in shouts, trying to be heard by one another over the music.

She was so animated. Artistry in motion. Of course, there were many like her, and he could wait, bide his time, enjoy others. But she was… Perfection.

Anticipation was everything. Waiting. Hoping. Fearing. Dreading. Praying.

Anticipation… How he loved it!

He watched her eyes now, so sparkling, so alive. In her, the eyes were the key to the soul, the essence, the vibrancy and incredible life within the woman.

And then he imagined those eyes again when she looked at him.

Anticipation. He had time. He would savor it.

He could see the beauty of those eyes…

When the light within them brightened. Not with excitement…

But with growing fear.

Then terror.

Knowledge.

He would watch as the light went out of them.

Then, she would be his. Entirely his.

# CHAPTER ONE

*Monday morning*

"Beautiful!"

Lying on the tomb, Avalon Morgan could hear Boris Koslov's comment, but she kept herself from smiling. Makeup artist Lauren Carlson—her friend from her days at college in Central Florida—had just finished touch-ups on Avalon as she lay on the tomb. Lauren was extraordinarily talented.

"Wow! Creepy."

"Beautiful."

"Wonderful!"

Those words came from a distance.

They were filming on Christy Island, and the heirs to the island—none of them with the surname *Christy*—had rented the island, the mansion and the cemetery to Boris for his movie. They had spoken almost in unison, though she thought it was Cara Holstein, probably standing with her husband, Gary, who had said, "Creepy." Cara's distant cousins—Julian Bennett and Kenneth Richard—had echoed one another's "Beautiful" and "Wonderful!"

While Cara Holstein, Julian Bennett and Kenneth Richard were heirs to the estate, they barely knew each other. Their parents had been cousins and, as happened, busy lives had kept that generation from being close. Now, however, they were equal heirs to the estate of Nolan Christy, the grand old patriarch who had passed away two months ago at the age of eighty-nine.

Avalon smiled, happy the group was enjoying the making of the movie…and her appearance on the tomb.

Avalon knew her skin was pale to start with, but with Lauren's artistic touch, she was beyond white, the perfect bride-to-be of the vampire king, Lucian LaCroix.

She also had long, naturally waving dark hair, and Lauren had lightly adjusted the waves to curls that fell around her face and down to the dusty tomb. Marks at her neck—discernible beneath the fall of her dark hair—were perfectly created puncture wounds, and a slender trail of blood extended just lightly beneath the marks.

In this movie, the vampires wasted very little blood.

"Yes! Beautiful," Boris Koslov repeated. He was silent a minute and added softly, "Perfect."

Avalon was certain Lauren was smiling. She kept her eyes closed, but she knew Lauren stood in the old graveyard next to the director of *The Two Faces of the Vampire*, and she was glad—low budget as this might be—that at least she was working on a film with a director who appreciated the work of his crew. Now, especially Lauren's work.

Lauren wasn't even supposed to be on set today. Cindy West, lead on the makeup crew, had been scheduled that morning. But she hadn't shown up for her call time, and no one had been able to reach her. Lauren, always professional, as well as helpful to her friends, had rushed in when Boris had called her, despite it being her day off.

Lauren was accustomed to working bigger budget projects. She'd done many movies with big-name actors and established directors, even heading up the makeup department for several. She was moving swiftly up the ranks in the field, and possibly had more experience than Cindy, who had been hired first.

Working on a cheesy B-movie vampire flick was not something Lauren would have agreed to if it hadn't been for her friendship with Avalon...and for Kevin Dunlevy, too.

Many in the cast and crew were friends before this filming had begun. Boris had been a visiting lecturer when they'd all been in college. Alumni often helped alumni, and other connections were made through the school. Kevin Dunlevy was the lead actor. He considered this to be his big chance; with the way the world of film was moving, it just might prove to be a cult hit. There were now so many venues for film, even if a movie didn't hit the major theaters.

Avalon had been offered a pretty juicy role, too. While the king of the vampires had many wives, she was his most beloved.

"The camera is loving this, Boris!" the director of photography, Brad Fallon, called out.

Brad wasn't a friend from college but had become tight with them all when they'd been hired for an internet show. A gangly blond man with a perpetual smile, he acted when needed for various projects, but his true love was working with the camera. Catching the light, composing the shot—everything working in unison was his dream.

Terry Jenson, production designer, was also a friend from school, and had done a fantastic job with the little area of the cemetery in which they were working, without doing harm to historic markers and funerary art.

Leo Gonzales, actor—tall and stalwart, portraying the detective—had taught a class in mime, which was not so important for this film, but a great learning experience that might well be useful at a different time.

Filming was proving to be a fun ensemble experience. It was an interesting script. Kevin was playing Lucian, king of the vampires, and he'd learned over hundreds of years to produce a blood strain that endured light, even the sun, and thus they could only be destroyed by one of two methods—a stake through the heart or complete decapitation. But rather than be bested by the cop who became his friend, by the end of the script Lucian came to rue his bloodlust. He would hide his past and become a scientist, working to cure all manner of blood-related diseases, at the end of the movie. Naturally, this meant there could be sequels with Lucian remaining good and fighting for justice and the American way...or reverting to his old ways.

All was set; Avalon waited for Boris to call out the rest of the cast who were in the scene and start filming.

But she knew he lingered, surveying the scene. Boris was still enjoying seeing his vision brought to life—he'd also written the script. "You're truly gifted," Boris said, and Avalon knew his words were for Lauren. "I knew you were good, but...well done," he said lightly, and Avalon could imagine him grinning. "Now I'm *not* going to have to throttle Cindy—I don't think she'd have done half so well."

Not showing up was not going to be good for Cindy's career. Boris could choose to let her go. He wasn't just the director and the writer—he'd used his own funds and a personal loan to fund the film.

"Thank you," Lauren replied. "But Cindy is very good, too, and I'm sure she had an emergency or something. She's very professional. This isn't like her."

Avalon cracked her eyes open. Lauren looked concerned. Of course, she did. Cindy was her friend—and she hadn't even bothered to call in sick. She had, however, been seen doing karaoke late the night before on Bourbon Street after she'd joined the rest of them for an evening drink. Still, failing to show up for work was not something she was known to do. Then again, she'd never been to New Orleans before.

"Cindy will have an explanation," Lauren said.

Avalon added, "Cindy is a good kid. She might have had her schedule marked wrong or something. She'll have an explanation."

"Well, thanks for coming in, Lauren," Boris said. "You are the best."

"The best!" Avalon told Lauren quietly, offering her friend a smile and a slight nod. Things happened; they didn't want Cindy's reputation marred, nor did they want her fired. But they were grateful for Lauren's skill.

Boris looked at Avalon again.

"Ah! She opens her eyes—crystal-blue eyes, framed so beautifully with bloodred rims," he said with a laugh. Then he turned to Lauren. "We're lucky to have you!" Boris said, "And, don't forget, I know you can do your own makeup. We have room for more brides. You'd make a beautiful bride, too. I know you don't wish to speak—I can make you a silent bride!"

"Thanks. I love creating on others," Lauren said lightly.

"Anyway..." Boris paused and glanced at his watch. "Time for the rest of my actors on set!" he said.

Avalon saw Kevin coming from the makeup tent, where there were also coolers filled with iced drinks and lawn chairs for those who were awaiting their call time. Lauren had finished with Kevin earlier, though there was little that needed to be done to enhance his appearance. He was tall and drop-dead gorgeous with wavy black hair, forest-green eyes and a perfectly honed body. He was, in truth, a stunning example of a human being. Avalon had once teased him that his sexual orientation was a serious loss to the women of the world. He had grinned and said, "But, hey, look what I'm doing for the men!"

Avalon and Kevin had been best friends since she'd begun studying at film school in Central Florida. Now, they'd all been out of school for several years, and had moved up to New Orleans, where there was more work available in filmmaking.

Lauren hurried off the set; Boris moved to his position and

shouted out to his cameramen. Moments later, Avalon was lying with her eyes closed again, waiting for her cue. Kevin—as vampire king Lucian LaCroix—came to her, assessing her form, then paused to place a kiss on her lips, just like Sleeping Beauty.

His kiss awakened her, and she rose, confused at first, then tearful and in denial as he reassured her, promising her that now, she could live forever. She was frightened, fascinated, torn and…

Hungry.

Then, the other vampires gathered around as she made her first kill, savored her first meal and became one with them.

Boris yelled, "Cut!"

They repeated the scene a number of times, then the actors stepped off set while the camera and lighting teams set up for the next angle.

Then they shot the scene from a few more camera angles.

The morning turned to afternoon. Avalon was always amazed at how a few minutes of movie could take an entire day to film. Lauren came in and did makeup touch-ups on the victim, then Boris released Lauren and a few other cast and crew members for the day.

Lauren waved to Avalon, and mouthed, *I'm out of here.*

Avalon didn't blame her. By the time they finished the group scenes and were back in their street clothes—certain Boris wouldn't want any special takes—it might be a while.

The cameras began to roll again, taking angle after angle of the vampires dancing among the tombs and statues.

"Cut!"

The assistant director called a final, "That's a wrap!" and reminded them all to check their call sheets for their times the following morning.

Kevin walked over and threw his arms around Avalon, hugging her and lifting her off the ground. He swung her around, set her down and kissed her cheek, then said, "Thank you!"

"Me?" she said.

"Walk with me a bit?"

"Sure. Then I need to get out of this makeup."

They strolled through the old cemetery. It was a fascinating place. The Christy family had once been incredibly wealthy. The mansion had been built circa 1799, and enhanced through the years, while the cemetery had welcomed its first burials when the Spanish had ruled New Orleans. They had built in the "city of the dead" style that had become so popular in New Orleans and much of the area. It was truly a gorgeous architectural gem, with all the atmosphere and decaying elegance they could possibly desire. The family had built several extravagant small mausoleums over the years since they had also allowed extended family and friends to bury their loved ones here. There were sarcophagus-style tombs—such as the one she had been lying on for the shoot—grand tombs, brick tombs and "oven" tombs in the walls surrounding the graveyard. It looked much like a smaller version of St. Louis Cemetery #1 just outside the French Quarter and was adorned with artistic angels and all manner of art, including a fine marble sculpture of two Civil War soldiers caring for a wounded dog, perhaps crafted to show that brothers had fought brothers in the horror of the war.

She'd learned the brothers were interred in the cemetery. One had fought for the North, the other for the South. The dog, so it was said, had been interred in the tomb, as well.

Boris had read about the death of Nolan Christy and how the property would soon be up for sale—for an exorbitant price that might mean it would take some time to find a buyer. Knowing that, he'd contacted the heirs, and learned they were open to renting while they waited. Thus, they had been able to film here for a very reasonable price. It helped that the heirs were interested in the movie industry. Connections meant everything in the film business—Boris had made sure to make a good one here. The family members—and Cara's husband, Gary—had all been delighted Boris was happy to have them present for filming, and they were welcome to be extras in the picture, too. They'd been thrilled to get to watch prep, design and filming. Avalon knew Cara and Gary intended to be in some of the final scenes.

Avalon turned, staring at the creepy old mansion, and wondered how she would feel if she inherited such a place.

"What are you looking at?" Kevin asked Avalon.

Avalon hesitated a moment.

In truth, she'd given a lot of thought over whether she should take this role or not. She had never wanted to come to Christy Island. There had just been too many strange happenings associated with the property. Of course, a friend had once told her every single place in and around New Orleans was haunted.

But the difference was that her friend didn't occasionally see the dead, as Avalon did.

Ghosts.

Avalon's connection to the deceased could make her life difficult, so she tried not to put herself in situations where she might be startled by a spirit.

And this place…well, it was almost certainly haunted.

But her friendship had won out. Kevin had wanted this role so badly, and had been so enthusiastic that she be on the project, too.

"The mansion!" she said in reply to his question. "I'm seeing shades of all kinds of things. Think Hitchcock, or the spookiest horror house you've ever been in. I heard poor old Mr. Christy was a loner to the end. He didn't want people in his house. No nurse—and certainly no assisted living—for him. They found him, dead, just sitting in his chair, staring at the hearth."

"Who found him? Not the family, right?"

"From what I've read? It was someone with the wildlife commission who had come out to ask about testing on the island. I think Cara and Gary Holstein are upstate—the Monroe area. Julian Bennett lives in Baton Rouge and Kenneth Richard is from Texas. Beaumont, I believe."

Avalon shivered. She was saddened to think of the old gentle-man dying alone in his chair.

With no one knowing. He'd been such a strange recluse.

*He'd probably just been a lonely old man. But she was afraid of see-ing his spirit.*

"So sad," Kevin muttered.

"And creepy. But you're right. Sad. Still, he lived as he wanted. I wonder if he left the property to all three of his closest—distant—heirs, hoping one might buy the others out."

"They all seem fun. Cara is a pretty little thing, isn't she? Skinny and kind of like a tiny terrier, but nice enough. And Julian's a good-looking dude with that dark red hair and his amber eyes."

Avalon raised her eyebrows, amused. "And Kenneth Rich-ard?"

"Okay, a little cuddly and round, balding, but he has been friendly and enthusiastic, too."

"They have made it nice to be here," Avalon said. Smiling at him, she added, "And working with old friends is pretty cool, too, though we have managed to do that a lot."

"Hmm, all our old friends? Are you thinking of taking off with the detective instead of the vampire?" Kevin teased. "That would give Boris a fluttering heart—he so loves his script!"

She grinned. Their friend Leo Gonzales, playing the detec-tive, was a prime example of what people usually referred to as tall, dark and handsome. He was also just a nice guy. He had never been a prima donna, and she knew, even if his star rose sky-high, he never would be. He preferred theater to film, but never minded working wherever, or doing whatever, in order to make a living at his craft.

"Hey, taking off with the detective would be preferable to being killed by him," Avalon said lightly.

"Have you read the whole script?"

"I have. I'm a goner."

"Well, I can ask Boris if—"

"No! Thanks. There are tons of local projects now. I've got a callback for that new TV series that's due to film soon. I love the character. She's kick-ass. Way tougher than I am, but, apparently, I have the look they want."

He smiled and nodded. "You look great," he said. "Considering we were all out on Bourbon Street last night."

"I left after that drink we all had together. My favorite music is often on Magazine Street or Frenchman Street—not that they don't have great bands on Bourbon. But I was tired. I knew it would be a long day today."

"I didn't even say good-night."

"That's because you were chatting with that cute guy from New Jersey at Pat O'Brien's!"

"Okay, so, yeah." He frowned. "I just don't see it, though."

"Don't see what?"

"Cindy not showing up. No matter how late she was out. She is usually so professional."

"She probably overslept."

"She'd still be up by now."

"I'm sure she's got a reason—and she'll make it up to Boris. She'll have an explanation. I'll admit I'm happy Lauren worked today."

"Well, anyway," Kevin said, pausing to sweep his arm around to indicate all of the cemetery, "I've brought you to my office here for a reason."

"Oh?"

"I just wanted to thank you, thank you, thank you!" Kevin said excitedly. "This part is going to mean so much for me."

"You're perfect for it. It's got nothing to do with me."

"Boris wanted you, too," Kevin told her. "I'm pretty sure we were a package deal."

They had wandered more deeply into the old place. It really

was so hauntingly pretty. Angels wept. Obelisks rose to the sky. Elegant tombs crouched in the lingering sunlight.

Looking ahead, Avalon paused. There was someone else in the cemetery. Playing a joke, or perhaps trying to surprise Boris, or something.

She looked back. She could see Boris, Terry, Leo and Brad were looking at a monitor, reviewing some of the camerawork. "Are they filming a backup scene of what we just shot?" she asked Kevin.

"No way. They got dozens of angles on everything. Why?"

"Then...who is that? What's going on?"

Ahead of them, slightly to the left of one of the grand family tombs, was a sarcophagus tomb, just like the one she had been lying on.

She blinked. *Was it a ghost, playing a trick? Enjoying the moviemaking, and being dramatic?*

No...not a ghost. Flesh and blood.

An actress was there, stretched out upon the tomb just as Avalon had been on the other.

Long white gown, dark hair...the palest flesh.

Curious, drawn, but feeling a sense of dread, Avalon moved toward the tomb. A thought weighed in her mind: had Lauren Carlson outdone herself again?

The woman on the tomb was stunning and terrifying.

No, Lauren had left.

Avalon began to run.

She reached the tomb, and the woman lying there upon it.

Flesh and blood...

Pinpricks in the skin at the throat.

The woman wasn't just as pale as alabaster death...she was dead.

Cindy West had an excuse for not being on set that morning.

She was dead.

Avalon began to scream.

★ ★ ★

*They just had to be filming a movie.*

The corpse could have so easily been a part of it—she was laid out beautifully.

Finley Stirling stood a slight distance away, watching as the medical examiner did his preliminary work, shaking his head as he looked at the corpse, then looking up at Finley next to Detective Ryder Stapleton.

Christy Island had no police force of its own. It was privately owned, and while other mainland facilities were closer, there had never been any crimes committed on the little island—so many years before, it had been put under the jurisprudence of the Orleans Parish Police Department.

The commissioner had called Ryder, who was with the NOPD. Ryder had called Adam Harrison at the FBI; he knew Adam had team members in the vicinity and the case was strange enough for Adam's Krewe of Hunters unit. Fin figured Ryder had asked specifically for one of his agents because the crime was macabre.

When Fin had received the assignment from Adam Harrison that morning, he'd learned Ryder thought his being called in on a murder an hour to the south and west of NOLA made no sense, either. But he'd been made lead in the investigation of the murder on the island, and that was that.

Fin knew Detective Stapleton by reputation: he'd worked alongside the Krewe on the recent "Axeman's Protégé" case. Ryder was a good guy—the kind of person who became a cop to help people and not for any kind of power trip. That he cared about his work showed; he was in his midthirties, just a bit older than Fin, but today he looked tired.

A murder in a cemetery. A corpse lain out like the bride of Frankenstein—or, in this case, the bride of Dracula.

The sun was falling when they arrived. And since the medical examiner had made it just ahead of them, they'd headed straight to the victim.

The Christy heirs and the actors and crew of the movie—*The Two Faces of the Vampire*—were rounded up in the grand foyer and great room of the Christy mansion, a house that looked like something out of a B horror movie without the help of a set designer.

Fin had known of the place, though he'd never been out to the island. Every school kid in Southern Louisiana knew about the pirate, Jean Lafitte, and his base on Barataria Island.

Christy Island wasn't far from Barataria Island, and Fin had often traveled the bayous and waterways around the area, having grown up in Houma, an hour's drive from the city of New Orleans. Kids told stories about it, especially because the last Christy had been considered a strange bird, a hermit who preferred his own company to any other and hadn't even met the heirs to whom he was leaving his estate.

Authorities hadn't been called until the afternoon and while they'd gotten here in record time, the day was fading. The sky was spectacular, as shades of red, mauve, pink and gold shot across the sky, casting down strange rays of light that seemed to add a gilding to the scene.

Dr. Conrad Houseman had been bending over the corpse; he stood, looked around and shook his head. He was around fifty, Fin thought, experienced and serious.

He turned to look at Fin and Ryder.

"Sad," he muttered.

"Extremely," Fin agreed. He knew the young woman had been part of the crew, and well-liked by the cast and her co-workers.

"This is preliminary," Houseman said, "but I believe she died sometime between two and four this morning. She wasn't killed here, but she was brought here almost immediately." He sighed. "See the puncture wounds? The killer managed to get those perfectly arranged on the jugular, bled her out…and then cleaned her up."

"You mean…she's missing all her blood?" Ryder asked.

Houseman shrugged. "Most of it, I'm going to warrant. She has only slight lividity, suggesting she doesn't have much blood in her. That color isn't makeup—that's her color…without much blood. What lividity there is suggests she was laid out on this tomb soon after death." He hesitated, appearing confused, and shrugged again. "They're making a movie here. I thought that directors shot at all hours. No one saw her until this afternoon?"

"Two of the actors were just walking through the cemetery," Ryder told him. "And they came upon her. The earliest call time for this morning was 7:00 a.m. and the owners aren't living here—they rented it all out to the movie company."

"Ah. So no one is on the island through the night?" Houseman asked.

"We haven't questioned the cast and crew yet," Ryder told him. "But the heirs hate the place—they're making all the legal arrangements to sell it and split the profits."

"Right, of course. Sorry. I just… I worked in New York City for twenty-plus years before coming down here and…still, I've never seen anything like this. Worse, I guess, but…"

"But not like this," Ryder said, finishing for him.

"I'll take her in now. This is as far as I can go here," Houseman said. "Go figure—they make a vampire movie, so someone has to get carried away. Well, it's an island. Maybe that will help you boys find her killer, though the good Lord knows, you have enough people with easy access to this place."

He walked away from the corpse, leaving Fin and Ryder.

Ryder shook his head. "The Axeman, and now this. I realize your team usually works serial killers or those crossing state lines—"

"We come when we're asked for help," Fin assured him.

"Yeah. And thank you for that. I've worked with Agents Tiger and Broussard before, but I appreciate any help I can get. This is…" He broke off, looking back at the corpse. "Not someone angry, killing someone for something they did. Not for greed, not for jealousy. Not in my opinion."

"Someone organized. This was planned out," Fin said. He was relatively new to the FBI, and to the Krewe, but he'd done his courses on profiling at the Academy, and he knew when to trust his gut.

"So it's got to be someone involved with the film."

"Yes, we're looking at them, the heirs to the estate, and caterers or anyone else they've had out here lately. Then again, I was in these waters in our little pirogue often enough when I was a kid—most people living in the area know about the island. Mr. Christy never asked anyone out here—I think he saw reps from the electronic company once fifteen years ago. But we're near Barataria Island, so it's a traveled area. People know about the cemetery and the house. They love to tell stories about old man Christy, and most kids are convinced the place is haunted. But the thing is…it had to be someone who could get close to Christy Island."

"They mentioned in their 911 call they'd all been out on Bourbon Street last night," Ryder said.

"She could have gotten involved with someone on Bourbon Street, but the chances of her running into a homicidal stranger who knew her and the island are slim."

Ryder nodded. He was still standing by the victim, as if someone needed to watch over her until she was gone.

She did look, even in death, sweet and innocent and so vulnerable.

Dr. Houseman returned with his assistants and nodded to the two of them, as if he understood why they remained.

"Let's get to the house," Fin said.

"Right."

They walked through a field of tombs, all of them either single small tombs above the ground, or larger mausoleum structures that housed many dead.

The cemetery, though overgrown, was beautiful. The tombs weren't in rows as they were at the St. Louis cemeteries or even Lafayette Cemetery. They were scattered. There were benches among them, foliage here and there, including small trees.

There were statues—typical angels, cherubs and more. Some were of human beings, some were of pets.

Menacing gargoyles stared down from the roofs of a few tombs. Others bore heralds atop them, and still others were ornately designed with carved lettering that broadcast a family name.

"How are so many people—sorry, dead people—here on a private island?" Ryder said as they walked.

Fin shrugged. "I believe the family first claimed the property right when the Spanish took control of the area—that was 1762. I don't know exact dates, but I know the original Christy and his heirs into the 1850s owned numerous plantations and had many slaves and then servants. The family never segregated in their cemetery, so you have anyone and everyone of every color and just about every religion intermingled here. They also allowed friends from the mainland to erect family mausoleums, which is why you see so many."

"Weird," Ryder said.

*You don't know the half of it*, Fin thought.

But he kept silent. Ryder wouldn't understand that some of the dead in the cemetery had lingered—and that they just might be able to help.

The mansion stood before them at last, right out of a Gothic tale. While built sometime after the turn of the nineteenth century, it was now a strange combination of architectural features.

Steps led to a grand porch—now decaying with chipped and grimed paint—and then to a front door with a Gothic arch. A small mudroom opened to a foyer, and the foyer opened to a massive parlor or entry, complete with a giant hearth. A fraying Persian rug lay before the hearth, and around it were numerous chairs and settees, easily changed about for small or large groups. The walls were covered with paintings of illustrious Christy family patriarchs from days long gone.

And the place was filled with officers, and cast and crew members.

"Where do we begin?" Ryder said.

"With the two who found her," Fin said.

"Over there—pick your poison. Beautiful actor or beautiful actress?" Ryder nodded toward the group at the hearth; two people were seated together on one of the settees, surrounded by the others.

Many in the group had tearstained faces and seemed to be asking their own questions of the seated pair and one another.

Before Fin could say it didn't matter, they were approached by the uniformed officer who appeared to be in charge. He nodded to Ryder and introduced himself to Fin as Sergeant Tim Ferrer. He was a solid man, early fifties, with a perpetually grim expression. He tilted his head toward the crowd of film crew.

"The two who came upon the body—Avalon Morgan and Kevin Dunlevy—are right there. He plays the lead vampire, and she plays his bride." The sergeant didn't look impressed. "The director is over there—Boris Koslov. The dead woman is Cindy West. She was head or lead or whatever on the makeup team. The others are…well, as you can see, a few are still in costume and makeup. Camera personnel seems to have gathered but a lot of extras and today's key girl on makeup were gone before we could get here."

"That's okay—we'll just need a list of everyone involved," Fin told him.

"I made them all stay until you two came."

"And we'll let them all go as quickly as possible," Ryder assured him.

"We did interview everyone," Ferrer said. "I divided up the group between four officers, so we'll have our notes."

"That's great," Fin acknowledged. As he spoke, he saw the lead actress was looking at him.

She was dressed like the corpse. She even had little red puncture marks at her throat. Makeup, he assumed. The killer hadn't just slain a woman and left her displayed, he had done his best to mimic a scene from the movie—a scene filmed that day, just before the discovery.

She started to rise, awkward and shaky, and yet stunning and ethereal in her costume and makeup, hair as dark as the coming night, and her eyes so blue he could see their color from his distance away from her.

She was looking at him as if...

Almost as if she knew him.

He didn't know her.

He would have never forgotten her. "I'll take Miss Morgan," he told Ryder, and he nodded his thanks to Sergeant Ferrer as he stepped toward the woman. At her side, the man rose, as well, quickly steadying her.

"Office and music room through the arch near the hearth," Ferrer said from behind him.

"Great," Fin said. He looked at Ryder. "I'll take the...music room?"

Ryder managed a weak grin. "Beauty and music—sure."

"I don't have to—"

"Kidding. Let's get started on this. Man, it has been one long day."

Fin couldn't agree more.

Although, it had to have been a much longer day for everybody waiting in that room.

Except one of them was a killer.

# CHAPTER TWO

Avalon still felt as if she was reeling, or living in an unreal, alternate universe.

Yet it had all been too real.

Cindy, lying there on the tomb. Stretched out in all her beauty, puncture marks at her throat.

Cindy.

Not tardy, not careless of others, but…dead.

Avalon had gone over everything with several police officers—not that there was much to go over. But now this tall, authoritative man in a suit was bringing her in to question her again; she knew he was going to do so the moment she saw him. She wasn't sure why. But he escorted her one way in the mansion while another, gruffer-looking man in a more casual suit brought Kevin in another direction.

"I'm Special Agent Finley Stirling," he said, introducing himself. "And I understand you and your friend—the star of the movie—were the first to find Cindy West."

He sat on the piano bench in the music room, indicating she should take the one old wingback chair. She sat in it.

She could still feel her makeup, as if it was grit that covered her skin. She longed desperately for a hot shower. For her own clothing. She wanted to be far away from the mansion and the cemetery and…

Death.

Avalon nodded, looking at the man who had come to speak with her now. What was he expecting? He could question her from now to doomsday. She didn't know more than what she had already said.

"We finished filming. Kevin and I are old friends. He just wanted to talk to me—to thank me for taking on the role. W-we've been working in the cemetery about two weeks."

"Right. And I'm curious about that. The entire island was rented to the movie company. But none of you stayed out here."

"Would you want to stay out here?" she asked him. "The house hasn't been dusted in—in years, I don't think. The sheets are probably glued to the beds."

"But you have a lot of expensive equipment out here," he said.

He was a tall man, who even looked tall sitting, though he was doing so casually. His hair was a dark blond color, not close-cropped, but neatly clipped to leave a striking golden thatch that just hovered over his forehead. His eyes were an intense green, dark as a forest. He didn't seem to be trying to intimidate her, and yet without trying, he was making her very nervous, even as he kept an even tone and seemed polite and curious.

She sighed softly. "I'm just an actor on this," she told him. "I don't own any of the equipment and, to the best of my knowledge, not much is left here overnight." She hesitated. "This isn't a major-budget epic, you know. I doubt if there will be any kind of theatrical distribution. We'll go straight to streaming and possibly a specialty cable channel, which is fine. But most of the financing on this is being done by Boris himself. Many of us are involved because we're friends from college or other projects, and it's a group effort." She hesitated. "And I've known many of these people a long time. No one is a... No one would ever want to hurt anyone, much less do something so horrible to anyone!"

She was passionate as she finished speaking, and she hoped he knew beyond a doubt that she was telling him the truth, that the murder was devastating to her.

"Do you have any enemies?" he asked her.

"Me?" She was startled.

"Cindy was laid out on that tomb just as you were. You were filming a similar scene not long before you discovered her." He indicated her costume.

"No, I don't have enemies," she said.

"No one jealous about your role?"

"On an ultra-low-budget movie?" she asked incredulously.

"You never know," he told her.

She shook her head. "No. No, there weren't even auditions for this—I didn't beat anyone out of a role. Kevin is friends with Boris. From what he was telling me, Boris wanted the two of us. I wanted to help Kevin—he's a great guy. And cheesy movie though this might be, he has a good role, and he'll look good on camera and it may lead to better things for him."

"What about the second makeup artist?"

"Lauren?" she asked, frowning.

"Might she have been jealous of another makeup artist?"

"No. Lauren took on this job just because of us. She and Cindy were friends." She frowned, staring at him. "I'm sorry, but...seriously? Someone killed Cindy, dressed her, carried her out there and laid her out. I like to think I'm fairly capable, but I doubt I'd have had the strength for doing all that, and neither would Lauren."

"Might have been a group effort," Fin said softly.

That angered her. She stared at him, assessing him as she was sure he was assessing her. He was probably just thirty or so, a few years older than her own twenty-eight. Maybe he'd been a tough kid who had needed to grow up and have a uniform and a badge. Except he wasn't in a uniform. He wore a black suit barely relieved by the white of his shirt.

He was carrying a gun. Of course, he was carrying a gun. She couldn't see it, but she knew he had it. His manner was polite and his questions did sound almost conversational…except that he was accusing her or suggesting that her friends could have done something like the awful thing done to Cindy.

"We're actors and crew! Not murderers. And why, in God's name, would we kill a friend and sabotage a movie? You think the whole cast and crew was in on it? Sure, let's be positive that this whole thing is a mess and we've wasted our time."

He shrugged, unaffected by her tone. "Could make the movie a massive hit, too."

"Oh, that's terrible. You're terrible. You don't know any of us! How could you suggest—"

"Listen, I'm sorry. You're on the island—your friends are on the island. And a dead girl—killed and left in a way that simulated a movie scene—is on the island. I have no choice. I need to ask you these questions. Now, hopefully, none of you would do something so cruel and horrible to one of your own. And yet, this island is rented to the production company, and, as you've said, it's a low-budget movie. There aren't scores of extra personnel running around—caterers or cleaners or security. *You* are the people on this island."

She shook her head. "But…it's an island. We're not in outer space. This place is easy enough to reach—by anyone with a little boat."

He didn't dispute that. "And with no one watching it through the night? Careless of the company, I think. Just the liability issue is great."

There was a tap at the door. He paused a moment before rising to answer it.

Avalon was glad to see Boris Koslov at the door. Boris was

in his forties, dark-haired and dark-eyed, lean and bronzed, and carried himself with a manner of confidence…and determination.

Of course, he had to be confident. He was accustomed to directing others.

"I'm sorry for the interruption," Boris said. "I just wanted to set a few things straight so that you'd know… So that you'd have more information while questioning my people. Please, you need to understand. This was someone from…outside. My people loved Cindy."

There was a catch in his voice.

Avalon watched Finley Stirling. She could almost read his mind, or at least she thought she could. Yes, he was thinking Boris might be a bit of an actor himself.

A man who knew when acting should be a subtle maneuver.

But the agent didn't give away his thoughts—if those were indeed the thoughts running through his head. He didn't chastise Boris for the interruption.

"Please, come in, join us. You may be able to help," he said.

Boris nodded and sat next to Avalon.

"Why is no one here overnight?" Special Agent Stirling asked him.

"Well, here's the thing. I don't advertise it, but I am here at night," Boris said. "I've been using the upstairs bedroom—in and out quickly. I bought new sheets for the bed. Had a maid in about three weeks ago, right when we were starting up. The heirs to this place want nothing to do with it—all they want is to sell. I don't have the money for a security team, but the bedroom I chose was right above our main filming location— the part of the cemetery that's closer to the mansion. No one else wants to stay out here. The locals are convinced the place is haunted. I don't think any of the heirs believe it's haunted— they just think it's filthy and creepy and none of them wants to put the money into restoring it. The decaying look worked for the movie, so…"

"So you were here last night?" the agent asked him.

Boris nodded.

"But I didn't see or hear anything!" Boris said, sounding dismayed. "I know that local kids like to take their fishing boats and pirogues out around the island, but most just like to look. In some areas, a haunted mansion and cemetery might be a draw, but there were a few times when Mr. Christy was alive that he knew about kids coming on to the shore, and he prosecuted them for trespassing. Due to that history, I felt pretty safe."

"You have a high opinion of your fellow man," Stirling said quietly.

"No. I know people do crazy things, sometimes, especially kids, for a lark. But I know, too, people don't like to get caught and go to jail. We've let people believe we do have a security force on the island and that there are cameras scattered about the property for security. Frankly, my cell phone works just fine out here, oddly enough, and I knew I could call for help at a moment's notice."

"And get help out here at a moment's notice?" Stirling asked.

"I didn't think anything would happen," Boris said. "We're a small production. There's no money in anything here. The cameras and lighting equipment are loaded out at night. The set decoration has a budget you wouldn't believe—we're using Halloween stuff drastically reduced." Boris went silent for a minute. "I guess that makes me your chief suspect. But I didn't do this. Cindy was… She was doing me a favor."

"Cindy must have met a psycho on Bourbon Street last night!" Avalon interjected passionately. "She was with us—with the group of us—and then she left. She was…happy."

"Inebriated?" the agent suggested gently.

Avalon couldn't help it—the question made her feel uncomfortable. She decided she would speak firmly, and truthfully.

"No. Not inebriated. She'd had a drink, but she was not drunk. She's an adult and she was having fun…and she knew she had an early call. I think she told Kevin she was making one last quick stop and then heading back to the hotel."

"And when did you go back to the hotel?" Fin asked her.

"Right after the last drink we all had together. Kevin was there…and Lauren." She paused, remembering.

"What time was it?" he asked her.

"About midnight, or maybe just as bit after," Avalon said. "Right?" she asked, frowning and looking at Boris.

"You were with them?"

"I was," Boris said.

"And when did you leave?" Fin asked politely.

"The same time as Kevin, Lauren and Avalon—then I drove from NOLA to Percy's Berth—easiest area this close to NOLA to use to get in and out. Cast and crew take a bigger boat than I have coming and going every day. I've rented a little motor-boat— it takes me about another twenty minutes to reach the island. All in all, the trip is only about an hour and fifteen minutes or maybe an hour and a half," Boris said.

"You got back here around two in the morning."

"Yes."

"And you didn't see a thing?"

"Nothing."

"All right," Stirling said. "I'm sure the police have already spoken with you, but I need a list of everyone involved with this production. Everyone. Boat-rental companies, boat captains and crew, food service…cast and crew. Everyone. And Avalon, if you would be so kind, I'd appreciate a list of everyone who was with you in NOLA last night—and every place you went." He stood up and smiled. "Thank you, and please, stay available."

Boris caught Avalon's hand, drawing her up with him as he asked, "Will we be able to get back to filming tomorrow? The movie is almost a wrap—"

The way Special Agent Finley Stirling turned to look at Boris gave Avalon goose bumps. The agent might not understand the costs involved in moviemaking. And still, the ice in his eyes and the slight arch of one eyebrow spoke volumes.

*A woman is dead, a friend is dead, and you want it to be business as usual?*

"Mr. Koslov, it's growing late." He looked at his watch. "Yes, nearly ten. So I'd revise that call sheet of yours—nothing will be happening out here tomorrow other than an intense investigation into the suspicious death of your crew member. Your friend, I believe?"

"Yes, of course," Boris said. "It's just that… I mean, we have to discover what happened to poor Cindy…" His shrugged miserably. "It's mostly my own money involved in this project. I could go under…and bring a lot of people with me."

"I hear it's all in the editing," Stirling said. "We'll release the island and your props and setting as soon as possible. It won't be tomorrow. Again," he added, his tone dry, "thank you so much for your time and your cooperation."

He opened the door, clearly indicating they should leave.

Avalon felt the emerald chill of his eyes as they swept over her. She wasn't sure why, but she wanted to fight against his contempt.

They all cared! Of course, they cared. Cindy had been murdered. They were in shock. It was all so bizarre that it remained surreal. A cheesy horror film—a horrendous murder.

She stopped, determined he was not going to intimidate her with a look.

"There are so many people you need to investigate. We—the cast and crew—were her friends, her coworkers. She was part of it all. You need to do your work and question not just us. Cindy was out on Bourbon Street last night. Someone might have met her then. Don't just think you can accuse one of us."

He gazed at her a moment before answering her. "I haven't

accused anyone…yet. I promise, if I had, you would know. Now, if you'll excuse me…take a seat out there. We'll start getting you all back to the mainland soon."

She went out, fighting a childish urge to kick him on her way past.

She felt as if she was drowning. As if great waves of water kept crashing over her, leaving her shaking and in disbelief.

Cindy was dead.

The waves washing over her turned colder and colder as fear set in along with the pain and loss of losing a friend.

"Soon" turned into hours and hours. Light was breaking when they were at last herded onto a boat to be brought back to the mainland.

They weren't warned not to leave town—they were just told not to leave the area. Fair or not, law enforcement blamed them. But that was something Avalon couldn't accept.

It simply wasn't possible that one among them could be a cold-blooded murderer.

*Tuesday morning*

Fin was both exhausted and wired as the sun rose. He and Ryder had worked through the night. There had been so many people to be interviewed.

In the end, while officers and crime-scene investigators continued the vast amount of their work, Fin sat with Ryder in the great room by the hearth, comparing notes.

"The director—that Boris guy," Ryder said. "He was here— he was here when she was murdered, or he got back right after. And if you ask me, low budget or not, that's weird. Who the hell would want to stay out at this place alone?"

"It's definitely not the Ritz," Fin agreed. "And yes, obviously that puts him at the top of the suspect list. And I can't help but wonder if the murderer would really hurt his own movie…or if it just might help it. Then again, I wonder if he isn't just too obvious. We're looking at something different here. It's not as if someone just had a beef with Cindy West. That was the work of an organized killer. He knew how he wanted to kill her, and he knew exactly how he wanted her displayed."

"Who knew better than the director?" Ryder asked.

"We're in a curious place," Fin said. "We could be looking at the heirs, too. There are a few places for sale in the French Quarter that are happily advertising 'haunted' along with three beds and two baths. To some, the events here would be a total turnoff—they'd never want to buy a place with such a recent history of tragedy. For others, well, buying a haunted island where such a strange and horrific event occurred recently would be like hitting the jackpot."

"True." Ryder kept his notes longhand in a folder. He pulled it out. "Interesting array of suspects. These people are old man Christy's descendants and heirs, and they supposedly just met recently. The last time any of them saw Christy was years ago, when they were kids. Not one of them checked up on him, visited him…ever seemed to care a bit. They all say they hate the place."

"I don't think he made any attempt to contact them, either. But, as far as this goes, the heirs were happy to rent to the production company—and the company *is* Boris Koslov—and would all hang around to watch the filming, friendly with the cast and crew. They're an interesting foursome themselves. First, Cara and Gary Holstein. She is an energetic little woman—midthirties, cute—and so energetic that…"

"She's annoying," Ryder said. "And he's a bit on the chubby side, with a goofy smile."

"She sells cosmetics—he owns a fishing charter company."

"With a boat," Ryder noted.

"Several boats, according to the info I got from my people," Fin said.

"There you go."

"That he owns a boat doesn't mean he's guilty of murder. Boris has rented a boat. Think of where we are—people own boats."

"Yes, but I'm looking at suspects who own boats."

"Which is important, of course, but we can't arrest people for owning boats."

"No. So then there's the other cousins. The one looks like a leading man. The other...doesn't. Unless it's as a leading man for a movie about not-so-good-looking people!"

Fin shook his head with a rueful smile. Ryder didn't pull punches. He was careful and respectful in public, but here, after a long night...

"Ugly doesn't make you a murderer, either," Fin reminded Ryder. But it was true—Julian Bennett was a tall man with dark hair and amber eyes who evidently worked out in a gym and cared about his appearance. He sold medical supplies for a living. In contrast, Kenneth Richard had a bit of a crook in his back, as if he was experiencing early problems with osteoporosis. He was balding, with tufts of hair growing randomly from wherever they chose rather than in a pattern. He seemed cursed with several knobby warts on his face, as well.

He had been earnest during the questioning; yes, he'd met Cindy West. She'd been lovely to them all, a beautiful, sweet girl. He'd even mentioned that Cindy had been just as nice to him as she had been to all the others.

Just as Julian knew he was endowed with assets, Kenneth knew he was not.

"Kenneth works for an oil company," Fin said. "Looks like he has a company boat issued to him. His work has to do with discovery and environmental dangers—he's often out in the Gulf."

"Another boat." Ryder sighed. "Back to the cast—I interviewed the 'detective.'" He paused to look at his notes again. "Leo Gonzales. He's one of the 'in' crowd. They all know each other from an arts college in Central Florida." He looked up at Fin. "He's a mime. He taught mime, and that's how he met these other guys. Boris was a visiting lecturer at the school, too." He sighed. "So they know each other. Not much to go on. And they're all convinced that Cindy West ran into some- one on Bourbon Street who did this to her."

"But who on Bourbon Street knew what was being filmed the following day?" Fin said.

"Exactly. Let's pray the medical examiner or the forensic in- vestigators come up with something. As it is, we have nothing."

"Well, we have an island. And there's a crew behind you, and a 'Krewe' behind me who will rip into the backgrounds of ev- eryone involved here."

"Do you want me to take the autopsy? Should we both go?"

Fin didn't hesitate. "I'll have you go in, if you don't mind. I'm going to walk around the island and maybe look further into the mansion."

"All right. I'll call you as soon as the doc is finished. I don't know how much more we're going to get from him. Precise instruments were used to make those puncture holes—holes that would allow for a woman to be practically bled out. That does make it look as if our medical-equipment rep might have something to do with this."

"It does," Fin said. "But we have no idea why any of these people might want to kill Cindy West."

Ryder shook his head. "Motives for murder—greed, jealousy, hatred, advancement, unrequited love."

"And obsession," Fin said. "Someone is relishing the fact that two agencies—and every law-enforcement officer in the south of the state—will be on this. They're savoring the media atten- tion it will get. For this type, the kill is the best moment, but it's also something to be enjoyed in all that follows."

"Killers like that might return to the scene of the crime," Ryder said.

"Not today and not now," Fin said. "But we should watch in the days to come."

Ryder rose, stretching. "Usually, in my world, John shoots Bill over a woman. Or a drug deal gone wrong. Or some drunk idiot takes a gun out on Bourbon Street. This kind of thing… well, I'm glad Adam Harrison sent you in on this."

"Teamwork," Fin said lightly. He wished that Adam was still in the city. It would be good to work with someone like him. The Krewe was a large agency now; Adam had a way of finding the right people. But those right people tended to be busy, off around the country, and only Finley had been here in New Orleans. He was from the area, which Adam thought to be a tremendous boon.

Yes, that had been it. He was already here, and no one else familiar with the territory was available.

He knew he should have confidence in himself; he *did* have confidence in himself. And there was a massive tech-and-research unit behind him.

Ryder was nodding at him. "Yeah, still…you guys are better at finding the freaks, you know?"

Fin shrugged and stood.

"I'm going to go around Bourbon Street after I've taken another look at the island," Fin told him. "I'll show Cindy West's picture around and see if anyone saw anything."

Ryder gave him a wave, and he was gone.

Fin walked to the center of the room. He acknowledged that he hated this case—because he hated being here. He remembered being a kid out with his dad when he'd first seen the decaying old mansion rising out of the foliage, trees and *tombs* on the island.

There were several hundred people interred in the cemetery. Mr. Christy had lived alone, with dozens of ancestors, friends of ancestors and even strangers—friends of the friends of his ancestors.

Fin stood in the house and closed his eyes, feeling the room. There was a miasma about the place. Too much had gone on for too long. He knew a few of the stories; he had met a few of the dead.

Now he was hoping one among them might help him.

But all he felt standing in the great room was that atmosphere of darkness, depression and oppression. If Christy's spirit had remained, that remnant of the man was not in his old house.

Fin headed out, walking down the long tile path and beneath the stone archway that led from the house to the cemetery.

As with most old properties, Christy Island had been owned by good people…and by cruel people.

He headed toward the back of the sprawling cemetery, to the place where Cindy West had been found. There were still forensic workers out, gathering every bit of evidence they could.

The dead woman was gone, and was now being prepared for her autopsy.

He paused by the statue of the two Civil War soldiers, standing by their dog.

Fin knew the story of the brothers, but as he stood there, he heard a soft voice. He turned subtly, aware of his visitor… and equally aware the cemetery was still filled with those who wouldn't see his old friend.

"You're all right, you're a distance from all of them, sugar," a soft, feminine voice assured him.

He smiled. "Vanessa…" he said softly.

She came and leaned against the base of the statue, smiling at him—a beautiful smile.

Vanessa's last name had been Christy. She'd never known if that had been because she actually *was* a Christy, since slave owners were known to father children among their household, or if it was simply the name of the man who owned her. Her mother had died when she'd been a child and no one else seemed to know the truth.

But it didn't matter to her. She'd been here when the Civil War had torn all asunder. She'd been born a slave but lived to be a free woman who had chosen not to leave Christy Island after the war—she had stayed on as a housekeeper, earning enough to see a grandson graduate from college. She had died at the age of fifty, but having lived during a rough period, she had maintained her beauty in death and she appeared to him as a slim woman, with skin a stunning golden color and eyes dark and soulful…and still filled with a strange light.

"It's good to see you," he told her.

She grinned. "I haven't seen you out here in years and years! So, what—you decided that you would be a lawman? Thought you weren't going to do that after you got in trouble when you were a kid."

Fin grimaced at the memory. "Big kids" had hidden a stash of drugs by a nearby bayou one day; an old pirate who still loved to go from NOLA to the smaller cities and out to Barataria Island over and over again had talked to Fin about it, disgusted because the "big" kid had been giving drugs to "wee ones." When the cops had come, Fin had been able to show them where to find the drugs, but not tell them how he knew. The authorities were careful because no one wanted anyone else to know he was the informant, but they had remained suspicious of him, and he'd made up a story about following the boys one day.

"Spirits making you look crazy stopped getting to you, eh, sweetie?" she asked him,

"I figured I'd use what I have," he said. "And, in fact, I was hoping—"

"You were hoping to find me and that I might be able to help you with this frightful business, right, my boy?" she asked.

"Did you see anything?"

She shook her head. "I was watching the filming—like the living!" she told him.

"But she was brought here sometime before all that began," he said.

"We don't just hang around our tombs, you know. Why stay where it's bleak and the memories are those of the tears shed over our deaths? We—Henri and me—slipped onto a boat with the director fellow, Boris. We were out, they were out—everyone was out."

"And when you came back?"

"I believe Boris went right to his room in the mansion and stayed there. I couldn't swear to it, but I believe that's what he did. Henri and I talked about changes in the world—things that do change and things that don't—until…well, almost until they started filming again in the morning. Honey, I wish to heaven that I could help, that I did know something! But you know as well as I do that little boats—especially little rowboats— can come right up just about any place on the island. Whoever brought in that dead girl did so from the rear of the cemetery. Maybe they were smart enough to stay away from the mansion, or the part where all the filming seems to take place. I don't know. I do know that I'll be on watch now. Though the place is teeming with police and the like."

Fin nodded, hoping not to show his disappointment.

"Where's Henri now?" he asked. He was referring to Henri Christy, a young man who had died in his early twenties from yellow fever in the early 1800s.

The two were fast friends; Vanessa had told him once that Henri had helped her when she'd first discovered she was not among the living…and yet still a bit of the earth.

"He's up at the mansion. He's fascinated with Boris—he wanted to be an actor when he was young, but apparently, that wasn't proper work for a man of his lineage back then. Anyway, honey, I promise you—I'll be watching now."

She turned to leave, and he quickly asked, "Vanessa, the whole cast and crew—or main cast and crew—were out on Bourbon Street last night, right?"

"Along with the 'family,'" she said, sounding a little bit disgusted. "You know, I realize I started life as a slave, and maybe that's why I have a greater appreciation for…a home. A real home. They treat this place as if it was garbage! A lark—money, and nothing more."

"Well, I didn't know Mr. Christy, but he was a hermit, and I guess he just didn't encourage people to care for him or his property. But the family was out with the cast and crew?"

"I don't know if you'd say 'with' the cast and crew. That foursome was out together, following them around. Oh, not that they're not nice. Crew members, cast…they're all very sweet. I've watched them working. But… I guess sometimes we just like our own friends, hmm?"

"Sometimes, maybe."

"Did you speak with the actress—the one the murder victim was laid out to resemble?"

"Avalon Morgan?"

"Yes," Vanessa said, rolling her eyes dramatically. "The raven-haired beauty. The bride of the beast!"

"Yes, of course, I interviewed her. Why?"

"She senses us," Vanessa said. "She looked right at me one day, right in the eye, and she smiled. She can't really just start a conversation in front of others. And I wasn't sure she even wanted to. But I know she saw me. She could be interesting. The girl is—"

"Don't say 'gifted!'" Fin moaned.

"Fine. Let's see… Cursed? How cruel a thing to say about those who can speak with us and help us."

"I didn't say 'cursed,' either," Fin assured her.

She grinned. "It is a gift, my friend. As is this time we remain here, seeking an answer, satisfaction, or just a way to give back to the living. None of us really knows why a few remain here on earth in whatever form this may be. There are those who feel us and know nothing more. Give her a try—I'd swear she also has the…talent! That's what I'll call it. I believe that's what your Krewe of Hunters refers to this sense as being. A talent."

"I did interview her. She cares deeply about all the people here. I don't believe she's a murderer, or that she'd abet a murderer in any way." Fin sighed.

"Then I'd get to know her better," Vanessa said.

"You think she knows who the murderer is?"

"No. But I think knowing someone else who has your talent might be a nice thing for you."

She offered him a weak smile and turned to leave.

He watched her go, fading into the shadows around the tombstones.

# CHAPTER THREE

*Tuesday afternoon*

"I think I can do it. I have to keep going, and then I have to hope…well, I have to hope that the police can solve this, or that people…" Boris broke off, wincing.

"Yeah, it's okay," Terry Jenson, his production designer, said wearily. "We have to hope people are such sensationalists they'll want to see a movie where a real murder took place during the making of it."

"Exactly," Leo Gonzales said. As one of the three main roles in the movie, Leo was going to be fine, and he knew it. And he could make more in a day doing some of his mime act out on the square than many did as extras on the film. But he was part of their group, and he cared about his friends.

"I can help edit. With the budget, you were pretty much going to be your own editor, anyway," Brad Fallon, the director of photography reminded him. "I have a pretty good eye for editing. No matter what happens, we can wrap the movie."

Avalon sat and listened as they discussed the events and what they were going to do next—and how to go about doing it.

They'd spent the night in numb misery and the morning moving; the hotel—in Kenner, much closer to the dock for the boat out to the island—was now too expensive.

The police had said they were fine to move into New Orleans for the next few days—they just couldn't go too far.

Thanks to a friend of Lauren's, they had moved into a house that was usually for short-term rentals. It had a beautiful court-yard, which was where they sat as they spoke. The house was right off the juncture of Dauphine Street and Bienville Street, easy walking distance to dozens of eateries and sites. Boris thought that might be important for them. While they were waiting to find out what was going to happen, they might get a little stir-crazy and need some distraction.

They were dealing with the loss of a friend.

And it was still difficult to take in. They couldn't go back to the island until the police and agents gave an all-clear. They didn't know when that would be.

And so, they were just…here. Discussing their futures.

"I can help edit, too," Kevin said.

"We're all thinking about the movie," Lauren said. "And Cindy is…being cut up. Dead. Given an autopsy. Are you all forgetting? We were just together!"

"None of us is forgetting," Boris said. "Not for a minute."

"We're distracting ourselves," Kevin said.

Silence fell around the table where they were sitting.

"Where is Cindy's family?" Terry asked. He had soft brown eyes and fluffy wild hair, causing his nickname to be "Shaggy." But he was a people person who tended to care deeply for others. While they hadn't all known Cindy well, they had all laughed and joked together during the filming.

"Luckily, they're dead," Boris said, and then he grimaced. "Wow, that didn't come out right. But at least they don't have to outlive their daughter. I've been told that a distant cousin is coming. I have the feeling we're going to be the people who care the most. She's been traveling a lot with work—she was lead makeup artist on a limited series that ended just before she started with me, and she was on a movie before that… I think we are her family."

"Then, if the cousin doesn't do right by her, we will," Avalon said, resolved. They were all silent for a minute. "But we don't… we don't know what we should do. And this cousin may know."

Kevin took Avalon's hand. "We'll wait and see. But if no one is going to care for her properly, we will."

Everyone was silent again. The doorbell chimed distantly.

They were the only residents at the time. The house had been broken up into seven units with a communal kitchen and entry.

They all looked at one another.

"Cops. Who else?" Boris asked.

Instead of walking to the front, he headed for the gate to the courtyard, opened it and stepped back.

"Officer Stirling," he said.

"Special Agent Stirling," their visitor said with a grimace, "but that's a lot of title. You're welcome to call me Tin."

"Uh, sure, thanks, and…please come in," Boris said.

"Thanks."

Their visitor came into the courtyard. He nodded to all of them as he found another chair and drew it up to the tiled table.

"You're all still together," he noted.

"Well, not all of us, but…um, yeah," Boris said. "But you, or Mr.—Detective—Stapleton questioned all of us. I'm not sure what any of us can tell you that we haven't said. We cared about Cindy. We were just talking about her. Do you—do you know what happens now?"

"Well, I'm not sure when, but the medical examiner will release her body to her next of kin. Ryder told me that she has a cousin coming, Myrna West."

"They have the same last name," Brad said, looking at the others.

"We just want… We want her to have a funeral. And to be remembered," Avalon said.

"Of course," Fin said. "I'll find out what I can for you. But now that you are all together, maybe you can help me. I'm trying to reenact your night out."

Boris sighed. "Well, we were all over. Some of us headed at one point to the Cat's Meow—karaoke lovers here, which I'm assuming you might guess." He pointed at Avalon, Kevin and Leo. "Actors, you know. They need a spotlight."

"Was Cindy with you then?"

"Yes," Avalon told him. "But we didn't start there. We were at Pat O'Brien's first."

"We were doing a lot of wandering," Brad told him. "I hadn't been to New Orleans or anywhere in Louisiana before this project. I think I'm the one who kept us moving."

"What about others in the cast and crew, or the family from the island?"

"Oh, well, yes, we ran into that group several times," Avalon said.

"That Julian Bennett—he's a party boy. Charming guy, and he likes to spread his charm," Lauren said. "He was meeting people everywhere he went. I kind of feel sorry for the other cousin—Kenneth is just…awkward. I think Julian was trying to help his cousin out, but every time he joined in on a conversation, well, the girls wandered off."

"They weren't with you, but they wound up with you in a number of places?" Stirling asked.

Avalon saw the others were as pensive as she was. They hadn't been thinking about who was with them when. Yes, they saw the Christy heirs often during the evening, but Avalon had been ready to go back to the hotel most of the evening—she'd stayed out to be with her friends, who all seemed to need the diversion. They worked long, hard hours…especially Boris, who was there for every minute of filming. And they'd learned early that they were in a business where knowing people—and helping friends along—could be very important.

No one else was answering, so Avalon spoke up. "The area we were prowling around is pretty small—I'd say we checked out places from Conti down to the Cat's Meow, all on Bourbon Street. And I think they were in the last bar we visited, though we weren't sitting together. At least, I think they were there. I believe I saw Cara talking to one of the bartenders, so maybe she was ordering for the rest of them, or maybe she wanted to keep going when the others went back."

"I saw her...and her husband," Kevin offered. "But I'm not sure about the other two—Julian and Kenneth."

"That's when Cindy left us," Lauren said quietly. "She was cryptic—gave me a wink and said she had one last stop to make. Before any of us could even ask if she wanted us to come with her, she'd taken off. We lingered a bit..." She shrugged. "Cindy was a responsible adult. I didn't have the right to tell her she had to stay with us. But I should have been looking out for her."

"We should have done something," Avalon whispered.

"But who in the world would have thought someone was out there, stalking her, stalking us?" Boris said.

"You will catch whoever did this, right?" Kevin demanded.

"We'll do our best," Stirling promised. "That's why I need your help. After she left the bar, none of you saw Cindy again, right?"

"Until we found her," Avalon said.

"And you were together the rest of the night?" he asked them.

They looked around at each other.

Avalon couldn't help feeling accused...and defensive.

"You're looking in the wrong place. Check out the hotel security tapes—we were at that little boutique hotel and they have security cameras in the lobby and the elevator."

"They are being checked," he assured her. "And, actually,

Miss Morgan, I'd appreciate it if you would do a little cruise of the area where you were last night with me."

"Me?" Avalon asked.

"Just Avalon?" Kevin asked, moving a bit closer to Avalon.

Finley Stirling nodded. "I need someone who was there, can't go asking questions with a whole group, and I think it's better when it's a duo."

"Lauren knew Cindy better—" Avalon began.

"No, Avalon, please!" Lauren said. "I don't think I can do it. It's too hard thinking that maybe we could have kept her with us."

Avalon forced a smile. "All right."

"Good. Thank you," Stirling said.

"Avalon?" Kevin said.

"I'm fine. I'll catch up with you all later."

She stood, not at all sure why he had chosen her, and more than a little nervous that he had done so.

He couldn't possibly suspect *her*, could he?

"I'll just get my bag," she told him.

"I'll bring her back safe and sound," he told the others. She grabbed her bag quickly, telling herself the faster she went, the faster she'd be through with the man.

Special Agent Stirling was waiting for her by the gate from the courtyard to the street.

She joined him and he opened it for her. "Miss Morgan."

"Avalon," she said, giving him a smile with no humor.

He headed toward the river first, leading the way to Bourbon Street. They walked in silence, then reached the street, where he paused, staring at her.

"You see the dead," he told her.

"What?" She blinked, not believing this man was saying the words to her. His sharp green gaze softened.

"It's all right. I talk to them, too. When they have something to say and choose to be seen. You're not the only one. It's just one of those special instincts people have that they don't discuss with others lest they be locked away."

Avalon froze, just staring at him.

They were on Bourbon Street, which was busy despite the time of day. People were passing by, laughing, enjoying themselves. A man was walking around with a sign that warned everyone they were going to hell if they didn't quickly repent; he was being ignored.

People didn't tend to be mean at this time of day.

Later, when a few had imbibed too much liquid pleasure in the bars, they could become surlier.

They were all a haze to Avalon.

"Look, it's all right." Fin sounded impatient. "I was informed by a friend at the cemetery that you were…gifted. A dead friend. Here's the thing—your talent may give us an edge up on what's going on."

Avalon turned and started walking down the street. He caught her arm. She looked at his hand, and then into his eyes.

He was sincere; he wasn't teasing her. He wasn't making it up, trying to get a rise out of her.

"I—I didn't want to film at Christy Island. I didn't want to be there… I knew there would be restless spirits. But Cindy being murdered… They might have been around, watching." She lowered her head. "I mean, no. I—I can't help!"

"All right," he said gently.

She'd wondered all her life if there were others like her, or if she simply had a strange touch that she just needed to accept. She'd learned early not to share anything regarding her strange encounters.

She looked up at him suspiciously. Finley Stirling looked perfectly sane. In fact, he might not like it, but he looked like the perfect law-enforcement agent—tall, built like steel, with those eyes that could seem to see to the soul, and a face that could register both empathy and dead-set determination.

*He was probably testing her. Maybe someone had suggested she was a little crazy, maybe he was doing this to see…*

"Avalon," he said softly, as if reading her mind, "please, believe me, I'm not trying to make fun of you, I'm not trying to grill you, I'm not doing anything to hurt you in any way. There are others. We seldom know about each other because we're such a small percentage of the world, and we, as humans, tend to mock or disbelieve that which we don't see or can't understand."

She inhaled, not knowing what to say.

"Come on—I know a quiet place a block down. Let's talk, and then we'll get started on our hunt through Bourbon Street."

She still didn't speak. He hurried her down to a small boutique hotel on Chartres Street, where there was a tiny, intimate café/bar. He brought her to a small table in the corner, then went to the counter and returned with two cups of café au lait and a plate of beignets.

"Um, thank you," she said.

"Do you like beignets?" he asked her.

"What's not to like? Two tons of sugar," she said, trying for a smile.

He smiled in return. "I knew it from the time I was very young. My folks had me see a psychiatrist before I went to first grade," he said dryly. "They're great, loving people, they just thought I took my imaginary friends a step too far." He offered her a rueful smile. "When my mom's sister passed away from cancer, she stood next to me and watched her own funeral, and then asked me to let my mom know she was okay and out of pain, but might hang around to watch out for others for a while. Both my parents were angry at first, thinking it was a weird thing to make up, but then Aunt Shelley asked me to sing this little song my grandmother had sung to them when they were kids. And then my mother believed me, and my dad even believed, but they warned me to keep it all to myself. It's a harsh world and people would mock me and maybe lock me up."

should have eaten the suckers—there'd have been a little less. Anyway, let's—"

The young woman behind the counter rushed over to them with dish towels. "I'm so sorry. I've never seen a gust like that—"

"It's okay, truly," Fin assured her. "And thank you."

He wiped his face and grinned at Avalon. "We'll just pay a visit to the facilities and—and you know, Avalon, they are great beignets. We should have eaten them."

"I can pack some up," the young woman offered.

"No, thank you, and not to worry." Fin looked across the table at Avalon. "We'll be back," he said quietly.

Avalon found herself nodding.

"Yes, thank you, we'll be back. I haven't been in here before, but it's great." She offered the young woman a warm smile. "We'll come back."

She knew it was time they began their hunt for whatever they were seeking on Bourbon Street.

Avalon Morgan had a good memory—which wasn't always the case when going back over a night on Bourbon Street.

Finley felt she seemed to have accepted him, and what he had said to her. She hadn't offered much of her own story, other than having met the ghost of a woman sent from the Alamo before the fighting began. But he didn't want to push; she was with him, she was being helpful, and that was what he needed.

They'd been to three places so far and he showed Cindy's picture to the staff at each, asking if they remembered her, and if they'd seen anyone watching her, or coming on to her.

"I'm amazed you remember this all so clearly," he told Avalon as they left the third place. Her phone was filled with photos of all the known players in the case, including pictures of Julian Bennett, Cara and Gary Holstein, and Kenneth Richard.

So far, at the three establishments they visited, managers remembered—vaguely—seeing the group, including the Christy family.

"I guess I wasn't feeling much like getting wild," she told him. "Don't get me wrong—my friends are great, and when you've been working sixteen-hour days many days in a row, you need a break. And I love Kevin and Lauren—we've been friends for years now. And Boris was great to all of us. With so many things happening out there now, it's still a very competitive industry. But a supportive one. I'm not making a lot of sense. Anyway, being out with them night before last meant a lot because we were getting close to a wrap and people had a break."

"How well have you gotten to know the four who own the island now?"

"The Christy family?" she asked, sounding surprised.

She paused in the street, looking at him. "I can't say I know any of them well, but they have all been nice, and they've been excited about the filming. They thought the movie having been filmed there would add value and prestige to the island as they're trying to sell it. I—I don't know what this will do. I'm sure the media is reporting on it already."

"Oh, yeah."

"I think it's…well, it's hard to get used to the fact that Cindy is… That it's not just something terrible that happened, but it happened to a friend."

"I know. I'm so sorry."

"It's strange. Lauren had just as much experience and she's valued in her field. She's a true makeup *artist*. Brilliant when making someone beautiful and equally brilliant when it comes to blood and guts and making someone incredibly horrifying or creepy. She and Cindy were similar as far as reputation and caliber goes, but neither cared who had the better title—they worked together well. They could give each other breaks."

"Nothing except friendship and support between them?"

Avalon nodded. "And I'm not being overly…gushy," she said,

after seeking the right word and not feeling that she'd found it. "They were friends, and this was one of the most supportive projects I've ever been involved in. Not that most aren't supportive, but this was mainly Boris's money. And a true group effort."

"Anything else about the family?"

"I don't know what else to say. They're three entities, of course, though four people. The money will be divided three ways—between Cara, Julian and Kenneth. Gary is a happy tagalong as Cara's husband. They seem to get along with one another—all three are glad that the others just want to unload the place."

"Were they following you the other night?"

"No...we weren't always at the same place at the same time. But often. I guess they were at the last bar, but Cindy was there, too."

"Want a soda, a cup of coffee—anything?" he asked her.

"I don't want a drink."

"Were you at Lafitte's?"

"Not last night."

"Let's stop in there now. Surely you could use a soda."

"If—if that's what you want." She looked at him suspiciously.

"I had a friend who used to hang out there," Fin told her.

"Used to?"

He smiled. "Yeah. He decided to go on. But there might be someone hanging around who could give us a hand."

"Oh," she said. Her eyes closed for a moment and he thought that she took a deep breath.

When she looked at him again, he thought that something in her had changed. His curiosity must have shown because she gave him a determined grimace.

"I've decided not to be a sniveling coward," she told him.

He shook his head. "Don't feel that way. Trust me. Ryder has been a cop forever, and finding Cindy got to him. It got to me. You lost a friend. And now you've discovered that you're not alone—that while rare, others have that gift of really com-municating with the dead. I don't think you ever were a snivel-ing coward—I think you've just had too much thrown at you."

That caused her to smile.

"No. But thank you. I have been a sniveling coward. And there's nothing I want more than whoever did this to be stopped, and if I can help with that, I guarantee you, I want to. So let's go to Lafitte's." She hesitated. "And we'll see if we can find a… friend."

Before they continued, Avalon heard the musical tone of her cell phone ringing.

She glanced at the caller, frowning.

"Is anything wrong?"

"No, no, but…excuse me a minute?"

"Have a seat out here. What would you like?"

"Soda water with lime, please."

He nodded and entered the bar area while she headed to one of the tables in the courtyard area. Inside, he ordered two sodas with lime and looked around the bar.

He had always loved Lafitte's—a major tourist destination, but, like Café du Monde, one with character and history, and in his mind, a lot of charm. Built between 1722 and 1732, it had sound reason to claim to be the oldest bar in business in the country. The Lafitte brothers had not owned the property, but it had been owned by one of their captains. While law enforce-ment and government agencies had often wanted the Lafitte brothers—and Pierre had faced arrest and imprisonment—the people of the city had generally welcomed them. The brothers brought goods to the city that might not have been obtained otherwise. And they were famous for the Battle of New Or-leans. It was likely that they did turn the tide; the British had expected poorly supplied and inexperienced resistance. Instead, the Lafitte brothers provided gunpowder, munitions and a crew of fierce men ready to do battle to defend New Orleans.

Approximately three hundred years of history rested in the walls. It was small and rustic, one of the few places to have survived two massive fires. Crooked stone and brick, a charming old hearth, wooden tables and barstools.

Fin ordered their drinks and headed out to the courtyard, where he ran into an old friend—off-duty patrolman Curtis Mason, who was leaving as he was entering.

Curtis gave him a welcoming smile, and then frowned. "Hey! You're still here, Fin. I thought you'd be heading back to DC. Oh, are you on that murder out on Christy Island? Hey, someone didn't kill a girl just to get publicity for the movie, did they?"

"You know how it goes, Curtis. We don't know anything yet. Early stages of the investigation."

"But it's an island."

"Yup, it's an island. With scores of people on and off it. At this moment, nothing is definitive. By the way, were you on duty here the night before last?"

"Yeah, I was, actually."

Fin pulled out his phone, drawing up a picture of Cindy.

The good thing was, since the murder had taken place on an island, only law enforcement had pictures of Cindy as she had been found on the tomb.

Reporters had come, but not until Cindy's body had been respectfully removed.

"I've seen her picture," Curtis said. "The thing is, even we beat cops know the killer could be anybody. How the hell do you catch someone who pulls off that kind of a thing? Had to be on the island, right?"

"Well, had to have been there to display the body, yes," Fin said. "But was he with the group on the island, or did he find out about the shooting schedule? The cast and crew who were out together that night think she met someone on Bourbon Street when she left them. Naturally, they don't want to believe any one of them is capable of such a thing. Like I said, we're in the early stages of this investigation."

Curtis nodded gravely. "I saw her that night."

"You did?"

He nodded. "I'm with the mounted police, you know, and Bourbon Street is in my patrol." He hesitated. "I almost spoke with the young woman in the courtyard—saw that she was with you, but she was on the phone. I saw her out with a group of people—the dead woman included. They'd been doing kara-oke—your friend has a kick-ass voice, by the way, and if I was from Massachusetts, I'd be telling you she is one *wicked* beauty. Seems nice, too. She smiled and excused herself when she walked by me. She an actress?"

"Bride of the vampire king," Fin said dryly. "Did you see any of them again?"

Curtis shook his head ruefully. "There was a brawl in the street this side of Bourbon, and I think they were closer to Canal—they were heading in that direction when I saw them. Trust me, I wish I could tell you more."

"Thanks, Curtis."

"Sure thing, Fin. I'll be on the lookout. For what, I'm not sure. But trust me. Every cop in the city will be on the alert."

Fin thanked him again and headed to the courtyard. The glasses he was holding were "sweating," so he hurried.

Avalon was sitting at a table, not on her phone any longer, but looking at it.

"Anything wrong?" he asked her.

She smiled and shook her head. "I love acting, I really do. But it's an iffy way to make a living. Unreliable, I mean. I do websites and promotion for writers and entertainers on the side. I got a curious request."

"Oh?"

"Samara Stella. Have you ever heard of her?"

"No."

"She has a place here, off Magazine Street." She hesitated, then shrugged. "She's a dominatrix, and has five girls in her employ who provide 'theatrical' encounters."

"She's a sex worker? Escort?"

"No, she's a dominatrix. I never judge anyone. Consenting adults are free to indulge in sexual encounters however they choose—is that the right way to say that? I mean, everyone has their fantasies or their idea of the perfect sensual or erotic situation."

She was flushing slightly. Uncomfortable talking about sex in any way with him. But she'd started—and she was going to finish.

"She wants me to do a new website for her. And kind of being here now, in limbo for a few days, it would be a good thing for me. I'm just not sure…"

"What kind of pictures is she going to ask you to take?"

"Oh, nothing…intimate. Just pictures of her and her employees."

"They are legal?"

"Yes, really she keeps it clean. Of course, she can't control what people do outside of her business, but at her place, people come to act out situations."

"She just wants you to do the website?"

Her flush deepened. "Well, she's offered me a job several times. It's just not… It's not my thing. I'm not into pain. Giving it or receiving it. Believe it or not, actors can be shy and withdrawn, which has nothing to do with this… It's just not my thing. Anyway, sorry—so beyond the point! Have you seen anyone who can help?"

"A friend."

"Who was it?"

"A living cop," he told her sardonically. "The city is on the alert. And, the thing is, we must start with the obvious, and that is someone who had continual access to the island and knew about the shooting schedule."

"That means the cast and crew."

"And the Christy family."

"Right. But—"

At a buzzing in his pocket, it was Fin's turn to excuse himself. It was Ryder calling from the morgue.

"Anything?" he asked quickly, casting Avalon an apologetic glance as he rose to take the call.

"Pizza," Ryder said.

"Pizza?"

"Yes, consumed about two hours before Cindy was killed. And the puncture marks—she was hit right where it mattered. The ME would say that in a far more eloquent manner, but whoever killed her did so with a very sharply pointed instrument and knew exactly what he was doing. She bled out—quickly, at least. Maybe we should be looking into the vampire cults in the area—there are some, you know. They 'donate' blood to each other and stuff like that."

"Yeah, we can look in that direction. Right now, I'm on Bourbon Street with Avalon Morgan."

"With Miss Morgan?"

"Yes, trying to follow the group's footsteps. I'll ask her about pizza. Anything else from the autopsy?"

Ryder was silent on the other end.

"Sexual assault?" Fin asked.

"Not while she was alive," Ryder said unhappily.

"What?"

He heard the detective sigh deeply. "The doc says there are no signs of…a fight. But there was sex involved."

"Oh, Lord. We're not going to put that out to the public," Fin said.

"No. I wish I could say it gives us a better idea of what we're looking for, but guys don't usually brag to other guys about the hot corpse they just slept with. Man, that came out horribly, but people don't wear this kind of thing on their faces, you know? And women are assaulted by all types of men—you have the guys out there who are charming, the guy-next-door types, who are absolute creeps. I attended at least a dozen lectures on profiling, but I'll be damned if I know how to recognize a killer like this."

"No other details have been let out, right?"

"Not by my guys. She was murdered—she was discovered, it was on Christy Island. That's all anyone has given out. My department won't say a word—it's officially turned over to you guys."

Fin was almost afraid to ask… "Anything else that the doc could give us?"

"Just what we already know, really. The killing was organized and well-planned. She has no defensive wounds. She was killed elsewhere, blood drained elsewhere, and then she was cleaned up, dressed and left on the tomb. Because of the blood loss, it's difficult for the doc to pinpoint just how long she was lying where she was, but he says in his 'educated' estimation that it all occurred—death and everything and then display—between the hours of two a.m. and five a.m."

"Okay, thanks. Anything from your forensic people yet?"

"No. Yours?"

"No. I'm going to check with Avalon about pizza places along the street until I find Cindy's last stop. And, with any luck, someone who can help."

"Let me know."

"Will do."

He returned to the table where Avalon was sitting.

She looked at him expectantly.

"Did you go in a group for pizza that night?"

"Pizza?" she asked.

"Pizza. Tomato sauce and cheese on a crust, sometimes with pepperoni and other toppings?"

She drew up as if indignant, but she was, in truth, smiling. Just a little.

"No, we'd all eaten dinner before we met up to prowl for good bands and fun places. People had finished working at different times during the day, so the plan was just to meet at eight thirty that night. I guess I wasn't that much fun. I was tired, and I've done the Bourbon Street thing before."

"You were tired and probably thought there were other places you could go." He grimaced weakly. "So, no pizza."

"No. Why?"

"Because Cindy's last meal was pizza."

"Oh. Okay, so…"

"There are a few places nearby. Let's head out again, if…you're all right with sparing the time today?"

"Yes, of course. You're serious, right?"

"I know you're not filming, but you just told me about your web design business."

"No, no, it's fine. Unless something happens or I'm needed again, I told Samara that I'd come by and we'd talk tomorrow."

"Pizza, then."

They left Lafitte's Blacksmith Shop and headed back down toward Canal. They stopped in each restaurant that sold pizza. It wasn't until they reached the third pizza shop that the girl at the counter called out to the manager.

"Miss Connor saw that poor girl," the young woman explained. "She told us this morning when they had her picture in the news. Wait just a second."

Miss Connor was a slim, attractive woman of about fifty with neatly coiffed silver hair, fluid movements and an easy way. She headed quickly toward them from the office to the back of the counter once she'd been summoned.

Fin introduced himself, showing his badge, and then introduced Avalon. He asked the restaurant manager if she had seen Cindy, and, if so, if she'd been with anyone.

The woman nodded. "I thought about calling the police, but from what I saw, they already knew she'd been out on Bourbon Street that night."

"She was alone when she came in here?"

"She was," Miss Connor said. "I think. Yes. No, I'm sure of it. And she looked tired—I've seen that look on others who come in here, you know? She was done with her night out, because morning comes, and morning brings work or other obligations. I was at the counter. I took her order. She was very sweet. We chatted a bit—she couldn't decide if she did or didn't want pepperoni. Loves it, but not great to sleep on, she said. But she needed food. She said she thought she needed a bit of something to soak up the alcohol—she had an early call in the morning and shouldn't have been out so late. But when she went out into the street…well, of course, I'm wondering now what I saw, or what I thought I saw."

"Please, tell us whatever it was."

"She was so nice—taking her food, thanking me, leaving a tip. So I was watching her, kind of, keeping an eye on her as she went out."

"And?" Fin asked.

The woman lowered her head for a minute, shaking it, before she looked up at them again.

"Miss Connor?" Avalon asked softly.

"A vampire," the woman said. "I thought I saw a vampire."

# CHAPTER FOUR

Vampire.

Well, yes, of course, it was New Orleans, and they had been filming a vampire movie.

But Avalon's first response was a protective one.

Kevin. Kevin had been playing the vampire. Kevin would be a suspect if they were talking about vampires.

"Miss Connor, you think you saw a vampire?" Fin asked politely.

The woman waved a hand in the air. "I'm sorry, I guess I figured I was seeing someone in a costume. And, at the time, it wasn't strange at all. It doesn't have to be Mardi Gras for people to run around these streets in costumes."

"Exactly what was he wearing?" Fin asked.

"Well, a cape, of course," Miss Connor said. "You know, the sweeping black cape."

"I see," Fin said.

"Dark hair—might have been a wig."

Determined to fathom how Cindy had walked down the street with a "vampire" and no one else had noticed, Avalon pressed, "He had dark hair and was wearing a cape and Cindy went right out to him…with her pizza?"

The woman gave her a somber nod. "Please remember, I was waiting on other customers."

"She came in alone, and went out to a vampire?" Fin asked.

Again, the woman nodded somberly. "I don't think she was expecting him. She left, and I think he called her back, and she started to laugh and walked over to him. As I said, at the time, I didn't think anything of it. Come for the right festival and you'll see people walking down the street in nothing but little cups over their privates and a lot of chains. Oh, don't get me wrong! A lot is beautiful, too, it's just that I don't think much of the unusual because…well, not too much is unusual to me anymore. But I'm pretty sure the young lady wasn't expecting him, but was pleased to see him. I can't tell you too much else. I have no idea about his face. I think he was wearing that cloak or cape over black pants and a vest and that—that he was dressed up for something. All I could think of was vampire. I mean, I suppose it could have been something else."

"And she walked down the street with him?" Fin asked.

Miss Connor nodded.

"Would you be willing to meet with a sketch artist?" Fin asked her.

"Oh, like I said—I was at the register, we were busy, I was just glancing out of the corner of my eye as she left and I noticed him. I mean, I can tell you for certain she didn't come with him but met up with him and while she was surprised, she wasn't displeased. In fact, she seemed happy to see him, and I think she was offering to share her pizza. I guess vampires eat pizza with no garlic," she said.

Avalon glanced at Fin.

"Sorry, sorry, it just came to mind, I mean… I am so sorry. I was horrified to recognize the young woman who had been killed!" Miss Connor said quickly. "I'm not sure how accurate

I can be at all. But yes, if you think it can help in any way, I'm happy to talk to a police artist."

"Thank you. Sincerely, thank you," Fin told her.

"Uh, would you two like some pizza?" she asked.

"No, thank you," Avalon said.

"Sure—thanks," Fin said.

"There are a few little round tables right there to the side," said Miss Connor, pointing. "Cheese, pepperoni—we have everything."

While Fin ordered, Avalon went ahead to take a seat at one of the tables crowded into the small shop.

"Sorry," he told her as he sat. "I'm hungry. I wore more of the beignets than I ate."

"So we're looking for...a vampire?" Avalon asked.

"Someone dressed as a vampire."

"Well, I can assure you—it wasn't Kevin! He was with me."

"Are you two a...couple?"

"Kevin is gay. He's an amazing friend, actor and man. He helps everyone. And as soon as she said the word *vampire*, I figured that you—"

"No," he told her.

"No?"

"It doesn't make him a suspect. Anyone can dress up as a vampire."

"Right," she said. She shook her head. "I still can't believe it was anyone involved with the film. I mean there were caterers and extras I never met before, and we didn't keep our filming schedule any kind of a secret. Boris was doing his best to be both within regulations, and within budget. But we were on an island."

"All of you left the island every night, and headed back by day," he reminded her.

She nodded. "Kevin, Lauren and I took the same car service back to our hotel. We were together the whole time."

"What about Boris? And the other actor—Leo Gonzales?"

"Boris and Leo were together—we couldn't get one of the big cars, so we took different cars."

"Leo is tall, and talented. A mime, right? A guy who could pull off a lot?"

She shook her head. "You're barking up the wrong tree there. Leo is gentle, and he loves what he does far more than money. He loves kids—loves to just play with them, creating doors or whatever out of the air on the streets. And unless he is purposefully doing a performance for money, he just does it to be a good guy and entertain kids."

"Boris…"

"Please! Boris put his everything into this!"

"And again," he reminded her, "that could mean he'd bring whatever attention he could to the project."

"That's just sick. And it's not Boris. He loves movies and he's great with people. He was friends with Cindy."

"Okay. What about the other guys, the set designer and the cameraman?"

She sighed. "Terry and Brad—"

"Terry found the tomb for you to lie on and together they did the storyboards for the scene?"

"Trust me—they're not crazed killers! Terry's horrified his work was copied in such a heinous and cruel fashion. I think he almost feels guilty. I'm telling you, I know these people."

"I hope you're right," he said softly.

She let out a sound of frustration. "I know I'm right!"

"As I said, I hope so. Anyway, we found what we were looking for—once Ryder gets here with his sketch artist, I'll walk you back."

She couldn't help the emotion churning within her. He now seemed so decent in so many ways; she'd recognized that he had something about him—more than his shared ability to see the

dead. She'd recognized the fact that he was infuriating her. She
was burning inside. But burning made her want to…

Smack him in the head—but also touch him, feel his skin,
sense the heartbeat beneath.

*Nope.* She couldn't think that way. "I'm perfectly capable of
walking myself back a few blocks. I know this city."

"You're from here?" he asked her.

"No."

"Where are you from?"

She gritted her teeth and didn't answer. Miss Connor was
walking over with a smile and a large cheese pizza.

Fin thanked her politely for the pizza and then thanked her
again for helping.

The poor woman just about drooled over him.

"I can't believe I can help in something so horrible, but if I
can, I'm very glad to do so. By the way, my name is Mindy."

"Thank you, Mindy," Fin said with a dazzling grin.

Avalon felt an even stronger desire to hit him.

Mindy Connor left them, and Fin turned his gaze back to
Avalon. "Sorry, so where are you from?"

"You don't know? You're the FBI."

"I don't know. But you're right. I can find out. It was really
just a casual question."

"Originally? St. Augustine. I still love the city. I went to
school in Central Florida. I know this city. I spent a few sum-
mers up here. I worked at the theater one year and did a series
of promos for the city another year."

"Where are you living now?"

"In a rental in the French Quarter."

"No, I mean, where are you living when you're not in a
rental room?"

She wasn't sure why she was annoyed by even his casual questioning and conversation.

"I don't know," she said.

He arched an eyebrow. "Okay."

"We were going to get through this project. Lauren has been talking me into moving in with her. She has a little house off Frenchman Street just the other side of Esplanade. She could use a roommate, and there is a lot of activity up here—for web design, and for movies and theatrical projects. Anyway, you don't need to walk me back anywhere."

She wondered if he was even paying attention to her. He seemed focused on the slice in his hands.

"You should eat—it's really good," he said.

"Where are you from?" she asked him, grudgingly accepting a piece of pizza.

"The Kenner area—near the airport."

"Oh!"

He nodded. "I grew up with all the pirate tales and stories about Barataria and Lafitte. And stories about the haunted island that Christy owned."

"I see. Is that why they put you on this case?"

He shrugged. "I was already here. And, yes, I'm sure my knowledge of the area had something to do with me being here."

She fell silent and bit into the pizza herself. She had several bites— it was very good—and then remembered it was Cindy's last meal.

She didn't have to explain her sudden loss of appetite; Detective Ryder Stapleton arrived with a young woman carrying a computer case. Fin rose and approached him, then introduced him and the young woman to Mindy Connor.

Avalon took the opportunity to slip from the table and go outside. She hurried along the street toward her temporary home, afraid Fin was going to follow her.

He did not.

She was surprised to feel something as she hurried along; not a tug, but something gentle like the stroke of a soft breeze against her arm. She turned quickly and saw someone she knew.

A dead friend.

"Dear one, are you okay?"

The ghost asking the question was Kathryn Anne McNeil, a young woman who had been, in her day, one of Jean Lafitte's friends. She must have been an unusually independent woman, for she had told Avalon that yes, indeed, they'd had a "heated" friendship, but he'd kept a woman named Marie Villard at his side and had several children with her.

Kathryn hadn't intended to be tied down in any way. She'd inherited a certain wealth of her own and loved the opera, which she did enjoy with Lafitte. Her place in society had allowed her to live as she chose. She had also enjoyed politics—had attended several events that had included Andrew Jackson—and the company of whomever she chose, when she chose. She'd died soon after the Battle of New Orleans, a victim of a fever that plagued the city, and was interred at the St. Louis Cemetery #1.

Avalon had met her during the months she'd been cast in a regional summer theater production of *Hamlet*.

Kathryn had told her that her first love was opera, but a play by William Shakespeare was hard to resist.

"I—" Avalon realized that she'd stopped dead in the street, something she had taught herself not to do when approached by spirits.

She started moving again, more slowly, and pulled out her cell phone to avoid the appearance of talking to herself.

"I'm...fine."

"No, you're not. You were on the island. I've seen the news. Oh, darling, I am so sorry! I hate to see you in discomfort. While I do love this city as I did in life, I do not wear blinders. It can be dangerous. I really don't think you should be running about alone."

They were in the French Quarter; it was still daylight. There were people everywhere.

Avalon paused in front of a store window and smiled at Kathryn. "I'm okay. Kathryn, there are people milling everywhere. And I'm headed back to the house where I'm staying. Thank you so much, but I'm fine."

"If you're so fine, why did you run away from that very fine specimen of a man?" Kathryn asked shrewdly.

She smiled and shook her head. "Because he's accusing my friends of murder."

"And you're so certain they're innocent?"

"Kathryn, I really am."

"I should have hitchhiked to the dock and popped on a boat over to the island," Kathryn said worriedly.

Avalon hesitated. "There are those who still haunt the island. Though I haven't met them. And none saw anything…to the best of my knowledge."

"The living look out for the living—not the dead," Kathryn said. She shook her head and then stared hard at Avalon. "I did see the man with the young woman who left the pizza shop."

"What?"

"There was a lovely band playing at the bar across the street. A jazz band. And I do love jazz—it didn't exist in my day, but the first time I heard Satchmo playing…well, that's neither here nor there. I was mesmerized, just leaning against the wall there, and I saw a woman leave the pizza parlor, see the man, start to laugh and then offer him pizza."

"Who—who was it, Kathryn? Please—"

Kathryn shook her head sadly. "I can tell you it was a man. He appeared to be tall, but I didn't look at his shoes. These days, you'll see men in lifts!"

"Kathryn."

"He was…well, I couldn't see his face. The collar of his cape stood up high. And I was listening to the music. I'd no idea that…well, darling, you must take care. And watch out for men—tall men who were on your island. Don't be there alone!"

Avalon sighed. "Kathryn, I promise. I won't go anywhere

with anyone alone. The police and the FBI are working on the case. And, trust me, they are suspicious of everyone."

"Nevertheless, I shall walk you to wherever you are going."

Avalon smiled and looked back.

Fin was not following her.

She wasn't sure if she was relieved…or disappointed.

"Sure, Kathryn. Thank you. So, what have you seen lately?"

"Well, I have been spending quite a bit of time at the Monteleone. I do so love that hotel, and while they've had no theatricals there, they have been having exquisite entertainment and I find the Carousel Bar to be a lively and wonderful place."

"It is wonderful, historic, beautiful…"

Again, Avalon looked back.

Then she tried to give her attention to the woman at her side. She smiled slightly as she saw some people shiver and look about, as if they had that "someone walked over their grave" feeling as Kathryn passed them by.

Some felt her; most did not.

And yet there was one thing oddly reassuring about the day.

She'd discovered that in having her sixth sense—or whatever it might be—she was not alone.

She had to wonder, too, why it couldn't work more conveniently. Why Cindy didn't come to her and simply tell her who had done this horrible thing.

Mindy Connor was right about one thing: she couldn't describe the man's face.

But she did allow them to have an image that might be shown through the media, and thus, alert anyone else who might encounter such an individual, or perhaps draw someone out who had seen the man's face.

Fin noticed when Avalon left; he was unhappy the minute she walked away.

But he had no right to stop her.

He sat with Ryder and the artist, and then, when his phone rang and he saw that Angela Hawkins was calling from Krewe headquarters, he excused himself and went outside to speak with her.

The afternoon was fading to dusk; night was coming. With the darkness on the way, a more fevered existence was coming to Bourbon Street.

More people on the streets, neon lights blazing. Music playing louder, and lovely characters stepping out on the streets to advertise the delights of the strip clubs.

"Anything on anyone?" he asked Angela.

"Parking tickets We've had our whole tech department on this throughout the day, and the best we can come up with against anyone—including extras, caterers, boat captains, et cetera—is parking tickets. But I do have something strange for you. I don't know if it's related or not."

"What is it?"

"Mississippi—two years ago. I'm sending you some crime-scene photos now. The killer was never caught. Often enough, serial killers are into display, but seldom so…designed as the murder you're investigating. This was similar. A young woman was found near a historic house close to Biloxi owned by a Civil War general in the 1850s, open to tours now. It's not a major destination, and they have one old caretaker who sits out at the gatehouse. No fencing or anything to stop anyone from entering via the surrounding woods. He came to work to open one day and saw a young woman in an antebellum dress sitting in the rocker on the porch. He went to ask her what she was doing there and realized she was dead. Her name was Ellen Frampton and she was from Minneapolis, but she'd been staying at a casino in Biloxi with friends. It's eerie, Fin. She looks like she's alive. He touched her, thinking she was being a wise-ass, or that something was wrong with her, and discovered that she was stone-cold. There was pressure on police from the state and all over, but the case dried up. May have nothing to do with your murderer, but you might want to speak with the detective who was handling the case. His name is Tom Drayton, and he retired last year, but he'd be happy to speak with you and share anything he has."

"How was she killed? Puncture marks?"

"Stabbed through the heart—then, apparently, cleaned up, dressed and posed."

"This is…yes, too similar. I hadn't heard about the case."

"The FBI wasn't involved. It was a local matter and bizarre as it was, the national media didn't take hold of it."

"Thanks, Angela. I'll look into it right away," he promised.

"I'm already following up, seeing which of your suspects—if any—was known to have been in Mississippi at the time. You have to remember, however, that it's an easy place to drive to, especially from where you are."

"I know. And thanks."

Fin still couldn't believe he hadn't heard about such a bizarre case. Then again…the murder rate was terrifying when known—approximately forty-six people a day in the United States.

But this one…

He ended the call and looked at his messages; there was the picture Angela had promised.

A beautiful young woman sat on a white rocking chair on a broad, columned porch. She was in a dress that emphasized the Victorian style popular during the Civil War—she could, in fact, have walked off the pages of *Gone with the Wind*. The dress was white with delicate green flowers and a broad sash that made her waist appear exceptionally tiny. She wore a sun hat that just shaded her eyes, yet showed the perfection of her lower face. Her hands rested on the wicker of the rocking chair.

He poked his head back in to get Ryder's attention, drawing him outside to show him the picture.

Ryder stared at the murder scene in silence for a full minute and then uttered an expletive.

"It could have been done by the same person. Our person could be a copycat…serial killers… I mean, he went two years before doing it a second time?"

"There is no telling what a killer's vision and needs may be. Our profilers have studied the worst many times, and there is no real guidebook to tell you—at this stage, at least—just what is going on here. We can't even say yet that these murders are related."

"But serial killers can escalate, too," Ryder said.

"And we're dealing with someone really twisted. They didn't catch whoever did it. I'm going to drive over and see the lead on the case. There and back tonight—ninety minutes there and ninety minutes back, hopefully."

Ryder nodded. "Keep me updated on anything."

"You bet."

"I'm going to get this sketch out—see if we get anything. Beyond attention seekers."

"Right," Fin said, and hesitated. "I still have concerns about that film crew and cast."

"I know where they are. I'll have an officer keep an eye on them."

"And the family—Cara and Gary Holstein, Julian Bennett and Kenneth Richard."

"Yes."

Fin started to turn, but then spoke again. "Ryder, Cindy West was made up and laid out to look just like Avalon Morgan did in the scene that was filmed right before Cindy was found. I'm worried about Avalon."

Ryder smiled. "Trust me. We'll watch out for her."

Fin nodded. "I know you will."

He'd been hunkered down at a guest house toward Canal and Rampart for the last several months; he hurried there and, without returning to his room, slid his car from one of the four parking spaces allotted visitors and headed out for I-10, calling retired detective Tom Drayton as he did.

Drayton answered immediately.

"I think it is the same son of a bitch," Drayton said. "And, trust me—I will do anything humanly possible to bring that monster down!"

That night, Avalon and her friends ordered dinner from a delivery service; none of them had the heart to go out. They ate together in the courtyard, and then split to different areas of the house.

Boris and Brad were going to work on the film, rewatching the dailies to see where they were, and if they could finish the film with what they had.

Luckily, filming scenes wasn't necessarily done in order, and therefore the final scene—when Kevin's character, the king of the vampires, had lost his beloved, Avalon's character—had been filmed several days earlier. It had called for only the two of them—an easy scene to film as far as set and direction went, harder for the actors portraying a mix of emotions.

Kevin and Leo had wanted to relax and watch a movie. A comedy, Kevin assured Avalon, when he asked her if she wanted to join them.

She was too restless for a movie.

Lauren and Avalon wound up in Avalon's room and talked for a while, but no matter where they started a conversation, it came back to their present circumstances.

"So, what's your plan for the immediate future?" Lauren asked her. "I can ask my friends. You know, there's always something filming here. I know you can get more work quickly. There's another horror movie starting up next week and—"

"No. Thank you. I'm fine for now. I'm going to work on a few websites. Have you heard of Samara Stella?"

"I have," Lauren said. "The famous—or infamous—dominatrix. She's very popular here, from what I understand. A few of the extras I worked on were talking about a visit to her place. They assured me that there was nothing too... I'm not sure that *kinky* would be the right word—she's definitely on the kinky side. But nothing illegal. They're performance artists—but they'll perform sometimes for an audience, drawing volunteers from it, and sometimes one on one. I find it a bit strange myself, but I understand there are high-powered men out there who feel the need to be dominated. Maybe that allows them to be cutthroat in business or something, I don't know. Or maybe a guy with a little meek and mild-mannered wife needs a little excitement without really cheating on his wife. Anyway, I've heard of her, and her place. You're...working with her?"

Avalon laughed. "No, I'm building her a website. She's seen some of the work I've done for friends—for actors, artists and some heavy-metal rock bands who may make Samara Stella look tame. Anyway, she offered a nice fee. Enough so I don't have to worry about the next month or so, at any rate."

"Oh, well, that's great," Lauren said. "But don't go getting involved with..."

"I'm not going to turn into a dominatrix. Or a pole dancer... though, wow. I have seen a few who have the best bodies known to man."

"Pole dancing is damned good exercise," Lauren said.

"Don't worry. I'm not going into the sex business."

"No nudity!" Lauren said firmly. "Unless it's HBO or a Spielberg movie and they're paying you the big bucks and you could wind up with a major award."

Avalon laughed again, glad for her friend. In Lauren's business, she was behind the scenes, and she was often able to hear a lot of the talk that was going around, for whatever any of it might be worth.

"Anyway, immediate future—I'm going to go see Samara Stella tomorrow. Want to come?"

Lauren yawned. "Maybe. For now, I'm going to bed. I didn't sleep much last night. I'm hoping I sleep more tonight. This whole situation is so upsetting. I didn't know Cindy that well, but we've worked together before. She was a really, really, good kid… It's hard to believe. So we all lie awake, needing sleep, wondering and being afraid. Avalon, do you realize, it might have been one of us? And she was laid out just like…"

Lauren's eyes went wide and her hand flew to cover her mouth.

"She was laid out just as I was, in the scene we'd just filmed," Avalon said, finishing for her. "I know."

"I'm sorry." Lauren sighed. "It wasn't us. And I feel bad, but also relieved. And we can't help trying to figure out what we're going to do about the movie, thinking about our own lives when Cindy doesn't have a life anymore, but—"

"It's what we have to do," Avalon said, determined. "And we have to do anything we can to find out who did this to Cindy."

"Well, thank you. I'm glad you're the one who went out with that detective today."

Avalon grinned. "He's not a detective. He's a special agent."

"Right. Well," Lauren said, smirking, "I'd say he's special. The other guy… Ryder. Nice, solid and I believe he knows what he's doing, and he's serious and has that bulldog look—I know he'll do what he can. But Stirling…well, I'd liked to have met him when we were just wandering around Bourbon Street."

Avalon gave her a dry smile. "Sure."

"You don't think he's attractive?" Lauren asked her. "Well, I mean, I suppose that's not something you think about at a time like this."

Avalon shrugged. "He has his qualities. I guess."

"A vampire," Lauren said.

"Pardon?"

"Well, you did find what you were looking for, right? They've been showing a sketch on the news, showing the last person she was seen with—a man in a cloak. They must be getting calls. I mean, we're not in the middle of Mardi Gras, and there may always be someone in costume on the street for theatrical reasons, or just for performances at Jackson Square or the like, but surely, someone noticed her with a vampire."

"I imagine the tip line is being bombarded," Avalon said. "We can only hope."

"I can't help wondering about it. Seems to me like someone who wanted to, I don't know... Maybe someone who really wanted to be in the movie."

"Or who wants to be a vampire."

Lauren shrugged. "Okay. I'm going to bed for real. Oh, um, just something I was thinking about—be careful with the dominatrix, yeah?"

"Be careful? She may be into stuff that doesn't particularly appeal to me, but that doesn't make her dangerous."

"No. But when I was working a few days ago, on the scene with all the extras, a couple of the young men—college boys, taking the gig for fun and to meet girls, and get out of a few days of math or whatever—were talking about Samara Stella."

"I think you mentioned that," Avalon said.

"Yeah, well, I forgot to say they were also talking about the dark web."

"I'm not doing a website for the dark web."

"No, of course not. But if she does have something on the dark web, she could be into some things you don't want any part of."

"People talk—that doesn't make things true."

"I know. Just...maybe I will go with you. Keep an eye on you."

"Sure! And there are a lot of great places on Magazine. We'll have lunch, maybe there will be some live music… Don't let me forget to bring my good camera."

"Kinky photos?"

"I think they're posing—dressed, more or less. She told me on the phone that bits of clothing were more tantalizing than total nudity. And they aren't sexual therapists or surrogates, they just liked to play at the edge and give the 'average' guy a bit of excitement."

"Okay, then…sounds cool. A walk on the wild side," Lauren said, heading to the door. "Really, really going to bed."

She blew a kiss from the doorway and went out, and then came back in quickly. "It's just us in this house, but lock your door!" she warned.

"Yes, ma'am," Avalon said, rising to do so.

She closed the door and locked it, glad that it was just their group staying in the house. The owner often rented out the rooms individually, but, as it had happened, despite the fantastic location and decent pricing, their group got the whole building because the owner had just had some of the plumbing overhauled.

She sat down and opened up her laptop, planning to work on possibilities for Samara Stella's website.

She paused, and then keyed in "dark web."

To her surprise, all manner of information popped up. There were sites, she quickly discovered, that needed special software to access. There were sites that had warning signs on them, and where she encountered login pop-ups needing passwords.

After signing in to her VPN and opening a new browser, she keyed in Samara Stella's name.

Nothing came up under her name at first.

She read down the page. She found herself fascinated.

Sex seemed to be the big seller on the web, and not just by women. She arched her eyebrows at the number of men who were selling "pictures and encounters" by displaying what they considered to be their very special "packages."

She was chuckling as she decided to add more key words to her search.

*New Orleans Murder… New Orleans Vampires…*

And things began to pop up.

Scanning the page, her eyes stopped, and for a moment she forgot to keep breathing.

There was a site called "My Fantasy Murder."

She was almost afraid to open the page, but was drawn to do it.

It couldn't be real; people couldn't think that way, and if they did, would they really share it?

Avalon read.

First, I'd stalk my prey. She'd be unknown, a goddess, but I would see her, and I would know. I would watch the way she moved, the way she breathed, the way her eyes would light when she laughed. I would be close enough at times to smell the sweetness that emanated from her supple flesh. I might brush by her.

Beauty knows no bounds. I have seen these goddesses in every ethnicity. Beauty covers the continents. True beauties are rare, but they come from every continent—they are Asian, African, Australian, South and North American, European…a little laugh here, okay, I've yet to encounter a goddess from Antarctica.

But I am good. I am a hunter, a stalker, and I know how to smile and laugh and charm. And I find my beauties…

Fantasy. So… I find my goddess. I am a gentleman, a rugged, charming gentleman. We play and we tease, and we drink, and it's divine. That's just it—it's all divine. I did say goddess.

I wait until we are so relaxed. She's at ease with me. I make it clear I don't expect intercourse…yet.

And when she is laughing, playing, enjoying me, looking at me with that divine sparkle in her eyes, I strike…

It's so beautiful. Watching her. Because she cannot fight—she knows and knows she cannot fight. And I hold her and assure her and watch the light slowly fade. She's in my arms—she's still warm. There's a perfect temperature and I wait for that…and then, I give her the divine ecstasy of my love. There is no greater high. When we are done, I take her so tenderly. I care for her. I lay her out in beauty. Eternal beauty. And it's all as it should be, ashes to ashes, and dust to dust, with all that is beautiful and divine in between.

Avalon felt as if ice water had been thrown over her to seep into her bones.

She sat back, as if the computer itself was as heinous as the words she read.

She stood, fumbling in her purse for her cell phone, and then for the card that Fin Stirling had given her. She stared at the screen as she looked at the card for his number.

She never dialed.

There was suddenly an explosion of color in the display on the screen, like fireworks going off; along with it came the sound of laughter.

The site was gone. She was looking at nothing but a blank page.

# CHAPTER FIVE

Detective Tom Drayton was tall, bald and as grizzled as an old oak. But he was still a spry man, who, even in retirement, had made certain to keep physically fit.

He lived just outside Biloxi in a comfortable little ranch house. Pictures of what Fin assumed were Tom's children and grand-children were abundant on the walls, the mantel and on the grand piano that sat in the living room. He greeted Fin grimly but with warmth, asking him in and indicating the dining room table, where he'd spread out the contents of several files—those he had retained, perhaps, because they were probably copies of those he had on a case that haunted him still, a case that had gotten away.

"Great family," Fin said, noting the pictures.

"Thanks. Four girls. All married, all with kids, and the old-est daughter's oldest son just gave me a great-grand." He was silent a minute. "Lost my wife three years ago."

"I'm sorry."

Drayton nodded his thanks. "Well, you know, I'd always fig-ured we'd spend our retirement traveling around, following the kids, you know? I have places to stay in Boston, New York, St.

Augustine, Denver… I can go all over the country. Anyway…" He paused for a minute, studying Fin. "That's not why you're here. This damned murder. I gave it everything. Probably tortured the poor girl's parents, grilled her friends, grilled every employee at the casino, looked at the security footage over and over again…and I came up with nothing. She'd been flirting with a croupier—brought him in, but he had at least ten witnesses swear he was off with them for a bachelor party when he left work. Went so far as to follow any security tape I could find, and yes, they were at a bar at another casino, all through the night. The kid was telling the truth—and he was devastated. Thought they'd be hooking up the night after." He shook his head. "Out where she was found…well, I don't know how well you know Mississippi, but you can go a lot of miles with just earth, trees and dirt paths. People come to Biloxi to see Beauvoir—you know, the last home of Jefferson Davis. It's just historic, you know. It's a beautiful old place. Me, I'm a mind that we don't forget history—that thing about repeating it, if you don't remember it, you know? Sorry…anyway, Biloxi is filled with casinos. So, a little history, a lot of gambling and spas. But it's a good city, too, you know—businesses, kids, families, schools. But, yeah, lots of casinos. And people everywhere… Who knows how she met the creep who killed her? Oh, and there are theaters and other places, so it looks like there are lots of weirdos running around, too."

"I wouldn't mind seeing the security tapes you're talking about," Fin said.

"It's getting late."

"I know. I'm sorry."

Drayton nodded and then said, "Well, when did late ever stop a cop? There are folks on down at my old precinct. I probably have a friend who will give us a hand—stayed tight with day and night captains," Drayton said. He shrugged. "I was a good detective—dogged. I found most people I was after. This one…

still bugs the damned hell out of me. And I can tell you…well, I'd just lost my wife, so I worked the hell out of it."

"I'm sure you did," Fin said.

"Have a seat. Everything is there, on the table. Look through it all to your heart's content."

Fin sat at the table, surveying the display before him. One folder contained witness reports. One contained the initial police report taken when Mr. Robert Fryer, the caretaker and tour guide at the General Amos Grimsby estate, had called it in. There was a report on the house itself; it was a Victorian mansion, built circa 1840, and lovingly tended through the years. An absentee owner—Kyle Howard, a descendant of General Grimsby—owned the house, but lived in Tacoma, Washington, and kept a room upstairs for himself and his wife when they visited. Robert Fryer lived in the old guard house and gave folks a tour when they came to visit. The house held period clothing and other memorabilia from the 1800s, including weapons, dinnerware and more. While the house was listed with the state as an official tourist destination, there weren't many die-hard Victorian or Civil War buffs who came through to call for more security for the place.

No cameras. Well, according to the police report, there were cameras, but they were just for show.

"Of course," Fin said to himself.

Another file had information on the victim, Ellen Frampton, a college senior—she was excited to be graduating soon and planned to teach. Her subject: history.

She might have been happy to head out to see the house, except that according to her friends, she hadn't even known about it. They'd all gone to tour Beauvoir, but the rest of the trip had been a spa day and Ellen had loved cheap, silly slot machines with bonuses that held great graphics.

Detective Drayton had been thorough. So thorough. Every

casino employee, it seemed, had been questioned. Her friends at college, friends from home.

There were more pictures of her as she had been found on the porch. There was no blood. But she hadn't died by puncture marks: she'd been stabbed through the heart with a pointed object.

Then he discovered the answer to the question he had not yet broached.

No defensive wounds, no sign of rape, but apparent intercourse after death.

"It's the same sick bastard!" he exploded.

"Pardon—I… You're sure?" Drayton asked, coming back over to the table.

Fin tapped at the report. "Cindy West was killed by two puncture wounds at the throat—this young woman was pierced through the heart. No blood at either crime scene, both women dressed up and displayed. Ellen loved history—she was found at a historic location. Cindy West was a makeup artist—she was found on a tomb in a cemetery where a movie was being filmed. She was laid out exactly as an actress had been earlier, working on a scene."

"It does sound like it could be the same guy," Drayton said. He sat suddenly, as if depleted.

Fin looked at the man and he shook his head.

"If I'd only caught the bastard, this wouldn't have happened again!" Drayton said miserably.

"Listen, you have here what we're going to need," Fin told him. "Your work is solid. I believe it's a stranger killing, and we all know that stranger killings are the hardest. Sir, your work is going to be very important to us."

Drayton nodded, as if a little mollified. "Well, come on now. I have us set up. We can see all the security tapes you want to see."

Fin thanked him. As he was rising, his phone rang. He glanced at the number and it felt as if his heart gave a little tremor of fear.

"Avalon?" he said.

"Yes, it's me. I'm sorry to bother you…"

"I told you to call me any time. Are you safe? Where are you? You're not in any immediate danger, are you? There's a patrolman near—"

"I'm fine. I'm in no danger. I'm in my room at the house in the French Quarter. My room door is locked, the main doors are locked for the night and the fence to the courtyard is locked. But I've just had a strange…incident."

"Go on."

"I mentioned to you that I was going to do a website for a dominatrix. Lauren said that some of the young men who had worked as extras on the movie had been to see her. I don't even remember the conversation, but the dark web came up, so I went on to see what it was… You need special software for the real dark web—and I don't have it, don't want to have it, but… I came across the most bizarre site, and then it disappeared. Fin…" she said, and he thought she had to be highly distracted to have finally used his given name. "Fin, a man was writing about his fantasy murder. And it was so creepy. He wrote, 'I lay her out in beauty.' It made me think of Cindy right away. I started to call you while it was up on my screen, but then it went down."

"All right—I'm in Biloxi at this moment."

"You're in Biloxi?"

"Yes, it's all related. It will be a few hours before I'm back. But speed may be important." He hesitated, knowing that he had to trust someone among her friends. "Find Kevin, please, and stay with him. I'm going to get Ryder to get over to you as quickly as possible with one of his tech people. That will be fastest, and I'm not a tech person. But, Ryder has great guys, as good as agency people." He glanced at his watch, cursing the fact that he couldn't be in two places at one time.

He was decent at working with a computer, but he was nowhere near expert enough to know if the content she'd watched could be found again or traced in any way.

"Avalon, please. Call Kevin to stay with you until Ryder gets there."

"Fin, I'm locked in my room in a locked house."

"Humor me."

"Okay. Maybe Kevin can find—"

"No. Even with Kevin, don't say what you've found."

"He's one of my best friends. You just said to call him."

"Yes. But we don't give out details of a murder and we keep what we can quiet. Obviously, I believe you, and I trust in your faith in Kevin. But people say things inadvertently. I'm hanging up, calling Ryder. Please, Avalon, just do as I say on this."

"All right, yes, fine!"

He ended the call and hit Ryder's number on his speed dial.

Ryder answered right away. He swore that he could get to Avalon in fifteen minutes, with one of the best techs in the business.

"He's going to want to take her computer, though," Ryder warned.

"We'll get her something else to use for now," Fin said. "This may be important."

"And it may be an idiot trying to instigate something on the internet," Ryder said.

"It may be."

"But we're going to look at it just the same. Gotcha."

Tom Drayton had been waiting politely by the entrance to the kitchen. He walked over to the table and asked, "You all right here?"

"Yeah, thanks," Fin said.

"Sometimes, we have to trust in others, you know?"

"Yes, I do," Fin said.

"It's hard."

"Yeah."

"You're welcome to take all these files. I'm not a cop any-more," Drayton said. "But I am here to help. Do you want to see some of that footage? We're set. It's a five-minute drive to the station. You can take your car, too, if you want to get on the road right after."

"I'll do that. And thank you."

"No. Thank *you*. I'll be a happier man if you get the bastard. No, I won't just be happier. I'll sleep better at night, feel some peace."

"This go-around, we have to catch him," Fin said, gathering the files. "You're sure?"

"They're copies—they're mine. Yeah, I'm sure."

Drayton was right about the proximity to the station. He was also right about his relationships. Fin was introduced to several of the officers on the night shift and then the two of them were led to a room with a good-size screen and an officer ready to run security footage.

Tom Drayton walked him through the tapes. He saw the croupiers, the casino guests…and the young woman with her friends, laughing with them, shaking her head at poker and craps, sitting down at a machine where different cats danced across the screen. There were shots from the elevator when she went to her room.

He had footage from the casino where the croupier who had been flirting with her at his table was partying with his friends.

There were more shots of the casino floor on the night that Ellen Frampton had disappeared. Fin watched, searching the crowds, but it was nearing the end of that footage when he noted something at the entrance to the casino.

A car drove up to the valet. And a man stepped from it. He was wearing a long dark coat, like a trench coat, long to the ground. He was wearing a baseball cap; the visor covered most of his face.

He never looked up. He was maybe five-ten—not as tall as

their killer, according to Miss Connor. But the man knew there were cameras, Fin thought, and he was careful that those cameras never captured an image of his face.

Tall… Maybe it was relative.

"There," he said.

"Right. But he never goes in," Drayton pointed out. "Look. He hangs around in front of the casino."

"Can you switch back to the floor?" Fin asked the officer running the footage.

In the other view, Ellen Frampton was at a machine. Then she looked toward the entry, smiling. She cashed out and walked to the front doors of the casino.

The waiting man asked for his car and drove out of the shot.

Ellen Frampton walked out smiling—and she also disappeared from the range of the cameras.

"I think that could be him," Fin said. "Can I get a copy of this?"

The young officer looked at Drayton.

"He's a Fed, working the case. Hell, yes, we can get it to him," Drayton said.

"If you can send it to our offices in New Orleans, that would be great," Fin said.

"Sure thing."

"Did you want to see the Amos Grimsby estate?" Drayton asked him.

"I do. But—"

"I'm at your service anytime tomorrow or whenever you'd like. Too dark now to see much out there, anyway, and I know you're anxious to get back to NOLA."

"Thank you," Fin said. He stood and nodded his thanks to the young officer, then shook Drayton's hand.

"Don't thank me—get him," Drayton said.

Fin nodded and hurried out to his car. At least it was late;

traffic shouldn't be too bad. Still, there was no way out of it—he had an hour-and-a-half drive ahead of him.

He called Ryder as he drove.

Ryder answered on the first ring.

"I'm here. All is well. Jodi Marsh, one of our best technical experts, is with me." He lowered his voice. "And Miss Morgan is just fine. She had a friend with her, waiting for me. She told him I just wanted to talk a little more about makeup and costuming for the women."

"Thank you. Ryder, I owe you."

Ryder laughed at that. "I don't mind being second fiddle on this at all. Are you heading back? Did you get anything?"

"Yes. I'll explain all when I see you. Ryder, I do think that this killer struck before—and it's imperative that we catch him."

"Right. Because if not, he will strike again. Get on back here."

"Going as fast as I can without getting arrested myself."

"See you here. I won't leave your girl until you get here."

They ended the call. Avalon Morgan wasn't "his girl." But...

She was bright, multitalented and had the sense to realize when she had stumbled upon something that might be extremely important. She saw the dead.

There was something about her. The killer had taken a victim and imitated her.

Fin couldn't help it. Every protective instinct in him was rising to the fore. She fascinated him.

That wasn't why he felt this urgency; he believed now, with all his instincts, that the two murders were related. That a clever, organized and very sick serial killer was out there. And Fin was afraid that he should have left Avalon Morgan out of his investigation—he was drawing her in far too close to a killer who'd slain a woman to imitate a scene Avalon starred in.

And that killer might just want the real thing.

★ ★ ★

It had been difficult for Avalon to ask Kevin to come sit with her while she waited for Ryder without telling him the truth as to why Ryder was coming.

But while she could easily resent Special Agent Fin Stirling, she felt that at least he had sound reasons for all that he said and did. It was too easy in conversation to let something slip—she and Kevin were all accustomed to being frank with one another and talking about anything.

She explained that she was just nervous.

"Why would this guy be questioning you at this time of night?" Kevin had responded.

"Because they want to catch this guy. Kevin, we have to catch this guy."

"Right. I know." Kevin shook his head. "I can't even begin to fathom what goes on in the mind of people like this. Remember Brett Thompson from school? He was in the animation program, but by day he was a cop. He told me about the first time he had to shoot someone. Killed the guy, who had a gun leveled at a kidnap victim. Still said that killing a man was the worst feeling imaginable. So, what is it in the mind of these people…? I get sick when I see roadkill."

When Ryder and the tech expert, Jodi Marsh, arrived, they thanked Kevin and let him go.

"You know, you can talk to me anytime, too. Day or night, middle of the night," Kevin had assured Ryder.

And then, after Ryder had gotten Kevin out of her room, she had given her computer to Jodi Marsh, and she had tried to describe the site she'd been on.

Jodi was in her midthirties, a slender woman with short brown hair and a wiry frame. When they first arrived, she was friendly, setting Avalon at ease, and had explained she'd been one of those kids who had been in the "tech wave" and she'd been obsessed with computers ever since.

She asked Avalon to explain just how she'd gotten to the site, and then she asked about it.

Jodi worked with the computer a long time, saying she was probably going to have to take it.

Naturally, Avalon was alarmed; with the movie on hold, her laptop was her source of income.

"Not to worry—we'll see that you're covered," Ryder assured her.

"How?"

"Not sure yet. Our FBI lead is on his way here."

A few minutes later, Ryder's phone rang. "That's Fin. I'm going to go down and let him in."

"There's a keypad—an alarm system at the door. It's changed every day since there are six rooms and people come and go," Avalon said. "I'll go."

She hurried out of her room and down the winding staircase to the communal room and the front door. When she opened it, Fin Stirling was waiting on the step.

It was a strange moment; she barely knew him and yet she felt someone who meant everything had come back into her life.

Her temptation was to throw herself into his arms.

She stood rooted to the spot, though.

And yet she had the odd feeling he wanted to reach out and draw her to him, as well. Hold her tight. Breathe with relief.

She'd never been in any danger, she reminded herself.

They didn't touch. But they stood there a bit too long, the air between them charged.

"Ryder and Jodi are here," she said softly. "Um, let me lock the door and set the alarm."

He stepped in, waiting for her.

She led the way to the staircase, up to her own room.

None of her friends had stirred. The house was almost eerily quiet. Ryder and Jodi greeted Fin; Avalon assumed they all knew each other, because, if she understood it all right, Jodi was with the New Orleans police. "I know how important this is," Avalon said. "If my computer can help, I want you to have it, of course, but… I'm supposed to be taking photos for a website tomorrow and my notes are on the computer and… Should I put that all off?"

"I'm on this now," Jodi said. "Ryder and I will take your laptop to the lab. I've got more tools there," she explained to Avalon. "We'll just work it through the night."

Avalon bundled her computer cable and handed it to Jodi. "I hate for you to be up all night."

"It's part of the gig," Jodi said.

"Don't worry about rushing on my behalf. I'll plan on just taking photos tomorrow. My notes are on the computer, but I haven't even met the client yet, and I'm… I'm a decent actress. I can fake what I don't remember."

"I'll get it back to you as soon as I can—it's a challenge now," Jodi assured her. "Ryder, ready to go? See you, Fin."

The two police officers left, and then she was alone with Fin Stirling.

"Want to tell me about it?" he asked her.

He took the chair in front of the dressing table.

She perched at the foot of the bed, facing him.

"The site was called 'My Fantasy Murder,'" Avalon told him. "It was decently written, which somehow made it more…horrible. He talked about choosing a beauty. He said that beauty came from everywhere—every continent except for Antarctica. He said he'd watch, he'd come close… I can't remember exactly. But he wanted to stalk his beauty and…it was sick! He talked about watching the light go out in her eyes and that he'd lay her out 'in beauty' and then…"

"Then?"

She winced. "I think he rapes these women *after* he kills them."

He stared back at her. She thought something was going on in his mind. Whatever it was, he was good at hiding his reactions.

"I hope they can trace that site," he said fervently.

She nodded. "Do you think that it's related?"

He sighed. "I think almost anything is possible. But, yes, this man who stalks beauty certainly sounds like someone who would display his victim." He paused a minute and then asked, "What the hell were you doing on the dark web?"

"I told you—it just came up in conversation. And I guess... Well, if I'm going to do a website for someone, I'd like to make sure the person I'm working for isn't... I don't know. Doing strange things on the internet."

"And?"

She shook her head. "I didn't find anything about the dominatrix."

"Please, stay off the dark web."

"It isn't my usual," she said. "Um, what were you doing in Biloxi?"

"Studying a similar case."

"Something like this has happened before?"

"Similar." He hesitated. "We're going to have to be careful about how we handle all this—we have to warn the public, but it's important to keep the details close. This web page you found—it could be someone just trying to be outrageous, and see how many hits he, or even she, might get. Then again, someone who displays bodies likes to draw attention to what he sees as his art." He leaned forward, his gaze serious. "You have to remember every person has an agenda. In his eyes, his desires are far more important than the lives he takes. He sees beauty, but he sees it as an end to his own needs, and he sees himself as more important than anyone else. Right now, I don't know if the website was a sensationalist who just likes to create havoc, or if he might be our killer. I don't know if the same killer struck before. We have extensive connections at the headquarters in

DC. Special Agent Angela Hawkins—our own research super-power—is seeing what else we can find. I'll be heading back to Mississippi. And I wouldn't mind at all if you'd come with me."

"I… Okay. I'll help in any way."

She wasn't sure she should go to Mississippi with him. There was a strange tension between them, and she was too aware of it now that he was here in her bedroom.

But she would do anything to help. She wasn't going to cower.

"Should I change my plans for tomorrow? Even if I lose the client, it won't be the end of the world."

"No. But can you see your client in the morning? I'm going to have a meeting, brief the police and other local agents on what we know…and what we don't." His tone softened. "Don't worry, there will be a policeman or an agent with you."

"I wasn't worried. I was going to go from the French Quarter to Magazine Street. I don't need to be followed every step of the way. And Lauren is going to come along."

He nodded, but it didn't seem as though he was agreeing with her.

"Will you be available about one or two in the afternoon? We're going to need to get out to the estate at least a few hours before dark," he said.

"Estate?"

"The body of a young woman was found about two years ago on a historic property—she was in antebellum attire, set on the porch of a seldom-visited site that is still registered and officially a tourist attraction. But it's not a major attraction—one elderly gentleman watches over the property and conducts the occasional tour. The security cameras are fake—the house is in the woods."

"Oh!" Avalon said. "Is that where you were today?"

He shook his head. "Not yet. I was talking to the detective in charge of the case. He's since retired, but the case still haunts him."

"He—he sees the dead, too?" she asked tentatively.

Fin smiled, shaking his head. "No, I mean…he's never really happy, he can't just live his life, because he can't stand the fact that he didn't find the killer. But, anyway, he'll meet us out there. He's given me everything he has on the case. I was with him earlier and watching security camera footage from the casino where the young woman was staying, reading witness reports and talking with him about it. Tomorrow afternoon, I need to speak with the caretaker/guide, and see where she was left."

"Are you hoping we might find someone—a ghost—who saw something, but didn't have the power to tell the detective?"

"That would be handy, but that's not usually how these things work." He grinned. "You know, my field director is a pretty amazing guy. My unit is an amazing place for a man like me to be. We know there are dead who linger. But every one of us also had to make it through the academy, and the logic, persistence and footwork of investigation always come first."

"But why do you want to see the estate, in that case?"

"I want to walk the grounds, see the porch—I want to know if there is anything else there at all that can help us."

"But… Christy Island was crawling with forensic experts and police…"

"And they collected dozens of prints and bits of trash that people don't even know they've left behind. And there's just one thing they've discovered."

"What's that?"

"That nothing they have found is out of the ordinary. Every print they took from any place in the mansion or on the island matches someone who was supposed to be there—the owners, and your cast and crew."

Avalon shook her head. "A killer like that would be careful. I never went through a police or agency academy and I don't pretend to know law enforcement. But even I can figure a killer like that would have worn gloves, that he would have been extremely careful to not leave a thing behind."

"Yes. But somehow, somewhere, he's tripped up. We need to find out where. I want to get back out to Christy Island, too."

She nodded. "And Cindy?"

"She'll be released soon. I believe her cousin has arrived."

"Will…well, I hope she'll speak with us. We want to make sure… I mean, if she doesn't have plans, we may be able to help."

"I can let her know. I believe I'll meet her at some point before we leave tomorrow."

She nodded. He offered her an encouraging smile.

"And thank you," he said softly.

"I didn't know Cindy that long or that well. But she was my friend. And I know to you that doesn't matter—no, I mean, I don't mean it that way! I mean to you, every victim deserves justice. Regardless of who they were."

She was sure she had sounded so horrible.

But he was smiling and inclining his head slightly.

"I understand," he said. He stood. "You should get some sleep. Tomorrow will be a long day for both of us, I imagine. Where would you like to be picked up? Here, or at your client's place?"

Avalon thought quickly. She'd asked Lauren to come with her, and they'd talked about finding lunch and a music venue…

"At the client's on Magazine Street, but then we'll need to drop Lauren back here—she's coming with me. The place is called 'Samara Stella's Theater of the Fantastic.'"

He nodded.

"You know it?"

He grinned and laughed. "Am I a customer? No. But I've been on Magazine Street many, many times and I've passed it."

"Ah. Well, as I said, we'll need to drop Lauren back here."

"That will be fine."

"Great."

"So. Ready to see me out?"

She nodded.

The hall was quiet; she realized it was about one in the morning, but that still didn't mean much of anything. Boris, Brad and all of them were accustomed to working long hours, often through the night.

But if any of them were up and together, they were silent.

She headed downstairs ahead of Fin. At the door, she keyed in the alarm to open it.

Fin Stirling stepped out. Avalon fought the sudden temptation to beg him to stay.

It wasn't that she was afraid. She had told herself that whatever came, she wasn't afraid. She'd learned to live with talking to ghosts, for God's sake!

And she was safe in this house with people she knew.

And still...

Fin lingered on the step. Again, there was a moment when they locked eyes, uncertainty and tension in the air.

Then he said lightly, "I'm going to stand here until you lock the door and key in the alarm. And then call me from your room."

She smiled. "You were just in here. Once I lock the door—"

"Humor me."

"Sure."

She closed the door, locked it and set the alarm.

The house was still dead silent, except for the light sound of the fall of her footsteps as she hurried back up the stairs.

She locked the door to her room and found her phone.

"All locked in," she told him.

"Thanks. See you tomorrow."

"Right."

She thought he was going to say more. The line stayed open a moment, then it went dead.

And she wondered if she was dreading whatever would come the next day...

Or if she wasn't looking forward to it a little.

Because whatever came, she would be with him.

# CHAPTER SIX

*Wednesday*

Fin stood in the local offices, prepared with video and every note he had. The room was filled with agents, NOPD and state police. He shared with them what he had learned—all they knew about Christy Island, the owners and the cast and crew of the movie. Boat captains had been vetted. Every possible stone was being turned, with the dirt beneath it investigated.

He was glad he knew so many of his fellow agents in the local office, and that he'd also worked so closely with the police before.

Then he shared everything he'd learned from Tom Drayton, and the possibility that this killer had struck before.

He was questioned as a matter of course, especially when he pointed out the drawing done of the man who had last seen Cindy West alongside the video surveillance from the casino in Biloxi.

"The clothing isn't the same," an officer pointed out.

"That's true—but the method of choosing victims might be

the same. We're working on recovering a site that appeared briefly on the dark web—"

"Fin? Sir!" Jodi Marsh had come into the room. "The site had a cherry bomb!" she said.

Everyone turned to look at her.

"We're still trying to trace the origin, but it was put up with a cherry bomb—that meant that it exploded, or disappeared, at a certain time. Whoever put it up knew to take it down in a way that would make it almost impossible to trace."

"Thanks, Jodi," he said. And he went on to explain what had been on it, to the best of his ability, aware he was paraphrasing what had been paraphrased by Avalon. He told the group his words were far from exact, but he gave the gist of the site. "The killer stalks his prey and loves beautiful women. But for him, the sexual gratification doesn't come until his beauty is dead."

"Necrophilia," someone said.

Another officer cleared his throat. "It is legal in Louisiana and a few other states," he said. "Even though I'm not sure how—"

"Murder is not legal," Fin said. "And, yes, there are still strange laws on the books...and not on the books. But the point of this is the girl was taken by a man. He murdered her, and she was young and had years of that life before her. She had spent the night out with friends drinking, so whether he plied her with more alcohol or not, we don't really know. She went with him willingly, so he might have been familiar to her. You've seen the sketch and have an idea of what his appearance was when he met her on the street. We believe he knows or stalks his victims, and one way or the other, has a good story or a good pickup line."

"The other murder was two years ago," an officer said. "Can we be sure that they're related?"

"No, but there is a chance."

"A victim every two years?" another officer asked. "Then..."

Fin knew what the officer was thinking. Thankfully, it might mean there wouldn't be a new victim soon. It also made him harder to catch.

"What we're sure of is this—Cindy West was working as the lead makeup artist for a low-budget movie being filmed on Christy Island. Everyone involved—from the cast and crew to the owners of the island—has an alibi for the time the murder occurred with at least one other person. Those alibis may be lies, but we haven't been able to prove that anyone has been lying. Boat captains, caterers and those connected with the island in any way have been questioned. She was last seen outside a pizza parlor on Bourbon Street meeting up with the man in the sketch. There was a murder two years ago near Biloxi where the victim was bled dry and posed in a chair in costume. We're following the lead on the person who wrote the site—with the cherry bomb. Now it's difficult here to tell you all to watch out for unusual activity. We believe the killer stalks his victims, so be aware of anyone who seems to be following a woman or watching her covertly. This doesn't mean we stop every man in the street who looks up when an attractive woman goes by—you are all smart. This is New Orleans. You've all learned to go for more dangerous crime amid chaos. Keep your eyes open, please."

Ryder spoke next and questions were posed and answered. And then, at last, the task-force meeting had come to an end, and all Fin had left to do was the scheduled press conference.

He was glad to be doing it himself; people needed to know to beware.

They didn't need intimate details, though, and at this time, he wouldn't inform the public of the murder in Mississippi.

As he spoke, he wondered why camera flashes had to be so bright and annoying when most cell phones could capture an image just as well.

But he managed to ignore them for the most part.

He was anxious for it to be over, and the afternoon to come.

★ ★ ★

People watched people.

Men watched women.

Women watched men.

He watched her.

Her every movement was lithe and filled with grace.

Her laughter was music.

He'd brushed by her for the briefest touch…

Her hair was silk, and her eyes were pure magic.

Anticipation was a sweet emotion. Dreaming filled the heart and mind with gladness, with purpose, with a love and desire for the future.

He could imagine her. Taking his time, enjoying the silk feel of her hair as he held her. He could imagine her eyes, the crystalline beauty of them as they met with his. The light within them, the fantastic light and emotion.

He could imagine…her. The warmth of her…

And the coldness, slipping in as he held her, as light faded, as she became his, really his.

Yes, anticipation, so sweet it was almost a taste upon the lips.

He watched. And he waited. Anticipation, so sweet, so savory…

Because he knew his turn was coming.

"Are you ready for this?" Lauren asked.

Avalon laughed. They were about twenty feet from the door to Samara Stella's establishment and Lauren looked uncomfortable.

"I'm ready, but are you? Lauren, you don't have to go in."

"I guess I just wonder if people think, seeing us go through that door, that we want to become part of a dominatrix…crew. Or worse! If they think we want to be chained up, or walked around on a dog leash, or… I don't even know what else."

"I'm not really too worried about people I'll never see again or don't know me from Adam…or Eve," Avalon said.

The words were barely out of her mouth when a middle-aged man stopped in front of them, staring at Avalon.

"You're…her! I saw you on that show. You were great! Oh, my goodness, I love Texas history, and…man, you played that woman well."

"I, uh, thank you," Avalon said. She smiled. "Thank you very much."

"Is it possible…? Would you give me an autograph?"

"Sure."

"And a picture? My wife isn't going to believe that I got to meet you!"

"Of course."

The man pulled out his camera and came to stand by Avalon, ready to do a selfie.

"Oh, please… Let me help you," Lauren said, grinning as she took the man's camera and stepped back.

"May I put an arm around your shoulder?" he asked politely.

"Sure," Avalon said. She smiled for the camera. He didn't have paper; he asked her to sign his jacket.

"That could ruin a perfectly good jacket—" Avalon said.

"Please."

She signed his jacket, chatted a minute longer and then said goodbye. At Avalon's side, Lauren was laughing. "They won't know you from Adam…or Eve! Well, at least I'm a behind-the-camera girl. They really won't know me. Oh, I can see the headlines—young, up-and-coming actress known for her work as historical figures seen entering dominatrix den!"

"Ha, ha, Lauren. How about young actress who doesn't want to be broke working on a website?"

"All right, all right. Hey, coast is clear—let's slip in."

Lauren said the words, but they both paused. Windows in front advertised the establishment with pictures of Samara Stella in black leather and lace, wielding a whip, holding a dog collar and bending low over a table filled with chains.

"Wow," Lauren muttered.

"All in a day," Avalon said. "You don't have to come in."

"Right. You bought me that great breakfast, and now I'm going to cop out on you."

"You really can."

"Open the damned door!"

Avalon grinned and opened the door. The reception area was sumptuous. A beautiful—and very well-endowed—blonde sat behind the counter wearing a leather halter top and studded leather headband. She smiled when she saw them.

"You must be the web designer! Or designers," she said.

"Yes. Hi. I'm Avalon Morgan, and this is Lauren Carlson."

"Pleased to meet you," the girl said. "Excuse me, I'll just call Miss Stella."

As the girl worked her interoffice phone, Lauren whispered to Avalon, "She looks pretty normal."

Avalon elbowed her.

A moment later, Samara Stella walked out.

She really was a striking beauty. Someone in her background had most probably been Asian; someone else had been African American, and someone else from somewhere in Europe. It all combined and created a stunning woman with bronze skin, flashing eyes that were a startling hazel—both the green and brown in them being bright—and long, elegantly straight hair in something close to pitch-black. She had a warm smile.

"Hey, thank you so much for coming! I've seen your work, sites you've done for several old friends, acquaintances and co-workers. Great stuff!"

"Thank you," Avalon said.

Samara smiled at Lauren. "And I know who you are, too. You did the makeup on the young child actor for that last comic-book-superhero movie. That was wonderful."

Lauren stared at her in shock for a minute. No one, outside of the business, ever paid attention to the credits.

"I… Thank you!"

The woman laughed. "Hey, I didn't start out this way. I was going to be a great Shakespearian actress. It just didn't work out—with me making a living, at any rate. Come on in and I'll give you the lay of the land, and you can tell me what my new site should look like."

Lauren glanced at Avalon with a subtle shrug. She was obviously liking Samara Stella far more than she'd been expecting she might.

They went through large black doors into the "parlor." A cushy black sectional sofa surrounded a shiny black table. Deep red cushions picked up the colors in the lush carpeting.

A large screen advertised the various pleasures to be enjoyed. Spankings were available, a special when they were "served" along with the drink of the day and the house chicken wings.

"You serve food, too?" Lauren asked her.

"Some of the best in New Orleans. My family includes Creole chefs, Cajun chefs and my one grandma, who made a killer meat loaf. Well, as she would say, she *prepared* a killer meat loaf—the animals 'made' the meat. Anyway, yes, we have a kitchen, but again, I wasn't making it as just a restaurant. This is New Orleans—competition is fierce. Not that there isn't enough room for countless good restaurants, but…well, I'm horrible at marketing. This way, I'm making a living. A good living." She grinned.

They went through other rooms that offered "stages," along with a few private rooms with various forms of equipment—feather whips lined the walls of one room.

"For the guy—or gal who is in to pretend," their hostess explained.

"I see."

"The 'theater' room is mine. It's our largest and we have some decent shows—some I just twisted after a playwriting class in college. Fantasies. Anne of Boleyn is about to go get her head chopped off, but rather than lament her fate, she beats down a guard and gets Henry the Eighth on a leash. It's an alternate view on history I would love to have seen."

Lauren laughed and Avalon realized her friend was having fun.

"Okay, I have a concern," she said.

"What's that?"

"Does the same person deliver the food…and a spanking on a bare butt?"

Samara laughed. "Come see the answer to the question. My mama 'beat' a few things into me herself before she passed. We're… I'd say we're one of the cleanest places in town!"

There were two food-prep workers in the kitchen, one a middle-aged woman with a quick smile, the other an older man, equally quick to smile; both were wearing gloves and apologized for not shaking hands. They were working on prep for lunch, which started around eleven thirty.

"My aunt and uncle," Samara explained. "Sophie and Taylor. And as far as serving goes…"

She brought them into a dressing room where several young women were getting ready for the day. One was dressed as Alice in Wonderland, another looked as if she was ready to take on the world like Wonder Woman…except in scanty leather biker attire.

"I serve food," Alice said, displaying disposable little white gloves.

"No spankings," Samara assured her.

"All right," Avalon said, surprised she was almost excited to come up with a website that would extol the food, along with all the aspects of the venue. "What we need to do is bring in the average person. For instance, honestly, Lauren and I wouldn't have wandered in. We need a menu that shows this as theatrical for those who just want fun, food, some drinks…and just a small step into the wild side. Then, of course, we need to show there are other delights to be had, too."

Avalon got to work. She took pictures of the kitchen and beautifully plated food, and poses of the girls in their very different apparel. Lauren helped, holding and angling the small light Avalon had brought, making sure the leather gleamed and the girls' eyes popped in their photos.

Then she, Samara and Lauren sat down and talked about the site.

It seemed that one o'clock rolled around too swiftly. Avalon was still speaking about the site when her phone rang.

Fin Stirling had arrived, and was standing outside.

"I'll get your guest," Samara said.

"Oh, I think he just needs us to come out—"

But Samara was gone. A minute later, she returned to her office with Fin. He was casual, in a soft charcoal jacket over jeans and a white tailored shirt unbuttoned at the neck.

"A two-minute eye-opener," he said to Samara as they entered. "I am anxious to see the site that Avalon creates."

"My aunt was *preparing* especially for you," Samara said, looking a little distraught at Avalon and Lauren and then Fin. "Do you have a minute?"

"Well, we are on the clock, but I don't think another twenty minutes will hurt if you won't mind if we eat and run," Fin said, smiling and polite.

Samara beamed, hit a call button on her phone and a minute later her aunt and uncle arrived, bearing trays of food.

The jambalaya was some of the best Avalon had ever eaten. They all raved over it, and Samara told them about a few of her other twisted history skits. When they had eaten, Fin apologized, saying they did have to run. They all bid each other goodbye, Avalon promising she'd send Samara a mock-up of what she intended.

Outside they headed to Fin's car with Lauren still exclaiming in wonder. "She's not what I expected at all! I mean, she may wield one mean whip, but…she's cool. She's still selling sex, sort of, but not what I expected. I—I had fun!"

"It was interesting, beyond a doubt," Avalon agreed. "And I think we need to emphasize the entertainment side and the food. And what's there for those who are a little more serious, though, honestly, from what I've heard…"

Fin glanced her way, grinning slightly, arching an eyebrow. "From what you've heard?"

"Samara's pretty mild, just playing at what she does. Which is fine—I mean, oh… I don't know what I mean. She advertises as a dominatrix, but I think it's really for tourists. It's not serious kink. Wow. Hmm. Okay, so… Lauren, what's your plan for today?" Avalon asked.

"Sleep!" Lauren told her. She sighed. "I've received several offers, projects needing more help in the makeup departments. There's so much going on in New Orleans right now. I guess I need to make sure it's okay to accept something, find out if Boris is going to need anything else…hey!" she said, turning to Fin. "Do I ask you?"

Fin nodded. "We just need people to stay in the area. I'd also ask you to be especially careful—whoever did this has something, a quality of friendship, that put Cindy West at ease. She was probably trusting and laughing until—until she died. Lauren, you need to make sure you're in public, and with people you trust."

He'd driven to the house where they were all staying; he pulled in front.

"We'll watch until you're through that gate," he assured Lauren.

Lauren smiled. "Thank you!"

She got out of the car and used her key to open the gate, stepping through it. When the gate closed and locked, Fin drove back out onto the street.

"I-10," he said. "And Mississippi."

They drove for a while in silence. Avalon stared out the window as the city turned to suburbs.

Then Avalon asked, "Are you hoping that maybe Ellen Frampton is…still there?"

He shook his head and glanced her way. "Would you hang around a place in the middle of nowhere where your body was discovered after you were murdered?"

"No, but ghosts do sometimes hang around cemeteries. Sometimes, the cemetery is like…hmm. A social club?"

"It's my belief—and I could be wrong—that those who stay do so to right a wrong, fix something with their family or loved ones, guard a place…and those I've known tend to enjoy *life*. They head for music, activity…and, yes, sometimes head back to the cemetery because it becomes a meeting place. I am hoping that we may see…someone. Or maybe you'll see what I don't see."

"Because you still don't trust my friends."

He glanced her way. "I mainly trust your friends, otherwise one of them would already be under arrest, and I'd make damned sure the rest of you weren't staying in the same house."

"Oh!"

"But we do have experts tracking the movements of everyone who might be involved over the last several years."

"Ah. Nothing on the website yet, right?"

He shook his head. "Cherry bomb."

"Cherry bomb?"

"I wasn't familiar with the term. Jodi used it—the site more or less exploded. You can't trace anything on it. You weren't deep into the dark web. Jodi is determined now to get in and find anything that resembles the site you described. And Jodi is good."

"I wish I'd thought to snap a picture of the page. But I've never seen anything explode in a…cherry bomb before."

"Because you don't play around on the dark web most of the time," he reminded her. "And don't start—Jodi is in tech, but she's a trained cop, too."

"I wasn't really planning a lifetime of exploring the dark web," Avalon said dryly. Then she forgot the bit of resentment she had felt. "The way he wrote…it was chilling. I can't imagine thinking that way. Fleeting, and yet so chilling."

"We will find this man," he said quietly. "This killer."

She nodded, not replying, and looked out the window as they traveled I-10.

"So. Where are you from?" he asked her.

"Florida," she said. "I was born in St. Augustine. We moved to Gainesville when my mom took a job down there as a professor. Then I went to school in Orlando because they have a wonderful program for artists, actors, musicians, dancers and more there. And since school…um, at the moment, I'm in transit. Lauren wants me to move in with her. And it's true that there is so much going on in New Orleans. She has had to turn down work. Lauren is really good at what she does."

"I imagine you're really good, too."

"Well, I hope so. I prefer theater."

"You'd love it up by me."

"Oh?"

"The founder of my unit is a man named Adam Harrison. He's filthy rich, by his own genius. But he's one of those people who spreads that wealth all over. He purchased an old crumbling theater and several of my coworkers have spouses and friends associated with it. There's a children's theater, too. It's great. I go whenever I can."

"Nice," Avalon said genuinely. It pleased her that he enjoyed the theater.

"Adam does a lot more, too. He gives money to more charities than I can count." He glanced her way with an awkward grin. "It helps us, as well. When a case calls for more than Uncle

Sam can afford, he's there. He's generous with his own money and very thrifty with Uncle Sam's."

"He sounds great."

"He is. It's kind of strange—the first Krewe case was here. As in New Orleans."

"Not so strange. They claim to be the most haunted city in the United States."

He laughed. "I believe that Savannah, Salem and maybe St. Augustine also make that claim. But, places with history…yes, well, a tumultuous history would provide more in the way of those who linger behind. Emotions that linger behind, horrors that linger…and good things, too."

"Does Adam Harrison see the dead?"

He smiled. "Only one, and his son was dead several years before Adam could see him. He'd always known Josh was special. When Josh was killed in an accident, he was with his best friend and something seemed to transfer to her… From then on, Adam had a talent for finding people with the talent. Anyway, he didn't establish the Krewe as a place for agents who saw ghosts—he'd have been laughed out of Washington. He established it as a unit to deal with the bizarre, like these murders."

"I see," she said. "I guess I can understand that."

"We've caught some flak over being labeled the 'ghost busters' unit," Fin said, shrugging as he stared straight ahead at the road. "But we have one of the highest solve rates to be found in law enforcement anywhere."

She grinned. "Well, you do have help sometimes, right?"

He returned her grin quickly. "Hell, yeah. And if we can put murderers away, I'm not at all adverse to any help we get."

"You're from here, you said?" she asked him. "As in New Orleans?"

"Kenner—close enough."

"And close enough to Christy Island."

He nodded, and then sighed. "Which means I'm aware of

how easy it is for someone to slip on or off the island. You can drag just about any small boat up on shore several places. When I was a kid, it was reputed to be haunted and most people stayed away. Kids will be kids. Teenagers from my high school went there fooling around, and Mr. Christy threw the book at them. People tended to give it a wide berth then—why would you want to get in trouble for stepping foot on such a godforsaken place, anyway? Haunted. Mosquito-ridden, often enough. And there were absolutely no reports of buried pirate treasure there, so why bother? Trespass where there are rumors of one or the other Lafitte brothers burying some gold or jewels."

"So…you've always lived here?"

He shook his head. "New York City for college, the academy and Virginia. I just came back here recently—and we're based in DC, or, technically, Northern Virginia."

"Ah. So. You'll go back there."

"For a base, yes. I'll always come back here," he said. "You?"

"I love everywhere I've lived. They're all home."

They drove in silence again for a while. She was surprised that it wasn't an uncomfortable silence.

Eventually he glanced her way and asked, "How did your picture-taking for your website planning go this morning?"

"Good. It wasn't what I expected."

"What were you expecting? A den of total debauchery?"

She laughed. "Well, Samara Stella does advertise as a dominatrix and I have friends who think that all of New Orleans is a den of debauchery."

He laughed softly. "I know. I have friends with kids who are afraid to visit. I sometimes need to remind friends that people procreate in New Orleans and there's all kinds of activities for children. Oh, there's a sign—we're coming up to the turnoff."

They'd exited the highway before reaching the exits for Biloxi. They were on a two-lane road that had been paved, but not recently.

"Where are we?"

"Not far from Biloxi."

"I've been to Biloxi! It's big, and busy."

"I said we're not far from Biloxi."

"Far enough."

"Exactly," he said softly.

They turned off the poorly paved road onto a road that wasn't paved at all. A road sign advertised the General Amos Grimsby Historic Site.

The dirt road led to an arch with two stone towers on either side of an iron gate. However, there was no fencing or wall around the property, just the gate that closed off the property from cars.

The gate opened as they approached it. Another vehicle was already there, a sturdy, no-nonsense truck.

Two older men stood by the truck, talking.

Fin eased up next to the truck and parked the car.

"They're waiting for us," Avalon noted. "Or waiting for you. Are we late?"

"Precisely on time," Fin said.

Avalon exited the car and joined Fin as he approached the two men. He introduced her to the younger of the two men. "Avalon Morgan, retired Detective Tom Drayton. And, sir, I believe you must be Robert Fryer?"

"I am, sir." He shook hands with Fin and Avalon and told them, "I read about that murder in New Orleans. Not much in the papers or on the news in the way of detail, but something about the reporting made me think that some things were being held back on purpose. I would have called Detective Tom here myself if he hadn't called me. I tell you, I didn't know the lass, but finding her..."

His voice trailed as he choked up.

"I understand," Fin said.

Robert Fryer looked at Avalon. "Are you a police officer, young lady?"

"No, sir."

"I recognize you."

"Avalon is an actress," Fin said.

"Oh. Right—I know where I saw you. You're dancing in one of those music-video things."

"Yes, for a group called Frankie and the Phish," Avalon said. She'd been one of several dancers; she was surprised the man had seen the video, much less recognized her from it.

She gave him a weak smile.

He was frowning. "Are you an actress and a psychic then?"

"No, no," Fin said quickly, and added, "Avalon was with a friend when they came upon the body of the woman killed on Christy Island. We're looking for similarities."

"Ah, of course," Fryer said, shaking his head. "I'm so sorry," he told Avalon.

"Thank you," she said.

"We believe, from what Tom has shown me, that we are looking for the same killer," Fin said. "I know it's painful, but if you'd walk us through the day you found her?"

Robert Fryer nodded. He pointed to one of the little gate-house structures. "That's my place. I came out, ready to open the house for the day. People don't come but maybe a few a month, and still, we are on the register, and I'm always ready to give a tour. I started up the walk there and looked at the porch." He paused to point again, indicating the cameras that looked out from the second-story balcony. "Those're fake, just for show. We don't get trouble out here. We probably should have an alarm system, but we had Waldorf until just before it all happened. Waldorf...well, he was a good-size shepherd and barked loud enough to be heard all the way to Biloxi if someone came at night. It was the strangest thing—the dog didn't bark by day, but he knew no one was supposed to be around at night. He made it to almost the ripe old dog age of sixteen and passed a few months before this happened. Anyway, I was walking toward the porch and… I just stone-cold stopped. She looked beautiful, young lady in a lovely Civil War dress, just sitting there, hat dipped low over her face, her hands just resting all pretty on the wicker chair. At first, I thought someone was going to take pictures and was just waiting for me to wake up, but the gates were closed. That meant that no cars came in close to the house, and I turned and didn't see one down the path. 'Miss!' I called out and got no answer. And I walked on up the path wondering then if she was passed out drunk, if some idiots had come in the night drinking down the road somewhere and forgotten she was with them. I walked up to her and touched her, and it was then that I realized she was dead. I almost fell off the porch. I didn't touch her again, or anything else near her, and I called the police. Officers came out and Tom arrived right after they got here. He had the medical examiner right behind him. Even then, it was bizarre. She was just pale and beautiful—I didn't know at first that she'd been stabbed through the heart, bled out and cleaned and then dressed up as someone might dress up a doll. Still get sick thinking about it—someone taking that poor girl's life like that and then—then…"

He stopped; Robert Fryer wasn't going to say more.

"Was anything touched in the house?" Fin asked.

"No, sir, and I would have known. I know this place like the back of my hand. I know every little relic in it. Whoever did this never entered the house—they just brought her through the woods and set her on the porch. I swear. Now, they had to have come through the woods because there is—and always has been—rough foliage by the gates. And I like to think I would have woken up with someone coming that close."

"There was no rain," Tom Drayton said. "But our forensic people couldn't find prints of any kind. Whoever did this was wearing gloves. They knew how to make sure they didn't leave anything behind."

"Tom, Mr. Fryer, would you mind if Avalon and I take a walk around here?" Fin asked.

"No, sir, I don't mind a thing that you do. I'd be happy to give you a tour of the house, if you'd like, too."

"Thank you," Fin said. "Right now, we're going to walk, if you don't mind."

"Be my guest."

Fin headed around the men and up to the porch, pausing to look at the steps, and at the wicker chair that sat near the door.

"This is where it was?"

"Yes, sir, just about," Fryer said.

Fin nodded his thanks and then looked at Avalon. "Shall we take a walk around?"

She nodded.

He caught her hand; she was glad of it. They started around the porch to the back of the house.

The size of the place was in its two stories, she thought. It might have been about five thousand square feet altogether, a perfect square. It didn't take any time to walk around to the back.

There was a bit of lawn, but not much. Forest stretched out behind it in all directions.

"Trees and trees and…a few gaps," Fin said, and pointed.

He started walking toward a narrow opening, drawing her along with him.

"Fin?"

He stood still for a minute once he had started through.

"It is a trail," he said. "Come on, let's see where it takes us."

They walked through brush and foliage.

The trail twisted and turned and finally broke out to a patch of earth with another trail behind it. He hurried toward it.

Since he still had her hand, Avalon had little choice but to follow.

He stopped again and pointed, and she could see through to the trail's end, where a narrow opening led to a paved road.

"He didn't come alone," he said.

"I can see what you mean or what you were looking for, but why do you think that?"

"I don't think one man could have come here and gotten through the trees and brush carrying her weight and keeping her so…pristine. I think he had help. The same on Christy Island. It's one thing to drag a body around. Another to create such a display. There isn't one killer. Or, at least, he has someone abetting him when it comes to disposing of—*displaying*—the body."

Avalon stared at him, and she felt a strange sensation of cold, thinking at first it was because of his words.

But then she heard a voice behind her.

"Miss?"

Avalon swung around, feeling the brush of a chill on her shoulder as the voice continued.

"There *were* two of them. Two of the monsters, all in black, carrying the poor wee lass through all this, so careful, and laughing and commending one another and warning each other they must take care. And then she was there, so young, so lovely… so dead!"

She and Fin had been joined by the dead.

Behind Avalon stood a girl of about eighteen wearing a blue dress that might have been a day gown worn by a woman of substance a century and a half ago. Her eyes appeared huge and blue, her hair was a soft brown, and she had a mournful look as she shook her head sadly.

"Forgive me… I felt something about you, miss. You see me…you hear me. You…" She paused, looking at Fin. "You both see and hear me!"

Fin bowed his head in recognition.

"We do," he said softly. "And anything you can tell us will help. Anything at all."

# CHAPTER SEVEN

"Alana Grimsby Howard," the young woman told them with a curtsy. Fin introduced the two of them, grateful Avalon had come with him.

The young spirit had seen something in Avalon. Something special, or "sensed" it rather, as she had said.

After the introduction, he explained he was with the FBI, and then thought he might have to explain the FBI to her.

But Alana waved a hand in the air. "I have been around a very, very long time!" she said. "Love my home," she explained to them. She let out a breath. "My father, wounded, came home to die. My husband, wounded, came home to die. Then there was fever... I know they whispered I didn't have the will to fight it, but they were so wrong—I was a mother, and I would have done anything to stay with my child."

"I'm so sorry!" Avalon said.

"It's all right, and we're here together now."

"General Grimsby and your husband have remained, too?"

The spirit nodded. "My poor father! Such a good man. He hated the war. He had always been a military man and my mother came from money. She passed years before the war, peacefully, in my father's arms. Despite his position, he was against what happened. He always hated the very concept of slavery—he said a human soul could not be owned. But he also loved his home, Mississippi… Anyway, the war took a toll, but I think maybe he stayed because he became such an ardent believer in a cause that wasn't his when it began, but became his. He believes we will all move on when all men and women cease to be cruel and hateful to one another and learn that God created all human beings."

"That may be a long, long time…" Avalon said dryly. Then she looked at Fin with dismay, clearly wishing she had bit her tongue.

"I think that we just have to pray that we keep moving forward on that score," Fin said, not wanting to crush her hope, yet wondering if such a day could ever come.

"The law must help us all move forward!"

"The law does help," Fin said. "But, as I'm sure your father knows, the law may be one thing changing the hearts and minds of some people is a monumental task. But it goes on. Some human beings are born…twisted. Some are taught a cruel way, but some are monsters, such as the ones who did this thing to the young woman who was left on your porch."

Alana nodded. "I was so—so horrified when they came that night. I didn't understand at first what they'd done, what they were doing…"

"When they came, was she…" Avalon faltered.

She looked to him for help. He nodded gravely to the ghost of Alana Grimsby Howard. "When they brought her, she was dead and dressed as she was found?"

Alana nodded.

"Might your father or husband know more?"

"I woke them when I saw what was being done. There were, sir, as you surmised, two of them. They were all in black. I don't know what they had on their faces, but they wore masks of some kind, made of material, and they formed to their faces. They wore black trousers and long-sleeved black shirts. They meant to blend in with the darkness."

Fin walked out to the road.

Ellen Frampton had been murdered two years ago. Two years of rain and storms had come and gone.

He studied the poor dirt road where they stood, anyway, mentally tracing back the way that it might lead out of the forested area.

Easy enough. The killers had taken I-10, just as they had, to reach the mansion. But had they come from the east or the west?

There had to be a base of operations somewhere; a place where they took their victims, where the women were killed and drained of blood and dressed like dolls for display.

But where?

He had to wonder where else these killers might have struck; with signatures so similar, they had to be the same. Or could it be worse, could there be more murders that they hadn't discovered yet?

Might there be even more than two people involved?

Aware that he was being watched by Avalon and Alana—the living and the dead, he thought dryly—he searched the road. He wondered how silly he must look as he thrashed through the bushes, long grasses and trees that grew close to the road.

The forestry service or road-maintenance crews must have kept the road open, and so they would have been over it several times in the last years.

But they would have kept the road cleared—they wouldn't have dealt with the heavy growth that encroached beside it.

"Fin?" Avalon asked softly.

He stopped and shook his head. He needed a team out there. And it might bring them nothing. He knew that Tom Drayton had ordered a forensic team out, but Fin didn't think they had

searched the road here. They had never known how the killers
had arrived to set up their victim.

"Fin?" Avalon said again.

"What are you looking for?" the ghost of Alana asked.

"I have no idea. Something. Anything. They can't be perfect.
I don't care what they know about forensics and law enforcement. They can't be perfect."

He was muttering; sounding a little crazed, he thought.
Maybe he was.

These killers couldn't get away with it.

His mind was racing, as well. One man had lured Cindy West
away when she had left the pizza parlor. One man was in the
video surveillance from the casino.

Were they a team?

Were there more of them? He thought about the murder fantasy website.

What else went on in the true dark web?

"Okay," Avalon said. She started fighting through the bushes
with him. He was happy to have her join, even though finding anything was a long shot. It was a thankless task and she finally stopped.

"We need to go back," she said.

"There has to be something—"

"We need to go back and get flashlights—that would help
tremendously. The undergrowth causes too much darkness."

He had been bending low over a thorny bush, and now
straightened.

She was right. And nothing was going to change in the time
it would take them to do this right, to do a thorough search.

"We'll head back."

He led the way, aware that Avalon followed close with the
ghost of Alana Grimsby Howard just behind her.

They wove through the path and back to the house. Tom
Drayton and Robert Fryer were on the porch. Tom was sitting

on the steps; Robert was sitting in the chair—the wicker chair where Ellen Frampton had been left. Maybe it wasn't the same chair. But Fin wondered.

Tom stood, looking at Fin anxiously.

Fin told him, "I think I know how the killer brought her here and I think he had help. We found a trail that leads to a dirt road—"

"There are a lot of dirt roads around here," Tom said, frowning.

"But not that many that lead to gaps in the forest," Robert Fryer said. He looked at Fin hopefully.

Fin nodded. He thought about where they were and remembered that with all his friends at the force, Tom was still retired.

"I'm going to get a team out there," he said.

Tom nodded. "Might be better you try to do it. They might just think that I'm…obsessed. Unable to let it go. And I think that… I don't know. I am obsessed. Best if you bring in agents. Fresh eyes."

Fin nodded and pulled out his phone. He called headquarters and spoke with both Jackson Crow and Angela Hawkins. Jackson would get him a team out there as fast as possible.

Angela was cross-referencing murder scenes from across the country, to search for anything that echoed this case. And she was getting someone in their office on the dark web, searching for sites like the one Avalon had so briefly discovered.

"What do we do now?" she asked.

He smiled. "Wait."

Robert Fryer stood up. He shivered slightly though the day wasn't cold, and Fin thought that he was feeling that Alana was near.

He opened the door to the house, indicating that they should come in.

"I'll tell you about the place, if that's okay. I don't think I can just sit, and it would be really rude of me to go watch a game show or read a book," Robert said.

"He gives a great tour," Alana whispered to them.

The house might not be important as having belonged to a president or a famous statesman, but it was a beautiful display of the Victorian era. Portraits of the general and his wife took precedence over the mantel in the large entry. The floor was hardwood, covered with handsomely knit rugs.

"The land came to the Grimsby family early in the 1800s," Robert Fryer said, compelled to give his speech. "Verne Grimsby, father of General Amos Grimsby, started the house in the 1830s—it was completed, as it stands now, by 1855. Amos Grimsby went to West Point and fought in the Mexican War alongside Grant, Sherman, Lee and Longstreet—all men on the same side at the time. Amos gave speeches against secession. He might have owned a lot of property, but he was never a planter. In his memoirs, he admitted that he should have upped and left because he didn't believe in the institution of slavery, but he was a Mississippi man born and bred. He was injured at Shiloh, and came home to die, just weeks before his son-in-law, Arthur Howard, was also injured—to make it home to die in the bedroom upstairs. Alana Grimsby Howard nursed both her father and her husband until both took their last breaths. She succumbed to a fever soon after herself, leaving her child, Ezekiel, to the care of a cousin who raised the boy. The current owner of the house is a direct descendant of General Grimsby who maintains the house as a historic venue, believing that the home showcases the Victorian era in the United States. If you'll follow me, you'll see the grand dining room, and the kitchen—a small area added in the late 1800s when the original kitchen, outside, burned down after an electrical storm. Please..."

Robert Fryer walked ahead of them, pointing out the woodwork on the dining table in the grand dining room that could sit up to twenty guests. There was a music room that offered a grand piano, a violin on a stand and a harpsichord.

"Grimsby was a great believer in education…for everyone," Fryer told him. "And his daughter, Alana, was a talented musician. She was adept with all the instruments here and was said to have the voice of an angel."

"I imagine that she did," Avalon said. "It's a beautiful home." He noted that she glanced toward Alana as she spoke.

Alana smiled.

"Well," Alana whispered to them, "the place is haunted. But not by that poor young woman. I believe…well, I'm not that experienced, but I believe she went on. I had to stay… I couldn't leave Ezekiel. He did grow to be a fine young man. I think he sensed me near sometimes, and his father and grandfather, as well."

"Her son, Ezekiel, had children?" Fin said.

"Ezekiel had four sons. He became a college professor and two of his sons went the same route—one became a state senator, and one went on to open a vocational school."

"That's wonderful. I know that Ezekiel's parents would have been extremely proud," Fin said, glancing at Alana, too.

Robert paused, shivering a little again, as if something inside him sensed Alana there, even if he couldn't pinpoint the cause of his chill.

"Impressive—and amazing that the house and so many articles from the family and the period remain here," Tom commented.

Robert Fryer nodded and added dryly, "You know, we had the occasional visitor—the true historian who was interested in people and lifestyles…and, sometimes, just the person heading from Biloxi to Vicksburg, still a buff, not just so rabid. But in the last two years, more people come. Now that we're haunted. I mean, we must be—by that young lady left to be discovered on our porch. I suppose it's good for the house. Great for the upkeep. But it doesn't do much for my faith in humanity." His shoulders sagged.

But then he beckoned them on. "Come on, you should see all the rooms. As I said, we keep care here. The house itself is such a fine example of the period and the rooms have changed so little. Even through the many decades, and family members moving off, of course. There was always someone, however, who saw to it."

He was still showing them the upstairs bedrooms when they heard the quick toot of a horn.

"That will be a team from the local office," Fin said.

"I'll get the gate," Robert said. "Unless you want to go with them and drive out to the road behind, where you think the killer got in from."

"We'll bring the team in, and I'll lead them through the back first," Fin said.

He headed down ahead of Robert Fryer, who passed him at the doorway to hurry to the old guardhouse to open the gate.

There were four in the forensic team—a man named Bert Nelson introduced himself as the head of the team.

He was familiar with the case, and he and his team members had done a quick study of the state police report from the time of murder.

"I'm not sure what we can do for you at this point, Special Agent Stirling," Bert said. He was a serious man in his late forties or early fifties with close-cropped graying hair and an athletic build. "They combed the porch and the grounds. The medical examiner tried to pull prints off the body. All was to no avail."

'I don't want you to try to find something here," Fin explained. "But I'd like you to follow me through a trail to a seldom-traveled dirt road that eventually leads out to a paved road and then I-10. There may be nothing, but—"

"There may be a serial killer at work," Bert said, nodding his head. "We heard about Christy Island. But, I'm curious—what makes you think you've found the right trail and the right road?"

"Process of elimination," Fin said. "There may be nothing—two years have passed. But I don't think they would have taken the same care where they parked to come through that they did on the porch. They wouldn't suspect that anyone would be able to discern just what they had done."

"Whatever it is, we'll search wherever you like," Bert assured him.

"Thank you," Fin said.

He introduced him to Robert Fryer, Tom Drayton and Avalon. In turn, Bert introduced them to the rest of his team.

"I'll take them through," Fin told the others.

"I'll trail behind you, if you don't mind," Avalon said.

"I will, too," Alana said softly, and it seemed that Robert gave a little shiver again. He didn't look in her direction, though he did look around as if just a bit puzzled.

"Robert and I will rehash what we can remember," Tom said. "We'll go back over every detail that we can possibly come up with."

"Thanks," Fin said. He looked at Bert. "You may want to drive around, but I thought that if you followed in this path, you'd understand the way my mind is working."

"Works for me," Bert told him.

Fin retraced his steps, followed closely by the others. When he reached the point where the trail split to the dirt road, he heard the others murmuring that it did seem like a plausible path.

"I'm going for the metal detector in the bushes, though what metal they might have lost, I don't know," a young technician said.

"Jewelry," the one woman on the forensics team said. "She might have had her own jewelry."

"Or a coin," the young tech speculated. "After all this time… something metal is all that might have survived."

Bert eyed his team. "There's always the murder weapon. There is the possibility that she was brought here, killed here in the road, cleaned here in the road and then displayed. Though I doubt that," he said. "I read the report—she hadn't just been wiped down. She was cleaned, as if bathed."

"That's right," Fin confirmed.

"We'll head back, get the car and bring our equipment here," Bert said. "We'll get a better lay of the land, though I think that they must have come off on one of the roads from I-10. They had to know this place, though. Had to know that it was quiet, and that the cameras were a sham."

"Anything that we can get will help—we need to stop these guys."

"We're going to move fast," Bert said, glancing at his watch. "At best, we have about two hours of daylight left."

He turned to his crew. "Let's move," he said, and the four of them quickly started back through the trail.

Fin remained where he was, noting that Avalon stood near the trail; she was alone. The ghost of Alana Grimsby Howard was no longer with her.

When the others had disappeared back into the brush and trees, he headed over to her.

"Let them get ahead a bit," she said softly.

He arched an eyebrow, but waited, as she had asked. A minute later, Alana reappeared, followed by a man of about her own age and an older gentleman; Fin knew that they had to be General Amos Grimsby and Alana's husband, Arthur Howard. Neither, however, was in uniform. They were dressed in formal suits with jackets, vests and ascots.

Alana introduced them quickly. "Father, Arthur, this is Miss Avalon Morgan and... Mr. Finley Stirling. Sir, I'm so sorry— I don't know or remember your proper title," she told Fin.

"Fin," he said, nodding to the two ghostly figures. "And, sir,

I believe you are General Amos Grimsby, and, Mr. Howard, I'm afraid I don't know your proper title."

"It was Lieutenant Howard," the younger man told him. "I go by Artie. You're with the federal government?" he asked.

Fin wondered if he was still leery of anything federal.

"Yes," he said.

"Thank the Good Lord that there is a federal!" Amos said, shaking his head. "I wept when Mississippi left the Union. States' rights! Atrocious. All economical, you know. And not that man has gotten any better. I do read, sir, and I listen, and there is solar power available, there are electric cars...but does it become law when something would better the world? No—not when great financial crashes might come from change. Why, man knows not to spew toxic waste into the water, but has he stopped? Not when the almighty dollar rules—"

"Father," Alana interrupted softly.

The general waved a hand in the air. "I'm sorry. You need our help, but you see there's an old stream down from the rear of the house, a beautiful area. Used to fish there when I was a kid, and when Artie came courting Alana, well, of course, I took him that way and it's still a favorite place."

"The general likes to sit there and contemplate the world," Artie said, a half smile on his face for the two of them. "He's watched every step of 'progress' since we departed, and I do admit, my father-in-law sees many evils in the world, and might even have some of the answers. I'm sorry—the point here being that we didn't see these men as Alana saw them. We did see them leaving and I don't even know how to describe their apparel. They were all in black." He frowned as he looked at his wife for a minute. "Cat burglars!" he said at last. "They were prepared for disappearing into the night. I don't know what the fabric was on their faces, but something that conformed to them, like opaque stockings for the face. It was impossible to know their ages, or anything else about them."

"We saw them as they left, walking quickly through the trail, complimenting one another on the scene they'd left behind," the general added.

"I hope that this helps in some way, though I don't believe we've given you anything," Alana told them.

"You have," Fin assured her.

"But you had come this way yourself—"

"But I couldn't be sure," he told her. "You've helped us immeasurably. And from what I've heard, you left behind a wonderful legacy."

"We were still wrong," the general said. "I knew it. I knew that what we were fighting for was wrong, but I went along with it because of my peers, my home, my state. But a man must always stand for what's right and what's wrong, when he knows the difference, even if he stands against an ocean of those who do not see. I knew right from wrong."

"You learned, sir. Many people do not. And, as I said, your heirs went on to do wonderful things," Fin told him.

He nodded. "Maybe any little bit done now may change the world. I do hope that in some small way, our being here can make even a tiny change for good."

"Sir," Avalon said, speaking up. "Any life is an extremely important life—these young women deserve justice, and your help may change the future for others, may allow others to live. Please know how much we thank you."

The general nodded.

"What now?"

"Maybe the forensic teams will find something. We can hope. And I'll go forward with this to the task force. We will find these people," Fin said.

It was a promise he could only do his best to fulfill. It was a sad fact of life: murderers sometimes got away with their crimes.

He couldn't let it happen this time.

He gazed at Avalon and reached out for her hand. "We'd better get back to the house. Tom and Robert will be waiting, now that the forensic team is here."

She took his hand.

"Thank you," he said again to the ghosts.

"We'll be watching," the general promised.

Avalon kept his hand as they left the ghosts in the woods and made their way back through the overgrown trail.

Once again, they found Tom Drayton and Robert Fryer on the porch. The two had been talking, it appeared, since they'd left.

"The forensic people just left with their vehicle," Tom told them. "I wish to hell someone would have thought to rip the forest and the roads to shreds two years ago. The concentration was here, at the house. At that time, though, we didn't know how they'd gotten in. There was emphasis on the porch and the house and the area surrounding the house."

"But that would be my fault," Robert said wearily. "I slept— I slept through it all."

"Hey, if you hadn't, you might have been a victim, too," Fin told him.

"Better me than that young lady," Robert said. "I've had a life. She had a beautiful road ahead of her."

"You couldn't have changed things," Avalon assured him. "She was dead when they came here. They just used this place for their shock value."

Tom nodded. "She's right, Robert. It was a done deal. Be angry, not guilty. You weren't at fault here in any way—you were used."

Robert Fryer nodded. "I know." He looked at Fin and handed him a sheet he had apparently written while they'd been out by the road. "Here's my contact information and contact info for Kyle Howard—the descendant who owns the house. He was down after the murder, and he was devastated, thought about shutting the place down. But he's a professor, too, kind that believes we need hold on to history lest we forget it. We closed for a month after the murder, but then reopened. Nice man if you think he can help any."

"Thank you," Fin told him.

"We're going to head back and wait to hear if they find anything."

"If the murderer knows that we're making this an active case again, they might be dangerous," Tom said. "I don't know if Robert should be out here alone."

"I agree."

"Hey. I do have a shotgun in the gatehouse if needed," Robert said. "I'm old, but my eyesight is still pretty good and can aim like a mother— Oh, whoops, sorry young lady," he said and winked at Avalon.

She was grinning. She walked over to Fin and set a hand on his shoulder. "Hey, this guy is young and well-trained, and even he knows that anyone can be taken by surprise."

"I'll get some rookie agents out here on shifts," Fin said. "They'll love it. You can give them free tours," Fin said.

"No need," Tom Drayton said. "I'm going to hang here with Robert for the next day or two—as long as that crew is working. Together, we're good."

"Yeah? I taped a bunch of the college games," Robert said.

"Fine way to spend an evening," Tom said.

"All right then," Fin said. "Avalon?"

She smiled. "Tom, Robert, thank you so much."

"A true pleasure," Tom said.

"Well, other than the circumstances," Robert said.

They headed to Fin's vehicle and then left the mansion behind them. He knew that the crew would search with the rest of the daylight they had and come back in the morning.

"Should you have stayed? I know you're just making sure that I get back safely," Avalon told him.

"They won't be able to search that long tonight. They'll grid the place and make their plans for tomorrow. I don't know this crew, but they seem to have it all together. They'll contact me. I'm going to report to headquarters. We'll find out if anyone among our suspects was in the vicinity two years ago."

"She might have been killed miles away...and brought out here."

"She was driven. She was taken from Biloxi and driven here. That will still limit the possibilities."

"And you still suspect someone in my crew," she said.

He let out a long sigh. "Avalon, there were dozens of people working on that island. People who knew the schedule, which doesn't mean it was one of your people—just someone who might have gotten hold of a schedule. Easier than you might think when you consider that these people really plan out what they're doing."

"So what is your plan now?" she asked him.

"I'm going to arrange to find out what is going on with the owners of Christy Island," he said.

"I believe they are still in New Orleans. Weren't we all rather ordered to stay?"

He nodded. "Yes. I think I'd like to see them on a social basis."

"Is that...allowed in a situation like this?"

He glanced her way. "Sure. You and Kevin and Boris and friends will arrange to meet with them. I'm just going to show up. I could call them back in for an interview, but there's no evidence against any of them and it would be unproductive. I want to see them out, and in action."

"You think one of them will start spouting out about killing a young woman and setting her up like a doll?" Avalon asked sardonically.

"Nope. Just want to watch them. Interact a bit."

"Forensics got nothing from the island?"

"Not yet. All we have is what the medical examiner gave us.

And it's not a lot to go on. We need to find out where she was killed, but that probably wasn't on the island."

"And how will you find it then?"

"By not stopping," he said.

They were silent again for a while. The sky darkened as they drove the I-10 westward. He glanced over at Avalon and thought that she was drifting to sleep.

She was.

He smiled as she began to lean toward him.

In time, she was asleep, her head rested on his shoulder.

He kept driving, sorry in a way that they were headed back to a house filled with her friends.

He realized how much he liked time alone with her.

She was…likable.

There was something giving and unique in her personality.

Even the dead knew it and came to her. That was a tremendous asset.

But he realized it wasn't at all why he liked being with her, and his reasons weren't good at all. He was growing far more than just appreciative of her raven-dark hair, sky-colored eyes and slim curves. The attraction he felt for her was growing by leaps and bounds every minute.

He wouldn't act on an attraction. He was a professional.

But he was also human.

# CHAPTER EIGHT

"Oh!" Avalon said, awakening with a start.

They were parked somewhere. She blinked; they weren't exactly in front of the rental house, but they were close.

"I'm sorry. Great travel companion I am."

She really hoped she hadn't drooled on his shoulder.

"It's okay. You probably needed it. And it was great of you to come with me. I really appreciate that you did."

"No, no. I want to help. I told you that. In any way that I can."

"Good. Invite me in," he said.

"What?" She narrowed her eyes. "You want to start interrogating my friends again."

"Hey, if they're innocent, what difference will it make? My real plan is to get us all out, and hopefully joined at some point by Cara Holstein, her husband Gary, Julian Bennett and Kenneth Richard."

Avalon glanced at her watch. It was almost eight. She wondered what the others were up to—they might not even be at the house.

"Fine. Come in. I don't know what anyone is doing."

It was easy enough to find out. Avalon headed into the house first and, hearing no one about in the public rooms, she headed out to the courtyard, followed by Fin.

"Hey!"

Boris was at one of the tables in the courtyard with Brad and Kevin, gathered around his computer.

They all stood to greet Avalon and Fin—each of them gave her a hug and nodded a little warily to Fin.

"Ah, you're back," Brad said.

Avalon truly enjoyed Brad, as a friend, as a cameraman. He knew how to get the best angles on a shot by being courteous and enthusiastic with actors, rather than ever ripping at them. Away from friends, he had a tendency to come across as awkward. He was thin and well over six feet tall, and seemed unable to make his length just be straight and still. With friends, he was easy and fun, intelligent and a keen observer, which, she supposed, was part of what made him so good with a camera.

"How was everything?" Brad continued. "I mean, it couldn't have been good. I'm sorry. I don't know what to say here."

Avalon wasn't sure what to say, either.

She didn't have to worry. Fin was at ease, and ready to put the others at ease, too.

"Mind if we join you?" he asked, reaching for a chair. "Well, I know you don't mind if Avalon joins you, but…"

"Please. Do join us," Boris said.

"Thanks."

Fin still waited for the others to sit before taking his own chair. Then he looked around the table, smiled weakly and told them, "Not sure what you do and don't know. There was a girl murdered a few years ago in Mississippi and left…displayed, as Cindy was. We took a drive over. Sad, sad case, too. Young woman, everything ahead of her… Anyway, we went out there."

"You think that whoever killed Cindy has done something like it before?" Boris asked.

"I do. Maybe more than the one time. We have people going through records from around the country, seeing what else might be related," Fin said.

Kevin looked at Avalon before speaking, and then he let out a long sigh. "I don't claim to know much about crime. But I watch a lot of television," he said. "Isn't it true that the first twenty-four to forty-eight hours are crucial in solving a crime? I mean, I know that investigations can take months, years, but...this is Cindy. This shouldn't have happened to Cindy!"

There was a note of pain in his voice that Avalon completely understood.

She looked at Fin, too.

"A lot of murders are domestic, and personal. Naturally, we look at those closest to someone in most situations. But this isn't your usual situation. Whoever did this was someone Cindy knew—but how well, it's difficult to tell. We believe that he met up with her on Bourbon Street when she left you all...but you know that. What we don't know is how well Cindy might have come to know the extras she was working with, if she was chatting and friendly with a caterer, we don't know." He looked around the table. Avalon couldn't tell if he was being friendly, or watching them all shrewdly for a reaction. "We do have a network of fantastic people who can trace a person's whereabouts through time, so we're seeing what we can find that way." He leaned forward. "And you all have known each other a long time, right?"

Boris, Brad and Kevin didn't need to look at one another; they stared at Fin and all nodded gravely.

"Anyway," Fin said, leaning back. "What are your plans for tonight?"

"Uh..." Kevin glanced at Avalon.

"Frankly, we don't have any plans," Boris said.

"We've just been working all day," Brad told Fin. "I mean... this sounds shallow, but we all still have to make a living."

"Not at all. If it helps any, I imagine the movie will do well, if you get it finished. The caretaker at the estate in Mississippi where the other girl was left told me that he gets many more people these days than he did before the murder."

They all just stared at him.

"People can be ghouls," Fin said softly.

Boris let out a sigh. "I put everything into this. My own production. I had so much faith. And I now I feel like...a jerk."

"You don't need to feel like a jerk," Avalon said.

"You didn't do it," Kevin said.

"No. And still, I feel it dishonors a friend if I get it into distribution, and dishonors others trying to make a living if I lose everything on it," Boris said.

"Let's catch the suckers who did this— that will help all of us, I think," Fin said.

"Right. What can we do?" Boris asked.

"I'm so glad you asked," Fin told him. "I need you to head out to dinner. There's a place on Magazine that would be perfect. Boris—you specifically are in contact with the Christy heirs, right?"

"Yes."

"Invite them to go with you."

"Okay," Boris said slowly. "I can ask..."

"They'll come," Fin said with assurance. "They're stuck in the city. They're enamored of the movies. They'll come."

"I— Sure," Boris said. "The one I've been in contact with the most is Cara—she gets the others to agree or disagree on anything. I'll give her a call. It's about seven thirty already, though..."

"How about eight thirty? That sounds like something everyone could make?" Fin asked.

"Um..." Boris looked at the others.

"Lauren is practicing alien makeup on Leo and Terry," Brad

said. "I'll run up and ask them if they can…clean up and be ready."

"Great. Thank you. Excuse me, I have to make a few phone calls," Fin said.

He rose and wandered away from the group, toward the gate.

"Who is he calling?" Kevin whispered to Avalon.

She shook her head. "Um, Detective Stapleton…or Ryder, as they call him. His headquarters? I don't know."

"Scary guy," Kevin said, looking at Fin.

"He'd have made a hell of an actor," Boris remarked.

"Yeah? You think so?" Kevin asked. And then he answered himself, "Yeah, yeah, rugged good looks, nice angles on the face, cool voice."

Boris shook his head. "I don't mean any of that. I mean that…his mind is turning constantly, and you can see it. But you haven't the least idea of what he's really thinking or feeling." He paused, grinning. "He could be after one of us—even one of us specifically. And we wouldn't know it."

"He seems to think that the family might be guilty," Brad said. He looked uneasy. "Me, too. I mean, they own the island, right?"

"But were they in Mississippi two years ago?" Boris asked. He winced suddenly. "I was thinking that this would make a good movie. My friend is dead, and…"

"Boris, it's okay. Call Cara," Avalon said.

Boris nodded, looking at her. "Do you trust him?"

"Do I trust that he wants to find Cindy's killer?" she asked. "Yes. Beyond a doubt."

"Okay, then."

Boris took out his phone.

Avalon was tired—it had already been a hell of a long day—but she stood restlessly and told Brad, "Let's go see what's going on with Lauren, Leo and Terry. See if they can clean up in an hour, or even if they'll come out tonight."

She headed into the house; the door from the courtyard to the house had been left unlocked—naturally, three of their number had been in the courtyard. She hurried in and headed up the stairs, Brad at her heels.

The door to Lauren's room was open. Leo was sitting on the bed, leafing through one of Lauren's books, and Terry was at her dressing table.

Lauren had finished with Leo, apparently. He'd been given the appearance of an extended head that went with his huge "bug" eyes.

Terry was done up in green. His hair was covered by a wig cap and he was an excellent approximation of a little green man. Lauren was surveying her work.

Seeing Avalon and Brad arrive, she asked, "What do you think?"

"Wow," Avalon said. "I hate to ask this, but do you want to do dinner on Magazine Street at eight thirty?"

"It's not just dinner," Brad warned.

"Fin Stirling wants us to go out and he's asked Boris to call the Christy heirs," Avalon explained.

"Oh," Lauren said.

"I can see that you've been busy," Avalon said. "And you can just say no "

"Never, not if it could help. Does he think that one of them might be…a heinous murderer?" Terry asked.

"I don't know what goes on his mind," Avalon said.

"Maybe he thinks one of *us* is a heinous murderer," Terry said.

"I don't care—obviously, we're suspects," Lauren said. "I'm happy to do anything. I just finished with Terry and it was all for fun practice. It will take these guys at least thirty minutes to get out of the prosthetics and wash up, but yeah, I think we can make eight thirty."

"And we need to eat, anyway," Terry said.

"But I need some pictures," Leo said. "For my portfolio. Brad, would you mind? Could you grab one of your cameras?"

"Sure. I'd be happy to," Brad said. "Come on down—it's dark outside, but the courtyard lights will be perfect for some great shots."

"I'd love some pictures for fun in this getup, too," said Terry.

"Come on down!" Brad said.

He headed out followed by "aliens" Terry and Leo. Lauren looked at Avalon, smiled and shook her head. "All right, well... I'm going to see what they get."

They hurried out behind the three men, heading for the courtyard.

When they stepped out into it, though, they discovered that apparently, neither Terry nor Leo had realized that Fin Stirling was out there.

Leo slammed on the brakes.

Terry crashed into him.

"Uh, hi!" Leo said.

Fin walked toward him, a slight smile on his face as he marveled at the makeup.

"Wow. That's amazing. Sorry, you both look amazing." He looked at Lauren. "You do incredible work."

Lauren was quiet for a minute. "Cindy was better at this," she said softly. "We'd both been talking about the fact that we'd been approached by a director considering doing a science-fiction movie. We would have taken the work...together." She shrugged, wincing. "I thought I should see how I'd do, but...not sure I can take the work now, anyway. I mean, that is the thing about being behind the camera—stars must vie for positions on big projects. We just need to...work."

"Well, you do exceptional work," Fin said. He looked straight at Lauren as he added, "I promise you. I won't stop. We'll find out who did it."

Lauren gave him a weak smile.

"So, pictures!" she said.

Everyone had an opinion on where in the courtyard great shots could be taken. They laughed about the idea of walking out on the streets in their makeup, but Kevin reminded them all that they were in New Orleans—people might not even notice.

Terry suggested that they could go to dinner as aliens.

Leo said an emphatic no—he was hungry. He wasn't going to eat in a prosthetic.

Avalon agreed to look like a terrified damsel in distress attempting to escape Leo's alien, but when they finished that shot, she excused herself to run upstairs. She'd forgotten until just then that she'd spent the morning taking shots for Samara Stella; she wanted to upload them into her computer, which Ryder had dropped off that afternoon while she'd been out.

She did so, and then stared at the screen, remembering the site she had seen.

And the "cherry bomb" that had removed it.

There was a knock at her door. She stood and opened it; Fin was there.

"Hey, are you all right?" he asked her.

"Fine. I just... It's been a really long day. I forgot that I accepted a job—I needed to get the pics I took onto my computer."

He nodded. "Be careful on that," he told her.

"Did your computer agent—Jodi—did she find anything?"

"She started and sent what she found up to headquarters. They're taking it from there, but, well, they found lots of things. Whether they've found our guy or not, I don't know." He hesitated. "Ryder has seen to it that the Christy heirs have been watched. They haven't done anything unusual. They're staying at a hotel on Canal Street now—all four of them. They went to a movie this afternoon, prowled the French Market and spent an hour or so with one another at Café du Monde. Boris reached Cara—I believe they're going to meet you."

"But you're not coming with us?"

"I am. I'm just going to show up looking for you once you've all been together for a bit."

"I see. No, I don't."

He smiled. "In a social setting, with you and your friends, they won't mind that I'm there, not after I've been accepted and greeted by you guys."

"Okay."

He lowered his head for a moment. "Angela found another possible victim," he said quietly.

"What?"

"Possible victim. Remains of a young woman were found in a bayou in Terrebonne Parish about thirteen months ago. It took a while to find this one because the remains had degraded, and we don't know if the incidents are related or not. I'll be taking a ride out there tomorrow, most probably, if you want to come."

"I—I don't know. I should be working on this, um, website. But, of course, if you think that I can help…wow. Okay, you want to look at the Christy heirs—but they're not even from this area, are they? And we're looking at Christy Island, and Terrebonne, which is, of course, so near, and then the Biloxi area. The Christy heirs are from—"

"Cara and Gary are from Monroe, Louisiana. Julian Bennett is from Baton Rouge, and Kenneth Richard is from Beaumont, Texas. Beaumont is the farthest…and not that far. Not far from Terrebonne Parish, and not far from Mississippi. Beaumont to NOLA is a four-to five-hour drive, depending on traffic. None of them would have needed a ticket to get on a plane—all of this is easy driving distance. I could be wrong. I believe that the only way someone managed all this was to be familiar with people and places. Not the kind of friends the family knows, but…"

"Well, the good thing is that should rule my friends out," Avalon said firmly. "I know them all very well." She hesitated. "What if you follow them and you find nothing on them?"

"Back to the drawing board. Until I do find the truth."

Avalon hesitated a minute. "I'll be happy to do whatever is needed."

He grinned. "Even spend time with me?"

She tilted her head. He was standing very close. The idea of shocking him, drawing him against her and applying the deepest, most evocative kiss known to man on his lips, absurdly occurred to her.

She didn't step away.

Neither did she touch him.

She forced a smile.

"I don't dislike you half as much as I did when we first met."

"Good. You're not half as annoying as you were, either."

"I was never annoying."

He grinned. "Well, at least you're not-bad-looking."

"Thank you. Nothing like being not-bad-looking and not too annoying."

His grin faded. "Seriously? You're something quite impressive. The dead can be...cautious. This afternoon, Alana trusted you." He smiled again. "Okay, not-bad-looking, and you have an incredible inner beauty. Anyway, thank you. You do help."

Avalon swallowed a little too hard.

"Thank you. Um, I need a minute before we leave. Oh, wait, you aren't coming with us. But then—"

"I'm leaving here when you do. I'll just follow a bit slowly. I'll let you all get situated and then I'll come in. Boris is going to welcome me and get me a chair."

"Okay, then..."

He smiled, turned and left her.

She closed the door. She hurried into her bathroom, stared at her reflection in the mirror and decided on a bit more makeup.

"I'm going through videos from toll plazas, checking car service and rental records. You name it, we're on it," Angela promised Fin.

He was keeping back a block or so from the six close-knit members of the cast and crew of the movie as they headed for the restaurant. He wanted to make sure that they were seated and had at least ordered drinks before he entered.

"Are you heading to Terrebonne Parish tomorrow?" she asked.

"I am."

"I've gone through what I could get from the sheriff's office there. I told them that you were coming. They said anytime— they would have the case files ready for you."

"She was dressed for a Roaring Twenties party?" Fin asked.

"Yep. Or the remnants of an outfit that was frilled and looked like a flapper's outfit. She had a band around her head." Angela was quiet for a minute. "The pictures I have are in your mailbox. When you have a chance...and here's the thing. She was never identified. There's a country bar out there that has decor like an old speakeasy and is, in fact, called the Speakeasy. The case jumped out at me because she was found in the bayou just down from the bar."

"And maybe she was set up somewhere by the bar, and something happened. Or maybe they got scared away before they had chance to finish their setup," Fin said.

"If she was their first, they might have panicked," Angela said. "God, I hope she was the first! If these are the same people, it's frightening to think of how long they might have been at this."

"Do we know anything else about timing on the cast, crew and heirs?" he asked her.

"Yes, and you're not going to like it."

"Tell me."

"Well, the heirs all live within possible driving distance of all the murder sites."

"Right. And?"

"When it comes to this murder? The medical examiner couldn't pinpoint the exact timing. But it was the same week that your close-knit group of rising artists was traveling to San Antonio for the internet show that they filmed."

"All of them?"

"All of them in that group staying at the house now—Boris Koslov, Terry Jenson, Leo Gonzales, Brad Fallon, Lauren Carlson *and* Avalon Morgan."

"Okay. Thanks."

"You don't want it to be one of them, do you?"

"Angela, I promise you, I want to find the truth—wherever it may lead."

"Right. Of course. I'll keep you up on anything I get. Any reports on forensic finds by any chance that I don't know about yet?"

"No, but at the mansion, there wasn't much good sunlight left. They'll start up again in the morning."

"And now?"

"I'm going to dinner."

"With?"

"My suspect list," he told her. "The entire list."

There she was, eyes like crystal fire, a laugh that filled the air with melody.

A smile that could rival sunlight.

Hair...softest silk. She was truly poetry.

*Wait...*

*He had to wait...*

So it should be.

He didn't want to wait. It was his turn. And he could watch her, envision her in his arms, feel her flesh as his hands slipped upon it, as he touched her, and touched her, tasted the sweetness of her flesh.

It was his turn.

And he hungered as he had never hungered before.

There had to be a complete plan, but that had been promised him. There had to be more than just the holding, the loving, the adoring, the moments that would live in his memory forever and ever.

There had to be the art, of course.

The artistry of display. The meaningfulness. All that mattered so very much. And it mattered that it was done right, that they could fulfill their dreams in all the time to come.

He reminded himself of the joy of anticipation.

Watching, stalking…feeling the air that was near her. Feeling the space where she had been, knowing that soon, soon…

Not soon enough.

The hunger was beginning to consume him.

The hunger to hold her, touch her, breathe her, taste her…

See those eyes on his. The color, the sparkle, the beauty in the depths.

See that fade…

And then have her as the warmth slowly left her body, and the fire filled his.


Her group took the St. Charles streetcar to reach the Magazine Street area and walked the few blocks from the streetcar down to the river.

There was a table almost ready for their group when they arrived; Avalon knew that Fin must have made the arrangements for them.

At this time of night, it wasn't easy to get a table for a group their size at any popular restaurant. "Mama Mia" was a comparatively new establishment, Avalon knew, and, as the name would suggest, it offered Italian cuisine. It also offered a little shop at the entry that sold food items such as olive oil and imported pastas, and T-shirts and kitchen gadgets with a NOLA flair. She noted salt and pepper shakers, gravy ladles and more that bore pictures of cute little chefs and the restaurant's name.

As they waited to be taken to their table, Avalon and Lauren wandered the little shop area. She was looking at a teakettle when she noticed a woman just down the aisle—simply dressed in jeans and a sweatshirt, hair drawn back in a ponytail.

The woman swung around suddenly and stared at Avalon, then smiled and laughed.

"Hello!" she said. "Small world, huh? I thought…never mind!"

Samara Stella had come to dine, too. It made sense—her place wasn't far away.

"Hi," Avalon said. She smiled. "You know, you do have a great restaurant in your own place."

Samara shrugged, smiling as well. "Note the name—Stella. It's my real name. I grew up with an Italian family, and the chef here prepares an eggplant almost as good as my mom's. They take care. There's nothing to ruin a good eggplant like getting a piece of the peel stuck in your teeth!" She shrugged and whispered, "I come over here often."

"Nice to have an endorsement before we sit down," Avalon said.

"Yes, the food is very good," Samara assured her. "And I'm sorry I'm so jumpy. I just had the oddest feeling… Like being watched, you know? I thought that someone was staring at me. I know it wasn't you. Maybe they weren't staring at me—maybe they were staring at you. Just a feeling. I'm sorry."

Avalon laughed, and the sound was a little forced to her own ears.

*She hadn't felt…anything. There were no dead wandering the shop.*

*But that feeling could come, too, when the living watched someone…*

She looked around: there was an older woman with a child in the room—a grandchild, Avalon thought—and they were both happily looking at a stand filled with stuffed toys. A few diners, also awaiting seating, were wandering about.

Her group was mostly milling by the hostess stand. Boris

was surveying a table filled with T-shirts with NOLA logos and silly memes.

She didn't see the Christy family yet, but they were probably on their way, out on the street, possibly.

Glass windows showcased the little shop, and the displays were attractive, with a rack at one end of the window spilling over with cute little stuffed chefs, crabs and crawfish.

Naturally, people would be drawn to look in from the street. Samara was now smiling at her. "Weird, I know, sorry. Anyway, how's it going? The website? Oh, I mean, I haven't given you any time, have I? I do like the idea of getting a little classy with the website. I mean, yes, we're a sex club, but I want to be a classy one, you know?"

"I think we're going to be able to create a good site," Avalon said. "One that you'll like. I was impressed by your place."

Samara laughed. "Want a job? You'd be nice and classy. I mean, do you want a job after the website? You're always welcome. Though I think people are paying you a sustainable wage for your work in film. Well, I told you my dream. It wasn't going so well. Parents died in a car crash when I was just graduating from high school and I clawed my way through state college and then… I just couldn't survive without twisting my talents a bit. I am still a showman, though—show-woman, that is!"

"What you've done is very interesting, and very smart," Avalon assured her. She studied Samara in her casual outfit, ponytail and clean-scrubbed face. She was so…

Normal.

She was a performer…and she had taken her business where she needed to go to survive.

"You're fascinating, and we're going to highlight the fact that you offer an amazing restaurant and fun performances. My favorite, I think, is your twisted history. Too bad we couldn't have really turned a few things in different directions."

"I agree. Hey, I see people craning their necks over these

aisles. I think your friends are looking for you. I'm on my way out. The osso buco is to die for, if you like that dish. I'll see you soon."

"Yes, and I'll send you all my ideas while we get it all going," Avalon replied.

She saw that Kevin, a worried frown on his face, was standing next to Leo, who was also looking anxiously around the store.

She hurried over to them.

Kevin gave her a hug. "There you are! Don't disappear these days—too scary."

"I'm sorry—I didn't realize how high the rows of shelves were," she said.

"Our table is ready. Come on." He took her hand and drew her close to him. "I'm going to keep you close to me."

A smiling hostess led them in. A long table by a window looking out on the street had been reserved for them. They had arrived before the Christy family.

Boris wound up at one head of the table; Avalon found herself between Leo and Kevin—her stalwart protectors, she thought. Lauren was across from Avalon, between Brad and Terry, who had managed to clean up except for the bit of "little green man" that he had missed on his left jaw.

Lauren noticed it as they were seated and took a snowy white napkin to dab at his cheek.

"I missed a spot?" Terry said.

"You're fine," Lauren assured him.

He grinned at Avalon across the table. "Personally, I think I should have come as an alien. Would have been fun—I'll bet you half the people on the streets would have thought that an alien had landed!"

"Possibly," Avalon agreed.

"Wrong seating," Boris said. "Terry, change with me?"

"I get the head of the table?" Terry asked.

"I need to be facing the door, ready to hop up," Boris said.

He looked contemplatively at Avalon. "Special Agent Stirling wants it to look like we're just trying to get back on friendly terms after the chaos and trauma, and let it look like we're totally baffled, have complete faith in them…"

"Good thing we have a few actors in this group," Lauren said. "I need to stay where I am. I'm definitely *not* an actor."

"Well, I am. Sometimes…" Brad said. "Okay, I'm usually an extra, but I can manage this gig."

Looking across to the entry, Avalon saw that Cara and Gary Holstein had arrived; they were at the hostess stand.

She stood and waved to them.

Cara, petite and slim, pretty in a flowery sundress, waved in return and pointed the table out to the hostess.

They were led over.

"You're waiting for a few more?" the hostess asked.

"Two more," Boris said.

The group stood to greet them. Hugs went around.

"There's a seat at the head," Gary said. "I'm going for it."

"He likes a chance to be head of the household," Cara said, laughing. "He always says I may be little, but I make up for it by being bossy, hmm, my love?" she said, hugging Gary.

"You really have to watch out for her," Gary said, nodding solemnly with a little smile. Then he grew serious. "You guys doing okay? I can't tell you how glad I am that none of us wanted to stay on the island. No one has been allowed back on yet, and if we'd had things there… Though now, it feels as if we're living in limbo."

"We are living in limbo," Boris said softly.

"I'm so, so sorry," Gary said. "We were devastated and can only imagine how you feel."

"Well, we thought we'd have a dinner to honor Cindy, and you were always so wonderful to us," Boris said. "We wanted you to be with us tonight."

"You know we're still behind you one hundred percent," Cara told him.

"Thank you," Boris said. "And, Gary, please sit there at the head of the table. You get to be the man tonight."

Gary grinned. "Cool. Whoops—I'll claim the seat fast. There's Julian. Mr. Handsome. Cara, how did you have a cousin so damned good-looking?"

She laughed. "Hey! Looks run in the family."

"I think they missed Kenneth," Gary said in a whisper.

Kenneth was right behind Julian. Avalon, still standing by her chair, watched as the two men came in; they'd been together, she thought.

*Were they a team? A team of killers?*

Kenneth may not have inherited the looks that Julian could claim, but he wasn't as bad as the teasing always made him sound. He was out of shape, a little on the pudgy side, but he had always been kind and enthusiastic when they'd been filming.

The two headed for the table and the greetings went around again. A waitress came; drinks and appetizers were ordered. Everyone asked what everyone else was doing, and the consensus was that they were all just biding time and waiting for the police to say that they could move on.

"Hey," Brad said suddenly. "Look who it is."

He stood up, waving madly.

"It's that... FBI agent," Cara whispered to her end of the table. "Special Agent Stirling. What's he doing here?"

"I guess he needs to eat, too. He's been damned decent to us. I'm going to see if he wants to join us," Boris said.

He hurried over to the hostess stand and greeted Fin, shaking his hand and drawing him in.

Boris led Fin to the table, where he looked around at all of them. "I heard this place was all the rage of new eateries in NOLA."

"Hey, you don't mind if we question you a bit while we eat, huh?" Boris asked.

"I just wish I had answers," Fin said.

"Draw up a chair," Boris said. He shifted Lauren's chair closer to Terry and his own chair closer to Lauren's, stealing a chair from another table to place Fin between himself and Cara Holstein.

"Thanks," Fin said, taking the seat. He looked at Cara Holstein, next to him.

"Is it...all right? Do you mind that I'm here? I don't mean to crash your party."

"No, no, of course, it's fine. We're glad to have you."

His hands folded before him, he looked around the table and focused at the end where the Christy heirs were seated.

"So. How are you all doing? What are you all up to?" he asked politely. "I heard a rumor that you're now considering keeping the island and opening it as a historic venue, a tourist attraction. Is that true?"

# CHAPTER NINE

Fin had heard the rumor ten minutes before joining the others at the table. He had kept his distance, watching the film crew as they'd gone in to the restaurant, and he'd waited, watching for the arrival of the Christy family.

Cara and Gary Holstein had naturally showed up together.

Julian Bennett and Kenneth Richard had then arrived together, laughing and loitering in the street, it appeared, as if they intended to make an entrance.

They made a strange pair, Fin thought. Kenneth had several years on Julian and had the look of a stodgy professor. Julian was more of a player—good-looking, quick to flirt, an outgoing man in every way.

They had claimed that none of them had known each other well prior to being named in the will. Nothing hostile, just the fact that they weren't first cousins, but rather that their parents had been cousins and life had been busy and they'd never really met.

Angela had called while Fin had watched and waited. She'd reported to him that the foursome had contacted their attorney to ask about licenses and requirements for making the island a state historic site.

A surprise to him.

And, obviously, to the others.

It seemed to Fin that his question brought about a few seconds of complete, stunned silence.

Then Lauren stood, stricken. "What?" she exclaimed.

The members of the Christy family looked awkwardly at one another.

Then Cara Holstein looked straight at Fin.

"Yes," she said softly. "Yes, but you must understand. We don't believe that we'll be able to sell it. We're going to be in massive trouble with taxes and…well, our attorney made us think about it."

"None of us really wants the wretched place," Julian said. "My dad hated his grandfather—said he was one of the meanest old men he'd ever met."

"My parents disliked him, too," added Cara. "That's why we seldom visited, and when my own grandfather died, well, I never went back on my own."

"Ditto to all the above," Kenneth told them. "He was known to be…weird."

"Interesting," Fin said. He saw that Avalon had probably given Lauren a little kick beneath the table; Lauren sat silent and pale. "I'd always heard he was an eccentric. I'd never heard anything about cruelty to his children or anything of the like." He lifted the water glass in front of him. "To justice for Cindy, and a better future for all."

"Justice—for Cindy," Lauren repeated.

The evening went on; Fin spoke to the Christy family mainly, keeping it all conversational, asking about their employment, their lives at home. He felt Avalon watching him now and then, wondering what he could possibly be getting from the conversation.

He was drawing Boris out, as well, talking about the art of filmmaking, the expense of sets, the ease when it came to simply working in a studio…and the expenses that were incurred both in and out of a studio.

It was Brad who brought up the murder again.

"Don't the forensic people have anything?" he demanded. "Someone was on that island in the middle of the night. They brought Cindy with them, cleaned up, dressed up…and they can't find anything?"

Fin smiled. "They have plenty. Footprints and fingerprints all over the cemetery. They all belong to all of you."

Brad stared back at him blankly.

"We were working there," Kevin said, confused.

"Yes, and that's the point. The footprints, fingerprints—DNA off a cigarette butt—"

"Kevin!" Lauren said.

"Yeah, yeah, I still have a cigarette now and then," Kevin said. He looked across the table. "So does Boris."

"This killer wouldn't have left DNA, fingerprints or footprints," Fin said. "Unless, of course, they were supposed to be there."

"You mean, as if one of us had done this. We—the owners of the island—or the film crew?" Kenneth demanded.

"We can't rule any of you out yet, I'm afraid," Fin said. "But we're looking into similar murders across the area over the last several years," Fin told them all.

"Because anyone could have come to the island," Lauren said. "Boris, you were staying there. I wonder if the killer knew it. I mean, there had been a few write-ups, saying that we were staying in a hotel during the filming. Maybe we should have all stayed on the island. Maybe this wouldn't have happened."

Cara Holstein made a snorting noise. "Have you really looked around the house? There are rats, roaches, spiderwebs! It's horrible. I mean, Boris got the one room cleaned up for himself, but…ugh. The place is horrible. It needs…" She broke off, shaking her head and sighing. "It needs so much work!"

"But that's all cosmetic," Kenneth said. "That's what made the attorneys come to us and suggest that there might be a better solution."

"Because people will want to come—now that a woman, brutally murdered, was found dead in the cemetery?" Kevin asked, his voice hard.

"We have to do something with the property," Julian said. "I don't know what is right and what is wrong, but our attorney told us that if we sell, someone else will just do the same thing. I mean, the structure of the house is sound—it's made it through dozens of wretched storms. But the way that it sits on that island, just about surrounded by the cemetery…well, it doesn't make for a great family home. The only reasonable bite we've had with an almost viable offer was from a freak from a rock band whose members have consumed spiders on stage, and even that… I'm just not sure what he'd do with the island. Sometimes, I don't care. Sometimes, I do."

"Heritage," Kenneth said. "Our great-grandfather was a bastard, but the house goes back before him, and…maybe it should be preserved. All of it—the good and the bad."

A waitress arrived at the table for their orders. Fin was about to ask for the étouffée, but he felt his phone vibrating in his jacket pocket and he quickly looked at it.

It was Ryder. The detective had texted him.

Meet me. Samara Stella's.

He knew that the detective had kept officers watching the Christy family, but he knew exactly where they were.

He excused himself to take the call; as he did so, he noticed that Avalon had her phone out…and was staring at it. She stood and glanced at the others apologetically. "I'm sorry, please excuse me for a few minutes. Website-client thing," she said, and started out of the restaurant.

Kevin started to rise. "What in the world—?"

Fin nodded at Kevin. "I've got this—got a call I have to answer, anyway."

He hurried out after Avalon, catching her in the street.

"Avalon, what're you doing? You don't just take off alone these days." He had her arm; he was holding her firmly.

She stared at her arm, and then at him. He didn't release her.

"I'm worried about your safety!" he snapped.

"Then let me go. Samara texted me, terrified."

"And Ryder texted me. Come on."

They walked across the street and down the block to Samara Stella's Theater of the Fantastic. The business was open, of course. The night was young in New Orleans.

A different young woman was at the reception desk. She was a brunette, tall and graceful, and every bit as attractive as the young woman who had held that position the day before.

She was distressed. "I'm afraid that we're not taking reservations right now—"

Fin produced his badge. "Where are they?"

The girl pointed.

They burst through the doors and headed for a room with one of the small stages. Samara was standing at the foot of the apron; Ryder was next to her.

"What's going on?" Fin demanded.

Samara pointed.

There was a divan on the stage, part of a scene, he assumed. And there was a woman on the divan…except that it wasn't a woman.

It was a doll or an effigy.

It looked exactly like Samara Stella…except that there was a knife through the doll's heart.

Samara Stella was there, as well, looking just like the girl next door in her ponytail, jeans and sweatshirt. She was pale as ash, and when she saw Avalon, she rushed forward, needing to hug her, and to be hugged in turn.

Ryder strode over. "Fin! I've been trying to tell Miss Stella that this isn't necessarily the Christy Island killer after her, but she ran out into the street screaming and she's... Well, I have a team coming, but we're back to where we were on Christy Island. There are dozens of people through here every single day. Prints are going to mean very little. I've been trying to calm her down." Ryder looked at him quizzically for a minute. "She said that she knew you. I guess I hadn't imagined..."

Ryder let his voice trail. He hadn't meant to be insulting to either him or Samara Stella, Fin mused. But the NOPD detective was thinking that Fin must have enjoyed a performance—perhaps even been part of one, getting a good whipping or something.

"Avalon is working on a website for Miss Stella," Fin said, shaking his head. "Ryder, you know that. That's how she found the site with the cherry bomb, the site that Jodi is still trying to trace."

Ryder looked at Avalon.

"Oh, yeah, I forgot. I see," he said.

Fin had no idea what Ryder saw, but Avalon didn't seem to care. She was trying to reassure Samara.

"He was watching me! Whoever did this was watching me—he wants it to be me. He wants me to be dead, just like this, on the settee!" she said.

"Samara," Fin said, extricating the woman from her fierce hold on Avalon. "Samara, please, we'll get people in, they'll figure out how this was done when you have a receptionist on duty, what back entrance might have been used...but this isn't that same. This is probably a sick bastard who just doesn't like what you do." He drew in a deep breath. "Samara, if the killer had been after you, he wouldn't have displayed a doll." He hesitated. "You would be dead. You would be the doll. This is so wrong and it's harassment, but I believe that it is harassment."

"But someone was watching. I know that someone was watching. In the restaurant, or from the street…someone was watching!"

"They were watching you?" Fin asked.

She frowned. "Yes. No. Avalon was there, too. I don't know. I felt it. There was someone there, and they were watching, and it was creepy, and it was… I'm so scared!"

Visitors had been shown out; Samara's employees and family from the kitchen and the other rooms had gathered in the room with its small stage and audience section.

"Samara," he said, "you're going to be okay. Whoever did this is gone. I'm here, Ryder is here, and soon, we'll have the place crawling with cops."

She tried to nod.

"I'm so scared. I'm never scared. But I'm so scared," she said.

"Hey. NOPD is on this," Ryder assured her, glancing at Fin. "This is a police matter, but Miss Stella was going on about you and…"

"It's all right."

"My people are good at what they do," Ryder reminded him.

"I know."

"I'm still scared!" Samara said.

The brunette receptionist came up to her. "Not to worry, Samara. You're not going home. You're going to come and stay with Benny and me." The brunette looked at Fin. "Benny is a cop."

"Benjamin Nolan?" Ryder asked the brunette.

She nodded.

"A good man," Ryder assured Fin.

"Samara, you'll go home with this young lady and not be alone. But now, we need to know more about the alley behind this place and who was here while you were taking time off across the street," Fin said.

"Close the place for the night," Ryder told the receptionist. "I'll get an officer to see you and Miss Stella to your place. Miss Stella, we'll get a team out here. You're going to be all right."

"You don't think that—that anyone is after me?" Samara asked. "You think it's just—"

"I think it's a prank created by a holy roller who doesn't like your form of entertainment," Ryder said. "But you don't need to worry—we'll investigate."

Fin looked at Avalon, who was studying the doll that had been set on the stage.

"What is it?" he asked her.

"It's obviously supposed to be Samara, but I've seen a doll like that before," she said.

"Where? When?" Fin asked her.

"About six years ago. I had a walk-on for it and managed a hell of a good scream. The dolls were used in a Halloween short—it was good. It went out to one of the major cable stations. It was used as a fifteen-minute filler. Say a movie they wanted to show ran an hour and forty minutes, or somewhere in that time frame. A filler like that allows a channel to keep to a two-hour format on it without putting in too many commercials or falling off a basic time schedule."

"You were in it? And you know the dolls?"

She nodded. "That was it—the name of the play. *The Doll.* The doll came to life and murdered people, but then the man who had created her realized that she had become more human than a doll…and he stabbed her and killed her, but then took the blame for the murders." She looked at him and hesitated several seconds, wincing. "Boris directed it."

"And you were an actor in it."

"I was in it, yes. And the doll…well, they start out plain. Fabricators, prop people and makeup artists can work on them.

They're very basic, readily available at a number of theatrical and film-supply houses," Avalon said.

"Who else was involved with this little film?"

"Not Brad—he started working with us in Texas. We were just out of school—Boris had lectured that year and Leo had also been a visiting guest artist teaching mime. Lauren did makeup and Terry worked as a set designer."

"Terry. So, he would have purchased the doll and created his own image upon the basic form?"

Avalon nodded miserably.

"Let me get this straight—I'm assuming that Kevin was in it?"

"Yes. Neither of us starred in it—I was the neighbor who discovered what was going on and Kevin was a victim of the doll. And Leo played a small part. But I'm telling you that the dolls can easily be bought—it's the work done to them that makes them funny, terrifying...or whatever. But seriously, you were at the house with all of us—you followed us here. You know that no one in my group did this."

"I do know that," he said.

"Then why are you—?"

"I'm not accusing your friends."

"It sounds—"

"I'm going to ask them to help me."

He swung around. Other officers were coming in; Ryder motioned to him that he had someone to bring Samara to the home of the receptionist so that Benny, the cop, could look after them both.

When they were gone, Ryder walked over to him.

"What do you think?" Ryder asked.

"I don't know," Fin said.

"A prank? By a self-righteous individual. You know, the kind who thinks it would be okay to kill everyone who isn't like them, let God sort them out."

"I think so. But it's strange and creepy."

"It wasn't the killer," Avalon said. "Fin said it—the killer wouldn't have made a doll up to look like Samara. The killer would have made Samara look like a doll."

"We're on this," Ryder told Fin. "I had dinner earlier—go back. Enjoy your social time with your nice long list of possible suspects."

"It's not a long list," Avalon corrected. "The Christy family."

Ryder kept his mouth shut and just nodded grimly. "Well, go eat. And keep in touch tomorrow. I imagine you'll hear back from Mississippi. Even if just to tell you they found nothing."

"Encouraging," Fin said dryly.

"The truth of it. Lots of hours and even more frustration," Ryder said. He looked at Avalon. "Maybe you should start looking around on the web again."

"I will," Avalon said.

"Ryder, she's in this deep enough—"

"Yeah? And she's going to Terrebonne Parish with you tomorrow, right?"

Fin gave Ryder a grim smile. "Yeah. She's going with me."

"Don't think it will change much if she tries the web again."

"You have an expert on it," Fin protested.

"But Avalon found it."

"Okay, you're right—we need to go eat." Fin gestured that he and Avalon should leave.

"I'm sure they're done eating by now," Avalon said.

"They'll still be there," Fin assured her.

It was strange to leave with the place so completely empty. As they walked back down the block, Avalon said, "You really think that was just a prank? Or, not a prank, but something like a hate joke?"

He looked at her. "Samara Stella hasn't been taking precautions—she's been walking around on her own, she's been in her place of business every day. If a killer wanted her dead—if *this* killer wanted her dead—she'd be dead."

Avalon nodded. "How awful. It's just so...strange." She turned to him fiercely. "You know none of my friends did this."

"Yeah. But I still need all the information on every possible place that someone might have gotten one of those dolls."

They walked across the street.

As they'd expected, their group had finished with their meal. But the table was now empty.

"Your night—social interrogating night—is ruined," Avalon said.

"Yes. Interesting," he said.

"How is that?"

"What if it was meant to be ruined?" he asked.

Avalon shook her head. "What? In your life, everything comes back to the investigation that you're working on. It must be hard to be so suspicious of people you just met."

He smiled. "Avalon, chill. I'm not after your people—other than that I'd like help from them. Should we just get some food to go?"

"You're coming back to the house with me?"

"I am."

"Fine."

At the restaurant, they ordered food to go. As they stood there, waiting at the reception desk by the small shop, Avalon shivered.

"What?" he asked her.

She shook her head. "Samara was here, but you know that. But when she spoke to me...she was nervous. Jumpy. Then she mentioned that it might be me they were watching."

"Yes, she mentioned it. So she was nervous, jumpy—scared even. And this was before she went back to her place and saw the doll."

"Yes."

"Well, she had people in the venue when the doll was placed—employees, customers. But there is a back door that backs out to an alley. People come and go through the back all the time, taking out trash, stepping out for a cigarette or to accept a de-livery. It's highly likely that the back door is unlocked most of the time and whoever did this, knew it." He hesitated, look-ing at her. "What happened tonight was a distraction. Maybe more. I wonder if this killer or killers aren't grandstanders. They do all this with the intent of creating alarm and confusion and they love watching the police and law enforcement trip over themselves trying to make a connection…or not making con-nections at all."

"And it might have been something else entirely."

"Yes. You just shivered. Do you feel that someone is watch-ing you now?"

"No… I just remember that she was frightened. And she isn't a frail person—she's not the kind of woman who jumps at a shadow."

The food came. Fin paid the bill and accepted the bag, then they headed out.

"You have a car here?" she asked.

He shook his head. "No. I was on the same streetcar as you and your friends. I can hail one of Ryder's people, or we can hop the streetcar back. Your call."

"Ryder's people are hopefully busy. Let's get the streetcar."

It was a nice night. The heat that could hang over southern Louisiana seemed to have lifted with the fall of night. The air was pleasant. Avalon remained thoughtful rather than shaken as she walked by his side.

She turned to look at him. "Terrebonne Parish. Is the police station we're going to in Houma?"

"It is."

"I wonder why this didn't come up right away—Christy Is-land just isn't that far."

"Because the body was so decomposed and degraded that it didn't seem similar."

"But maybe it is?"

"Everything is a *maybe* right now. But I'd like to head back out to Christy Island after discovering what I can at the Houma station."

"And you want me to go."

He sighed. "I don't want to take advantage of your willingness to help, Avalon. But, yes. If you want."

"Oh, I want. I want to find out the truth behind all of this. I want whoever did this to Cindy to be put away forever, the key thrown in the middle of the Gulf. I'm ready."

They passed shops and restaurants—the Magazine Street area was also alive and brimming with life despite the hour.

Several passengers awaited the streetcar. They didn't speak as they boarded and the trip back down to the stop for the French Quarter didn't take long.

It was nearing midnight by the time they reached the house. Still, Fin followed her in.

"They might have all gone to bed," Avalon told him.

"Let's see. I think we should find Boris. And I'm pretty sure I heard voices in the courtyard."

Avalon gave him a fierce frown but opened the door to the courtyard.

He was right; none of the group had gone to bed. Boris, Terry, Brad, Leo, Kevin and Lauren were all seated around one of the tables. A few had cold drinks in front of them. A few were drinking coffee despite the hour.

"So what the hell happened?" Boris demanded, seeing them and jumping to his feet.

Kevin stood, too, and he and Boris each grabbed another chair. Lauren stared at Avalon, seeming to demand answers.

Avalon lifted a hand, shaking her head, leaving the explanation to Fin.

They sat in the offered chairs and unpacked their take-out from the restaurant. Fin was hungry, and their Italian dishes were still delicious despite traveling. He and Avalon ate while the others asked questions and Fin tried to answer.

When Fin finished telling them about what Samara Stella had found in her theater, Boris looked at Avalon. "It was one of those dolls made by the Richter-Olsen Company?"

"Yes. I believe other companies create something similar, but it did look like the same kind of doll we used in that short film years ago."

"That's where it would come from?" Fin asked. "The Richter-Olsen Company? Where is it? Where is their factory?"

"There's one not far from here," Kevin said. "As you can imagine, New Orleans is a place where fabricators can go crazy. They're doing a lot of film here now, and when they're not doing film, we have not just Mardi Gras, but Decadence Fest and a dozen other festivals. Wig shops, costume shops and prop shops all have plenty of business. But…wow. I mean, this can't have anything to do with—with what happened to Cindy, can it?"

"Probably not," Fin said. He saw that Avalon glared at him. "But you never know. So how was dinner?"

Leo let out a sniff and shook his head. "Did one of them blurt out the fact that they were really crazy killers? No. Gary—I guess he's the brains in the operation—mainly talked about their session with their attorney. None of them are rich on their own, but none of them are starving, either. Apparently, they've been convinced that some cleanup could turn the island into a remarkable moneymaker."

"Cara acted as if she was a bit ashamed of the idea—she liked Cindy, said she was beautiful and sweet, and they'd talked about makeup and the island. She said that it was devastating, but they couldn't make anything bad in the past go away. All any of us could do was move forward," Kevin told them. "She was concerned, though."

"Julian wasn't," Lauren said. "He was a jerk. Said it was their island and they couldn't help the fact that the police and the FBI were incompetent. You know, he seems to think that he's God's gift to women and I have news for him—he's a jerk."

Brad laughed. "He asked Lauren out. Seemed shocked when she said no."

"I wasn't rude!" Lauren said. "He's just…full of himself." She managed a laugh. "And he's not even an actor."

"Hey!" Kevin protested. "I'm an actor—and I'm a doll!"

"You are," Lauren assured him, laughing.

"What about me?" Leo asked.

"You're okay. Sometimes, I like you best as a mime. You're quiet that way," Lauren said.

"Whoa!" Leo protested.

"We're getting off course here," Boris said. He looked at Fin. "Seriously, we hoped you two were coming back, but there were cop cars on the streets, and we saw officers running around and people milling, so…we tried to draw them out. Cara, Gary, Kenneth…and Julian. All we got was teary-eyed malarkey from Cara, swagger from Julian, business from Gary and a bunch of nods from Kenneth. He seems the least concerned. What his cousins want to do, he's okay with it. But he is anxious to see the place cleaned up. Wants the cops or the FBI or whoever is keeping the entire island in crime-scene tape to finish up. He says if…" He paused, a frown wrinkling his features.

Kevin picked up the thread, and said flatly, "He said that if you idiots haven't come up with something by now, you're not going to. I think Kenneth wanted you at dinner—he wanted to make you give him his island back."

"And, of course," Leo added, "Cara also talked about the movie—getting the island going so that Boris could finish the movie."

"She had wanted to be an extra in the last scene that needed to be shot, but Brad, Terry and I have figured out how to edit the thing so that we have all the footage that we need," Boris told him.

"Did you tell her that?" Fin asked.

"I... No. We all said that we just had to wait to see what the future held," Boris said. "We didn't know if you wanted them to think we were going back, or what?"

"You didn't really think that any of them *would* just admit to killing Cindy, did you?" Lauren asked, wide-eyed.

Fin shook his head, smiling. "No, but you never know when someone might give away something about themselves, where they've been, how they feel...what makes them tick. I'm sorry for the way it turned out and I thank you all sincerely for your help."

It was late. And he wanted to head out to Houma early and leave them plenty of time to get to the police dock and get a ride out to Christy Island by midafternoon. He stood up. "Thank you again."

"We want it solved, too," Boris assured him, standing.

The others stood as well.

Fin looked over at Avalon. She gave him a forced smile.

"Eight a.m.?"

She nodded.

Boris walked him to the gate.

"Don't worry. I'll lock and bolt it the minute you're out. And, yes, there's a nice high wall around the courtyard here, but people can crawl walls. I'll also make sure that the doors to the house are securely locked."

"Thanks," Fin said.

"You really think this is a serial killer?" Boris asked.

"The scariest kind. Someone who stalks prey, who knows patience, who has studied forensics. Yeah, I think there's a serial killer at work."

Boris nodded and lifted a hand in farewell. Fin headed out down the street to his car.

He paused, looking at the house. He hated leaving. He realized that he didn't want to believe that anyone in the movie cast and crew was involved.

But they just might be.

And they were living together.

He pulled out his phone as he reached his car, putting through a call to Angela to tell her about Samara Stella and the doll.

Angela was assuring him that she'd hunt down the origins of the doll when a loud scream echoed down the street. He turned and ran.

Right as he reached the rental house, Boris was swinging the front door open for him, clearly having intuited that Fin would be rushing back, and wanting his help with whatever had caused that scream.

Kevin, Brad and Lauren were standing helplessly in the courtyard.

"What's going on?" he demanded.

"I don't know—that was Avalon."

He flew up the stairs and burst into her room.

She had a tablet that was lying on the ground, the screen bright...but empty. She had her hands pressed to her temples. She looked at him in horror and seemed almost unaware that she had screamed.

"Avalon?"

'He was on it again, but this time... Fin! It wasn't just words... They filmed it! They filmed the murder of that poor girl, Ellen Frampton. Oh, God, Fin, if it wasn't her, just how many people have they killed?"

# CHAPTER TEN

Avalon still couldn't believe what she had seen.

She didn't want to believe what she had seen.

But it had appeared real. Just seconds of film…

A knife going into a woman's chest, coming out, going in again…

Blood spattering the camera…

And then gone.

Her scream had drawn everyone in the house.

Along with Fin, the rest of the group crowded into the hallway, and partially into her room.

It was chaos. She had frightened everyone, and standing there, she knew that she hadn't realized what the scene had done to her, just how loud and terrified her scream had been. But it had been horrible.

"Who does that? Who kills someone brutally and films it? These are monsters—"

"Wait, wait," Boris said. "Avalon! You're in film. You know that something like that can be faked—what you saw had to have been faked."

Lauren was looking at her with sheer terror in her eyes.

Boris was skeptical. It seemed that Brad and Terry were equally doubtful, too, while Leo and Kevin looked more worried.

"Can you play it again?" Brad asked her. "If Boris and Terry and I look at it, maybe we'll be able to figure out if it was something faked. I mean, who would put that on the internet? The cops would be all over them."

"People record almost everything these days," Lauren said.

They all looked at Fin.

"It depends on your definition of a snuff film. Are they made and distributed by anyone legitimate? No. But rumors do exist claiming that some serial killers have filmed their victims." He was quiet a minute and then said, "What Avalon saw, I don't know." He was looking at her worriedly.

She'd been so angry when she thought about what had been done. Lives so brutally stolen. Beauty, youth and promise—taken. She'd been determined that she wasn't going to be afraid.

She'd just turned on the tablet—thinking she might stumble upon another thread where someone had written about his longing for murder—and navigated to the same website she'd found before.

She hadn't really expected to find anything. She wasn't ready for what she saw.

Fin picked up the tablet off the floor and looked at it, but didn't touch it.

"We'll give this to Jodi," he told her.

She nodded.

"Really. You should stay off the computer," Lauren said firmly. "Off a tablet. You shouldn't even look at your phone, except to answer it if it's ringing."

"She's right," Kevin said, looking at her with concern.

"It's hard to do a website if you don't get on a computer," Avalon said.

"Then give it a few days. Samara isn't going to be concerned about refreshing her website right now," Boris said.

"I promise you, she's not," Leo said.

"All of you—I'm sorry. Go to bed, please!" Avalon said. "It is late. This was crazy. I was trying to distract myself. Trying to be useful. I… Go to bed!"

She looked at Fin.

"Sorry," she said.

"There's a sofa downstairs," he said. "I'll be on it."

"What?" she asked. "No, we can't have you do that—"

"I've slept on many a sofa."

"I like the idea of you sleeping downstairs on a sofa," Kevin told him. "It makes me feel safer—not that this person has been attacking men, but you never know. And there are people who don't like that I'm gay. Just as they don't like women like Samara who don't hide their own sexuality."

"Works for me," Lauren said.

"I guess your acting, lighting, tech friends aren't the most macho," Brad said sadly.

"Has nothing to do with macho," Fin assured him. "I've just had a lot more practice and, most importantly, I carry a weapon that I'm licensed to carry and trained to use."

"Works for me," Boris said.

"I can sleep on the couch and you can have my room," Kevin offered.

"I'm able to sleep anywhere, Kevin. Thanks for the offer," Fin said. "I will accept a pillow and a blanket, though—thanks."

Avalon had already gone for one of the big, puffy pillows on her bed and tossed it over to him. She headed to the closet for a blanket.

"All right. I may sleep tonight," Lauren said.

She went over to Fin and gave him a kiss on the cheek, turned to grin at Avalon and hurried out.

"All right then. Maybe we'll all sleep better tonight," Boris said.

He saluted and headed down the hall. Bit by bit, they all went, until Fin was left there, and he looked at Avalon as she looked at him.

"We still have to drive out early, right?" she asked.

"We do."

"But what about your clothing, changing, a shower—"

"I'll head out at seven and be back by seven thirty," he assured her. "I'm not staying far from here. We'll be fine. Just... go to bed."

She nodded. She felt as if her face was filling with color, and she wasn't sure why, other than that she'd had that temptation to throw herself at him again. He was there. At the door to her room. It was late; it had been a long and shocking day, and she shouldn't have been thinking about him as a man at all, just as an agent, and she wasn't sure that she didn't still mistrust him. Was he worried about her after the scream, or was he here because he didn't entirely trust the cast and crew?

Did any of that matter?

He was going to be sleeping right downstairs.

"Lock your door," he told her. "I've got the tablet—not sure it will help any, but I'm going to have an officer pick it up. Want to give me the alarm code so I can lock up after?"

"Today it's...um, two-eight-seven-nine. It changes all the time."

"Lock your door when I go, anyway."

She nodded. "Right. Sure. Okay. I will. I promise."

He stood outside of the room...and waited.

She walked over, then closed and bolted the door. Only then did she hear his footsteps recede down the hallway and thump as he headed down the stairs.

She had to get some sleep; she knew that. But images kept rolling in her mind. She couldn't forget being at the Grimsby house, meeting Alana and her father and husband, thinking that they had been such fine people, lost too early in life. Now, they wanted to help find justice for another young woman—also lost way too early in life.

The doll at Samara's place had a knife through the heart.

Ellen Frampton had been killed…with a knife through the heart.

And, for a moment, she had seen images that had seemed damned real of a knife being thrust into a woman's heart.

Samara had been afraid of being watched. Or that Avalon was being watched.

Maybe none of it was related. Maybe all of it was related.

She lay down, thinking she'd fall asleep maybe, and just shower in the morning.

It all kept going through her head.

Shower now.

She showered, keeping the water nice and hot, and then slipped into soft flannel pants and a big cotton T-shirt; it wasn't cold at all, but the air-conditioning in the house was set cool, and she was more accustomed to keeping a place a bit warmer.

She cuddled her remaining pillow, and still lay awake, staring at the ceiling. She concentrated on it being a white blank and…

It didn't work at all. She thought about the events, about herself, about the future, and then again, she came back to screaming when she'd seen the images—when she'd sworn to herself that she wasn't going to be a coward. She wasn't. She was going to do anything she could to help with the investigation.

Even knowing that meant a return to Christy Island.

And still, the moving image she had seen so briefly played through her mind, along with sorrow for the young woman she hadn't known, Ellen Frampton, and a deeper sense of loss for the woman she had known, Cindy West.

At length she got out of bed. She was being ridiculous, but ridiculous was okay—she could maybe get a few minutes of sleep.

Padding lightly on bare feet, she hurried down the stairs.

Fin was lying on the sofa, his hands folded behind his head on the pillow. He had heard her coming, and sat up as she came down.

"What happened?" he asked, his tone deep and anxious.

"Nothing. I'm sorry. I just… Do you mind if I stay down here with you? I won't say a word, I'm just going to curl into the chair and…"

She broke off as he stood up, sweeping out a hand to indicate she should take the sofa.

"No, no, I'm sorry. I just haven't been able to fall asleep. I won't bother you—we both need to sleep. I can close my eyes and catch at bit almost anywhere, just—just not alone tonight. I'm sorry—please don't get up."

"I'm sorry, but you have to take the sofa."

"But I don't want—"

"Make me happy. Take the sofa. Trust me, I lost my mom, but I'm not haunted by her. But if I let you sleep on a chair while I was on the sofa, I swear, I know she'd come back."

Avalon smiled.

"Really—"

"Really! Please. Loved my mom, but I like to think of her, and my dad, up having a great poker game in the clouds somewhere. They were good people, but serious about manners. Please, take the sofa."

Avalon walked over. "Now I feel guilty."

"Don't."

"Not to worry. I don't feel guilty enough to go back up to my own room."

She lay down on the sofa with the pillow beneath her head. She closed her eyes for a moment, and then opened them to reach for the blanket.

He was already drawing it over her.

"Thank you," she said.

"Not at all."

"I guess I'm starting to think you're really not so bad at all," she said.

"Yeah?"

"Yeah."

"I almost like you. Maybe even a lot," he told her.

Eyes still closed, she smiled. This was hardly the heated, sensual exchange she had imagined somewhere in the dark back burners of her mind.

But then again…

It was nice.

"Maybe I could push it a little," she whispered. "I almost like you, too. Maybe even a lot," she told him.

She heard him as he settled into the big upholstered chair. It was good, just to be near him.

Just to feel sleep taking her…

Of course, she did have a bed upstairs; they'd both fit in it.

She decided it was a really good thing that she was deep enough in the falling-to-sleep stage not to have the energy to rise and suggest such a thing.

Her room was private…

But she didn't relish the thought of explanations in the morning.

Then again, though he might like her, how humiliating would it be if he turned her down?

It didn't matter; the sweet release of sleep fell all around her, and she knew nothing again until she opened her eyes, hearing voices in the kitchen, and knowing that it was morning.

*Thursday*

Avalon woke up and glanced quickly to the chair, but Fin was no longer seated in it. Swinging her legs over the side of the sofa, she collected the pillow and blanket that she'd given Fin from her room.

As she stood up with her bundle of bedding, Kevin came to the parlor communal area.

"Hey, sleepyhead. I was supposed to wake you in five minutes if you didn't get up."

"I'm up."

Kevin was staring at her, grinning.

"Is something in the air? I don't want to criticize, but I'd go for something maybe just a wee bit more daring than plaid flannel."

"Kevin!" she said.

"You could do much worse, you know?" he said.

"Kevin!"

"Hey, if you're not going to listen to me, who will you listen to? He obviously cares about you—"

"He doesn't dislike me anymore," she said.

"And I see something in your eyes when you're looking at him. Oh, come on, my delightfully straitlaced friend. Walk on the wild side. Take a few chances with being human."

"I am human."

Lauren came in and stood next to Kevin, crossing her arms over her chest as Kevin was doing. "Hey there. What, did you have a lot of long, soulful discussions after the rest of us went to bed?" Lauren asked.

"I told her she could do much worse."

"Oh, and she has!" Lauren said. "Remember Rock Bentley?"

"Back in college," Kevin said, nodding. "Prettiest boy you'd ever want to see."

"Except that you could never appreciate his beauty as much as he did," Lauren said. "Luckily, she nipped that one in the bud."

"Yeah, I think he was ticked off—he wasn't accustomed to women getting tired of him."

"Then there was Dixon a few years ago," Lauren added, remembering.

"Now he was a nice enough guy. I think they're still friends. No chemistry—that's what she told me," Kevin said sagely.

"I'm seeing chemistry all over the place here," Lauren said. "And if she doesn't see it soon…well, I'm available!"

"If he weren't straight, I'd be available!" Kevin said. "I really like him. Confident enough so that he can be friends with anyone, careful of others…and, I bet, if anyone can solve this thing, it's him."

"And they're both a little weird, huh?" Lauren said. "Makes them perfect for each other."

Avalon stared at the two of them, shaking her head.

*Of course, neither of them knew the half of their "weirdness!"*

"Are you two done?" she asked.

Boris came on in, grinning at her, too. "You know, you have a perfectly good room upstairs with a perfectly good bed and guess what? A perfectly good door with a lock that locks."

She groaned and turned to leave. "Guys!"

"Yeah, you'd better get up there and get ready. He had some coffee with us and said that he'd be back for you, that we should make sure that you're awake."

She nodded. By then, Leo, Brad and Terry were also in the room, all of them staring at her…and smirking.

"I'm awake. I'm getting ready! If you all will quit laughing at me and let me excuse myself," Avalon said.

"Wait—we're not laughing at you," Lauren protested. "We're happy for you!"

"And wait," Leo said. He disappeared and reappeared almost instantly with a cup of coffee for her. "We're your friends, remember. We just think it's cool if…"

"Leo is trying to let you know that we've given Special Agent Finley Stirling our nod of approval," Boris told her.

"Now if he'll only give it back to us," Leo said. "Anyway, maybe I'll entertain some kids on the street today, if anyone wants to come with me."

Lauren nodded. "I'll do your makeup. More practice for me."

"You have a job offer, here, in the city. I don't believe anyone would have a problem with you taking work that's in town," Boris told her.

Lauren shook her head. "I'm sticking with you guys a bit longer. Eventually, I guess, we'll all have to get going, but…hey! Avalon—get going! Maybe you can help our boy solve this thing and let us all try to get on with life."

Maybe. Avalon wasn't sure. It seemed that strange events just crashed down on other strange events, and they might all be tangled up, and they might not.

But she smiled at them all, shook her head and headed for the stairs, now balancing the blanket, the pillow and her cup of coffee.

She paused at the foot of the stairs. "Thank you all for your blessing. But you will note the flannel, me on the sofa, him on the chair. I was just…unnerved. I needed company."

Lauren laughed. "Could have come to my room."

"I don't know, Lauren. You're pretty cute," Kevin teased. "But Agent Stirling is hot."

Avalon let out a groan and hurried on up the stairs.

Fin knew it wouldn't take him long to get to his place, shower and change, and get back. Still, when he'd woken up, he'd delayed leaving.

He'd waited until Kevin and Lauren had been awake and moving, along with Terry and Boris.

He didn't believe that any of the cast and crew were involved. It was natural that Avalon should fight against that idea, but he had learned that during an investigation, all possibilities had to be considered. So, while he wanted to believe that they were innocent, he needed to make sure that several of them were awake before he left.

He had an instinct about Kevin—the man really cared about

Avalon. He was equally convinced that everything about Lauren was honest, and all reports pointed to a man, or two men, being the perpetrator.

He'd seen many things. Not "just about everything," because the evil that could exist in humanity never ceased to surprise him. But, in this case, he had an instinct about Lauren, and he prayed that he was right.

He'd just come out of the shower when his phone rang. He'd thought that it might be Angela. But it wasn't—rather, it was the crime-scene investigator in Biloxi, Bert Nelson.

"Thanks for calling me—you have something?"

"We dug and dug, and while we can't be sure when this was lost, we did come up with something in the bushes right off the road."

"What did you find?"

"It's a medallion. Not a necklace, just a medallion—a souvenir. Naturally, we investigated where it might have come from originally. I'm sending you pictures, front and back. There's a popular rock band out—been hitting the charts about three years now—called Pauly's Pariah. These medallions were one of their promo items, given out at their concerts. I went back with Tom Drayton and we searched through records trying to find out if Ellen Frampton had been to a concert given by the group, of if any of her known friends or associates had any connection to the band. We found nothing. Also, whoever handled the medallion last was wearing gloves. No prints whatsoever, wiped clean. That's what we found."

"Thank you. It may just lead us somewhere we need to go," Fin told him.

He ended the call quickly, anxious to get the information to Angela, and not sure that it would have gone through all the official channels yet.

He reported to her and she promised she'd take their list of characters and find out who might have been at a Pauly's Pariah concert, or been involved with the band in any way.

He was already in the car, on his way to pick up Avalon, when he got a call back from Angela.

"Anyone?" he asked.

"Interesting group of characters, actually," she said.

"Oh?"

"Boris Koslov directed a video for them just about three years ago."

"Three years ago?"

*He'd just left Avalon at the house with Boris Koslov!*

"Just about. And while some of it was filmed here—at a pretty old mansion with a phenomenal ballroom and staircase—a lot of it was filmed outside of New Orleans, out near the Chalmette Battlefield. But, Fin, he's not the only one who had something to do with them. There's video of the making of the video—Lauren Carlson was doing makeup for the band, and Terry Jenson was working on the set design. But one of our new people, an absolute wizard with facial-recognition software, ran footage of people in the audience, extras hired to dance and cheer on the band. Julian Bennett can be seen in one of the crowd scenes."

"Thanks. Can you find out where the band is located now? I understand that they've become popular in the last few years, so I imagine they could be anywhere."

"Yes, they could be. But they just came off tour and Paul Mc Masters, the lead singer, is from Houma, so it's likely that he and his main bandmates—brothers Sean and Perry Adair—are with him. There's about two weeks before they're due to be working back in the studio and the studio they use is in New Orleans."

"Thanks."

"There's more."

"Yeah?"

"Avalon Morgan is in it, too."

Everything seemed to circle around.

Avalon. He knew that Avalon had not had anything to do with what had happened.

But Boris…

Boris seemed to be just about everywhere.

"I'm going to get Jackson and Adam working on finding the right connection for you to get to visit with them, if you wish. Then again, maybe Miss Morgan has an in with them."

"I'm heading to Houma now and the police station there. As soon as I pick up Avalon. I wanted to get out to Christy Island, too. We'll see if we can get it all in—if I can contact the band members—or if Avalon does have an in and can arrange for me to see them or at least one of them."

"Right. I'll get back to you on that. But I was about to call you about another piece of this puzzle. Officer Jodi Marsh has been working with our computer tech people here, trying to trace the writing—and the image—that Avalon saw."

"And?"

"They found something on the dark web—not traceable yet, but we'll keep at it."

"And?" Fin asked.

"A fan seemed to have loved what was written. Of course, we aren't sure it's what Avalon saw, but it sounds close, if not. Even with the dark web, you can track down certain things but not all—if someone was at a public venue and hacked into someone else's internet, we're looking at another whole skein of possibilities. I've sent you what Jodi and our team found. They're like dogs with a bone. When you're good at this stuff, a challenge like this is a puzzle that has to be solved."

"You're good at this stuff."

"Not like these guys. I know you're in a hurry but take a minute to read what I'm emailing you. You know the people involved—you've seen them all in action. Something may click."

"Wouldn't that be great?" he said.

"You will get there," Angela said softly. "Read what I sent you."

They ended the call and Fin pulled off the street before opening his email from her and reading what Angela had sent him.

It was titled "My Fantasy Murder."

First, I'd stalk my prey. She'd be unknown, a goddess, but I would see her, and I would know. I would watch the way that she moved, the way that she breathed, the way that her eyes would light when she laughed. I would be close enough at times to smell the sweetness that emanated from her supple flesh. I might brush by her.

Beauty knows no bounds. I have seen these goddesses in every ethnicity. Beauty covers the world. True beauties are rare, but they come from every continent—they are Asian, African, Australian, South and North American, European...a little laugh here, okay, I've yet to encounter a goddess from Antarctica.

But I am good. I am a hunter, a stalker, and I know how to smile and laugh and charm. And I find my beauties...

Fantasy. So... I find my goddess. I am a gentleman, a rugged, charming gentleman. We play and we tease, and we drink, and it's divine. That's just it—it's all divine. I did say goddess.

I wait until we are so relaxed. She's at ease with me. I make it clear that I don't expect intercourse...yet.

And when she is laughing, playing, enjoying me, looking at me with that divine sparkle in her eyes, I strike...

It's so beautiful. Watching her. Because she cannot fight—she knows and knows that she cannot fight. And I hold her and assure her and watch the light slowly fade. She's in my arms—she's still warm. There's a perfect temperature and I wait for that...and then, I give her the divine ecstasy of my love. There is no greater high. When we are done, I take her so tenderly. I care for her. I lay her out in beauty. Eternal beauty. And it's all as it should be, ashes to ashes, and dust to dust, with all that is beautiful and divine in between.

He sat in silence, chilled to the bone. While Avalon had tried to remember the words that had been in the essay, she'd been upset, she'd seen it so briefly...

She hadn't quite described just how disturbing and *sick* the written words were.

He felt himself anxious to get to her again.

He needed to get Avalon, get to Houma, continue the steps of his investigation. Go through the day. And when the day was done, with just possibly more learned from the Houma sources, he would read the words again, and think of the people involved. Think of who he knew who might write in such a manner.

Luckily, the street space he had left behind forty minutes earlier was still there; he parked the car and hurried to the house, telling himself it was ridiculous to think that anything had happened in the time that he'd been gone.

But Boris had been on the island when Cindy West's body had been displayed on the tomb.

And he'd directed a video for a band, and one of their promotional items had been found near the site of another display.

There was another dead girl who had been found in waters of the bayou...

And Avalon was in the house with Boris.

So were others.

He couldn't shake the feeling that Avalon might be a target.

Avalon had showered the night before, but showering was a good way to wake up.

She didn't take long; when she closed her eyes, she saw again the flash of death she had seen on her tablet the night before.

The knife, the blood, the human being.

She emerged from the shower and dressed for the day, thinking that she needed most to be practical. They'd be in Houma, and then they'd be back on the island.

Police were taking shifts, watching over the forensic crews

who were still combing the place. She figured that they'd finish soon.

And then what?

She couldn't imagine the place where their dead friend had
been left displayed on a tomb becoming a tourist attraction.
And yet...

That was why they sometimes saw the dead. Saw those who
stayed behind. Because history brought with it the good, the
bad and the heroic.

And the very ugly.

The heirs hated the island. They just wanted to get rid of it.
According to them, none of their parents had cared for old man
Christy; he had lived in solitude and died in solitude.

She wondered what he had really been like.

That was something she needed to ask Fin about—he seemed
to be able access information on just about anything.

Because if there had been something off about the old man...

Maybe that something had come through to his heirs...

*No, no, no,* she told herself. The sins of the fathers did not
come down on the sons.

She looked at herself in the mirror. No fear in her eyes. Clothing—serviceable.

She was going to be strong. And if seeing the ugly might
mean getting to the end of it, she was ready.

She glanced at her watch. Right on time. Fin would be there
any second.

While she felt constantly torn in his company, there was one
thing she believed: he was passionate about finding Cindy's
killer. And he saw the dead, too. She didn't have to pretend with
him. Now if only she didn't have to pretend that she was feeling
such a growing attraction to him, as complex as that seemed to
be, she'd be just fine.

What the hell.

She *was* an actress. Right now, she wanted to be as helpful as humanly possible, as strong, as courageous—and, dammit, she had the same passion as Fin to solve Cindy's murder.

He had said that he wouldn't stop.

Well, neither would she!

# CHAPTER ELEVEN

Fin rang the bell, and somehow schooled himself not to bang on the door. He needed to compartmentalize—push the web page to the back burner. The investigation today—with Avalon at his side—should be foremost in his mind.

Kevin opened the door, smiling in greeting. "She's up—she's ready. We even made her drink a cup of coffee."

"I'll run and get her for you." Lauren waved as she headed up the stairs.

"Kevin, you know about a group called Pauly's Pariah, right?" Fin asked casually as he stepped into the living room.

"Oh, sure, yeah—you must have heard of them, too. Come on, man, you're an FBI agent—not the walking dead!"

Fin grimaced and had to laugh. "Hey, I like music—tend toward rock and jazz."

"They do that song, 'Hold on to Me.' That's the one that made them popular. And they're very theatrical. I was jealous—Boris directed a video for them. I couldn't be in it—I was working on Broadway at the time, and man...okay, it was as a horse's foot, but I was on Broadway."

"I have heard of the band—you're right. I know that song. But Broadway is great," Fin agreed.

"Yeah, but the band is getting really good. Lauren worked with them, and…yeah, Terry, too. That's the promise of being a struggling young actor. Sometimes it's feast, and sometimes it's famine." He grew quiet. "That's the thing, you know. You work so hard. Boris had such dreams for getting his movie made. And if it was a hit—cult hit, being horror and B budget—we'd have all benefited. You haven't seen the video, huh? Because, if you had, you'd know it."

"I'd recognize their work?"

"Maybe. But you wouldn't miss Avalon."

"Ah, of course. Avalon was in it, too."

"Yeah, as the object of the lead singer's affections. YouTube it—it will come up. She does websites for other people, and never really pushes herself enough. But it's a cool video, really. Anyway…aha! Speak of the devil…or devil-ette or -ess? She appears!"

Avalon was coming down the stairs. She was wearing leggings with a long knit jacket, hair pulled back in a single braid, as if she was ready for anything.

"Devil-ette?" she asked Kevin.

"In the very best way," he said.

"Okay. We're off. If we're going to be late, I'll call."

"We're going to be late," Fin told Avalon, then turned to Kevin. "But we'll keep you posted so that you don't worry."

They started out and she paused, turning back to Kevin. "You guys be careful, okay?"

"We'll stick together like glue," he promised.

"Watch Lauren," Fin said. "Don't let her be alone."

"You think—"

"Ryder has cops watching, but who knows right now? Don't let Lauren be alone, hit 911 at anything suspicious, inside the house or out."

He had Avalon with him but felt a pang of worry at leaving the others alone.

Avalon arched an eyebrow, then Fin bid Kevin goodbye, thanking him for making sure that Avalon was awake and ready to go.

As they headed to his car, he called Ryder.

She was clearly listening as he asked for officers to make sure that the house and all inside it were safe during the day and when night fell.

"All right, what the hell is going on?" she demanded as they reached the car.

He didn't answer her as he opened the passenger side door for her, but asked, "How well do you know the band Pauly's Pariah?"

"I was in a video for them. It was a good-paying gig—and I have Boris to thank for it. He called me because he remembered me from when he'd lectured me as a student. He's done great things for me, really. And others."

He didn't reply, just walked around and took his seat on the driver's side of the car. He felt her watching him as he started the car and rolled out into traffic.

"Fin!"

He sighed. "We're not sharing this yet, and it may mean nothing, but one of the band's souvenir medallions was found on the road out behind the Grimsby Estate," he told her.

"A medallion?"

"Right. It has the band engraved on one side and a spectral figure on the other. I have a picture of it on my phone—"

"I don't need your picture," she told him. "I have one."

"Boris, Terry and Lauren were all on that shoot, too," he said.

"Wow. I guess you and Kevin had a talk."

"I didn't need to talk to Kevin."

"That's right," she said. Her voice was hard. "You're the FBI.

You know everything. Well, if you know everything, who the hell killed Cindy!"

He didn't reply.

"I'm telling you that I know Boris. He's a good guy."

"Okay."

"But he's still under suspicion."

He didn't reply.

"Look, I was practically the star of the damned video. I should be under suspicion. Then again, maybe I am," she said. "Maybe I spend my days with you so that you can break down my defenses and I'll admit that I'm really a serial killer, or a procurer, or a criminal mastermind…"

"You done?"

"Yes, I'm done. At least you haven't had Boris locked up yet."

That could be coming. He didn't say it.

Silence fell between them. "Houma. I've always enjoyed Houma. There's a super bookstore in Houma," she said. "Bent Pages. I spent a lot of time there before and after filming on the video. They chose Houma because it's where Paul McMasters is from, but you probably know that. The city isn't too big, and it isn't too small. There's also a plantation—Houmas House. Beautiful homes and property."

"I grew up not all that far from Houma. In fact, the owners of that bookstore probably thought that I was a ghoul. They were always ordering books for me when I was still in high school, books on criminology."

She was silent again and he told her, "You, Boris and Terry aren't the only people involved with Christy Island who can be seen on that video."

"Oh?"

"Julian Bennett was there," he revealed.

"Oh! I—I never saw him."

"I haven't seen the video yet. I just learned about this between the time I left and the time I came back for you. We should watch it again—maybe you'll notice something."

"I hate watching."

"Why?"

"I never watch myself on film—not unless I have to."

"Why?"

"If I'm horrible or see what I should have done differently, it's too late to do anything."

"I don't think you're horrible very often," he said.

"Thanks for the faith." She sighed. "I wish you had that much faith in Boris."

"Are you sure that *you* do?" he asked her.

"You need to concentrate on the family. Or on... I don't know."

"They're being watched," he assured her.

It took a good hour to reach the outskirts of Houma, a bit more to arrive where they needed to be. Avalon remained wary, but not ice-cold. She obviously cared for her friends.

He didn't want to talk about the fact that their computer techs had found a copy of what he thought she might have read. Not yet. He needed to go over it, word for word, himself.

Eventually, he had to show it to her.

Once they arrived at the Houma police station, Fin introduced himself at the reception desk and then waited a moment for someone to arrive to help them.

It was a serious older man with a cap of snowy white hair who met them, introducing himself as Captain Wayne Tremont. "Glad to see that you're taking an interest in this. We bring the case up again at just about every meeting, but we never have a new lead. We don't have any old leads. As I'm sure you've heard, all we know is that she was dressed in one of those Roaring Twenties outfits, which wasn't a surprise. The Speakeasy is still out there. Mort Jones—who owns the place—was devastated about the girl and almost closed. But here's the thing—he has a fun place. Young people like it. We're not a big party town like New Orleans. The Speakeasy allows for young adults to get dressed up in something other than the ordinary. You know how it goes. Some people like a nice quiet bar for a Friday night drink and maybe dinner before they go home. Others are itching for a bit of fun on the weekends. Anyway, I told Morty that you might be out. First, though I'm sure you've gotten everything on your email, I thought you'd want to see our records on the case. Pictures and notes as they were taken by the detectives on the case. I'm sorry that they're not here to help you. One died of a heart attack about a year ago and the other moved down to the Caribbean. Says his excitement now is watching a dolphin jump out of the water and he likes it that way."

"Thank you," Fin said.

He'd introduced Avalon as a consultant on the case; she'd accepted the introduction and been polite to the captain, but she was keeping quiet.

He led them into a meeting room. Folders had been strewn across a large table, allowing him easy access.

The crime-scene photos were already up on a large screen.

They were grim.

"She's still a Jane Doe. I'd have thought that somewhere along the line, we might connect her to a missing-persons case, but it hasn't happened," the captain told them.

Avalon stood by his side, staring at the screen. "Are you okay with this?" he whispered. She seemed a little pale but said nothing and displayed no emotion. Fin gave her shoulder a gentle squeeze of support.

There hadn't been a lot left of the young woman. The flapper outfit was in shreds, barely covering her body.

Much of her flesh was gone; the skull remained, and the bones had detached.

"She was floating in the bayou. A shrimper called it in."

"Where might we find the medical examiner's report?" Fin asked.

The captain pointed to one of the folders.

The body had been too degraded for the medical examiner to determine if there had been a sexual assault. Knicks on rib bones suggested that she had been stabbed. The state of decay had prevented him from knowing if she'd had defensive wounds.

There was an image of what the woman might have looked like, done by a forensic artist from the victim's skull. She had been in her late twenties or early thirties, dark-haired, pretty.

"How could no one know who she was?" Avalon whispered.

"She might have been working the streets," Fin told her. "Even in Houma. And when young women are working the streets, friends are sometimes afraid to come forward. Even when the police announce that there will be no retribution. And they don't always keep in contact with their families. She might have been from anywhere."

"What do you think?" Captain Tremont asked. "I've read up on that murder you're working out on Christy Island. In my mind, that island should have fallen under the jurisdiction of Terrebonne Parish, but... I guess lines were set long ago and it's not like there was really any kind of law out there...or, until now, any kind of law needed." He shrugged. "But if you need anything from us, anything at all, you let us know."

"I will, and thank you," Fin said.

He sat down to read the files. Avalon sat, as well. She didn't seem to be able to stop staring at the screen.

"Was she found with any jewelry?" she asked Captain Tremont.

He shook his head. "If she was wearing any, it's down in the muck, or in the gullet of a seabird of a fledgling gator, I imagine. I guess we're lucky that...well, that she wasn't more broken up."

Fin looked up at Captain Tremont. "What about this restaurant and bar? The Speakeasy. Do they have 1920s displays, any kind of a place where a murderer might have displayed her?"

The captain thought about that.

"Well, when you go in, to get to the bar, you go down a little staircase so that it really looks like you're in the bowels of a 1920s basement. There are sofas and chairs, and it's dark and the bartenders dress in suspenders and cotton shirts. The women working—bartenders and waitresses—wear flapper dresses and bands with feathers in their hair. But for display…she wasn't displayed. She was lost in the bayou."

"How close is this place to the water?" Fin asked.

"Oh, right there. Some of the fishing and shrimping boys like to tie up at the dock and go in for a drink before heading in for the night. There's a path—just dirt and gravel—that leads from the dock right up to the place." He hesitated. "It's estimated that she was in the water from two to four weeks before she was found."

Fin studied the files a while longer; he was surprised that Avalon quit staring at the screen and started reading through them, as well.

"You'll excuse me," Captain Tremont said. "Take your time— all you need."

There didn't seem to be much more that he could discover. The detectives had questioned customers, workers and everyone they could think of. They had sent the forensic artist's likeness for the victim across the country, to be compared to missing-person reports.

They had done all the right things.

But they had nothing.

He looked over at Avalon. She stared back at him, shaking her head.

"How do people do these things?" she whispered.

He stood, shaking his head, then gathered the folders, leaving them in a neat pile. He looked at her. "Let's go see this place. The Speakeasy."

She nodded. "Do you really think this can relate? I mean, she was probably dressed as a flapper to go to the bar. We don't know if she was…assaulted when dead. She was found in the bayou, possibly stabbed. She might have been… Say she was a sex worker—out with a john who got carried away. Maybe she made him angry. This could be nothing—".

"It could be nothing. You didn't tell me—are you friends with any of the members of Pauly's Pariah?"

She shook her head. "No. Not really. They were fine, they were nice…and I do like their music. But… Hold on. Paul did give me his phone number and wanted me to know I was welcome backstage if I happened to be in a city where they were playing." She made a face. "He…um. He was nice enough, and he asked me to join him for dinner, but I was uncomfortable. He's married and it would have felt wrong—it was just him, not the group. It might have been just dinner, but… I don't know. I made an excuse. I do have his number."

"Will you try calling him?"

She nodded. "I will, but…"

"I don't know what we'll get. Maybe nothing."

She nodded. "And out on the island…"

"I don't know. But if we don't just keep going, we'll never get where we hope to go."

She put through the call. She greeted the singer and reminded him who she was, made a bit of friendly small talk. Then she looked at Fin and mouthed, *What do I say?*

"Tell him the truth—and that we won't take much of his time."

She brought her phone back to her ear, but apparently, Paul McMasters was talking to her. She was nodding, as if he could see her, and she said softly, "Yes, and thank you, and I'm so sorry, that's why I'm calling. I'm working with an agent on the case and…long explanation, but we won't take much of your time, if you could just spare a few minutes…yes, we're in Houma now. We can be there in a matter of minutes."

McMasters talked on the other end for a few moments and she hung up.

"Apparently, he'd already heard about us. Well, you. His agent contacted him because someone high up had contacted him, and…anyway, he was expecting to see an agent. And he's happy to see me."

"Great. Thank you."

She looked at him. "You had contacts reach out already."

"They may or may not have worked. We would have had to have gone through red tape and worse—time—to arrange a meeting."

"Oh. Okay. Aren't you going to ask me where we're going?"

He smiled. "I'm the FBI, remember? I already have an address."

Fin had to admit that while he loved music and had been to his share of concerts, he wasn't sure what to expect. Pauly's Pariah had become a popular group. He had no idea how much money they made, if that might have changed an easygoing musician, brought about a lot of security, or what.

But Paul McMasters was staying at his mother's house. It was a fair-size old farmhouse, but not a mansion by any means.

The man was on the front porch when they arrived. He came down the steps to greet them, giving Avalon a hug when she emerged from the passenger's seat and then coming around to shake Fin's hand. He had shoulder-length light brown hair that was well kept, a slim, wiry build and an easy manner.

"I'm not sure how I can help you, but, hey, come on in. My mother makes the best Arnold Palmers in the state and beyond."

In the house, they met his mother, an attractive woman in her late fifties or early sixties, his teenage sister and his grandfather.

They were offered lunch.

It was nice to see that while Paul McMasters might be all the rage on stage, he was simply Paul when he was home, and he seemed to appreciate his family. He explained that his wife's dad had just had surgery, and she was over in Arkansas with him for a few days.

There was no polite way to refuse sandwiches and fruit salad. Not a bad idea, really. They needed to eat.

But the McMasters family also knew that Fin was FBI and that he and Avalon had come for a reason, even if his little sister seemed to be more in awe of Avalon than she was of her brother.

They sat outside on the patio at a tiled table with a little umbrella alone after interacting with the family—all had discreetly left the table.

"So, tell me. How can I help? I didn't know Cindy West," he told Fin. "But I do know Boris and Terry and Lauren—and Avalon. We were still starting out and, in this day and age, you have to have video," he said. "We made a good team—the product was important to all of us. We didn't have a big budget, and Boris wasn't demanding. But we were legitimate! And we wound up with a backer, so everyone wound up being paid fairly. And that video helped bring us to the public." He sat back, serious as he looked at Fin. "Sorry, that was round-about. I just mean that I can't see how I can help, but I'm more than happy to. This hurt people who were good to me."

"We're being careful about what goes out to the press," Fin said. "But, in truth, we're afraid that there is a serial killer at work. A young lady was left in a similar way in Mississippi—killed, cleaned, dressed up and left at a historic estate. We're afraid that a victim found near the Speakeasy might also have been someone this killer—or killers—managed to coerce away with them. In this instance—"

"The Speakeasy Jane Doe," McMasters said. "I read about it in the paper—they sent out a picture of what she might have looked like a while back. I remember—my mom still has the paper delivered. I remember seeing it on the counter. So sad. You know, we played at the Speakeasy when we were starting out. Have you been there yet?"

"No," Fin said. "But we will take a ride out there."

"The owner is a super nice guy—promised him we would do a ticketed event for him sometime in the future. And we will. We never forget the people who helped us when we were a garage band." He paused to laugh. "We really were a garage band. Or a carriage-house band, I guess. We used to practice in what is now the garage and was once the carriage house and barn. It's a bit from the house—that kept my parents from going insane when we started playing. Especially when we decided we were getting good enough to test out a few amplifiers."

"How did you find working with Boris?" Fin asked. He saw Avalon's eyes narrow, but she didn't say a word.

"Boris?" Paul said. "Love him. I don't believe we'd be where we are now if it wasn't for that video. Don't get me wrong— I have faith in our music. But there are many talented people out there, and some will be able to go farther than others with their talent because of luck or good fortune…or good decisions. That video was a chance for all of us. He was amazing to work with." He was quiet for a minute and then sighed softly. "If he's in trouble now—I know that he largely financed the movie he was making himself—I'd be more than happy to help him out. So would the band." He smiled and turned to Avalon. "And this lady was perfection. Well, I can imagine you know that, if you've seen the video."

"He hasn't seen the whole video," Avalon said.

"I'm sorry. I didn't know about it until earlier," Fin said.

"Bring it up on your phone. I mean, well, we have a small screening room here now, but if you just want to get a quick look, you know. Pull up YouTube. It's still the first video that will come up under Pauly's Pariah."

Fin nodded, taking out his phone, and did as had been suggested.

It was a good music video; the fantastic with the realistic. A historic home had been used with the set design to create the appearance of a castle. Paul McMasters, singing, seemed to be enjoying the good in life, but longing for the most important thing—the right person with whom to share it. Avalon was in the dream sequence. Beautiful in a flowing ballroom gown, she danced with him in a sweeping circle until he simply held her at the end and the dream sequence faded into reality. Then there was a shot of the band on stage…and the extras dancing by the stage.

Julian Bennett was in that scene, dancing with a half-dozen young women to a different tempo, hot and heavy.

"Avalon was super—she taught me to do the Viennese waltz for that segment," McMasters said. "And she didn't whine once when I stepped all over her."

"Avalon is remarkably talented," Fin said. The sequence had been amazing, and she'd embodied a sense of beauty and fantasy.

"Terry Jenson did the set?" he asked.

"Yeah. He and Boris are exceptionally good together," McMasters said. "Most of what we needed was lighting. But Terry is great at set design."

"Boris has a vision—Terry has ability to deliver that vision," Avalon explained. "Boris, Terry—and then Brad—have been great working together."

"What about the extras used here—the audience. They were paid—that wasn't a live performance?"

"The extras were paid—it was not a real live performance," McMasters said. "We have to be careful. Some people get carried away when they gain an audience. I can say for Sean and Perry and me, we're not…hmm. I don't know what to say. At live concerts we've had panties thrown at us onstage, and sometimes, security has to stop overzealous fans… Don't get me wrong—I am so appreciative of having made it to where we're surviving nicely as a band, but... Sorry. Long explanation. I guess you were looking for a simple yes or no."

"Did you know any of the extras?"

"Oh, sure, a lot were friends of mine, of Perry, or Sean."

Fin played the video again, freezing at the frame with Julian Bennett.

"You know this guy?"

"Julian. Nice enough guy. Comes down from Baton Rouge. In fact, I met him several years ago at the Speakeasy. Hey, you must know him, too, right, Avalon? He and his family own Christy Island. I didn't know that before—I don't think it meant anything to him. I guess any of us who grew up in this area just thought of Christy Island as a creepy place owned by an even creepier old man. Julian's last name is Bennett—I never associated him with Christy Island."

"But you met at the Speakeasy?" Fin asked.

"I think it was there. We don't have that many venues nearby." He leaned back.

"Pretty sure we all hung out there after the video, too, with Boris and the crew."

Fin nodded politely. "You've been very helpful, and I appreciate it."

"This was really nice of you," Avalon told him.

They went back through the house and said goodbye to his family. That took a while.

When they were in the car again, Avalon said, "I think he would have gone with us out to the Speakeasy if we had asked him."

"I think that's possible," he said.

"But you didn't ask him."

He looked over at her. "Well, I'm going to have to ask *about* him," he said.

"Ah, of course. But you can't be serious. I mean, Paul might be in a rock band, but he's even more apple pie than I remembered."

"You always think the best of everyone."

"And you think the worst."

"It's my job. And I don't think the worst of everyone, I just leave the possibility open that we're not all what we appear to be on the surface."

"You found him to be suspicious?"

"No, not really."

She shook her head and looked at the road. Then she frowned. "I never saw Julian Bennett that day. Not that I remember. But the sequence I was in was filmed at the house. We danced across the hall or the makeshift ballroom. When they were shooting the crowd scene..." She frowned. "I was with Lauren. We were both free to go—the live-performance scene was the last thing they filmed, and I even like the song, but I'd heard it so many times that day I was ready to leave. We saw all the extras as we were leaving, but I never noticed Julian Bennett."

He was thoughtful and he looked at her. "Boris and Terry have acted as if they first met him when they came to Christy Island."

"Maybe they didn't notice him at the video shoot, either."

"Terry might not have been around once the set was decorated, but Brad does a lot of the editing with Boris from what I understand. Boris had to have seen Julian, at minimum in the footage. And if they all partied together at the Speakeasy once the filming was done, they must have been introduced to Julian then."

"Did Boris ever tell you specifically that he didn't know any of the Christy family?" she asked, and then added, "Oh!"

"What is it?"

"I'm curious. And you have a way of knowing everything. Or the FBI has a way of knowing everything..."

"We have access to records. We don't spy on the average man."

"Right, sorry!" she said.

He sighed. "What is it that you're curious about?"

"Nolan Christy."

"Old Nolan? He's dead."

"Right. But he scared people away from the island. He was a loner. What was he really doing out on that island?"

"Well, growing old and dying for one," Fin said.

She made a face at him. "His heirs say that their parents—his grandchildren—hated him. They had to have had their reasons."

"I'll have Angela see if she can dig anything up," he said. "Why? You're expecting to discover that he was luring women to the island and murdering them there?"

"Maybe."

"You would think that there would have been a number of missing-person reports."

"Hey, they still haven't identified Jane Doe, pulled from the bayou near the bar."

"True," he acknowledged. They drove alongside the bayou for another mile or so before coming to a fork in the road. Fin followed his navigation and turned to the left, heading along a paved road with signs that advertised the Speakeasy. Written below were words that warned, *Know the password, and please, SHHH!*

"Do you know the password?" Avalon asked him.

"Maybe," he told her cryptically.

He really didn't know; he had to check his email to see if Angela had supplied it for him. But whether he knew it or not, he was getting into the place, and he had a feeling that it was easily guessed—the venue needed clientele to survive.

After he parked, he looked at his phone.

Yes, Angela had talked to the man, and yes, Mort Jones would be waiting for him and he had his own special password.

He paused by the car, surveilling the space around him, and the restaurant.

A path led down to the water. The slow-moving bayou drifted beautifully by in the sunlight of the dying afternoon. Docks right below the restaurant offered space for ten to twenty small boats, less space for bigger shrimpers. A small grassy slope made its way down from the restaurant to the water and the docks. A tile-and-gravel path provided a walkway.

He looked at the Speakeasy. There were a few period all-weather lounges beneath an arched overhang by the entrance. The outer wall was white, but there had been a picture painted on it of a young woman in a 1920s sheath dress, lounging imperiously on a settee, a cigarette cradled by a long cigarette holder in her hand as she looked with disdain at the world around her.

He paused, thinking about the dead woman.

Lost to the water; deteriorated, decomposing, decayed.

But maybe the plan had been to dress her up, leave her in the front, posed on one of the period sofas there, down to the cigarette holder in her hand.

Had something gone wrong?

Perhaps someone had come upon him...or them. It was easy enough for them to charm and abduct a woman; maybe they weren't so tough, though. Fin had a feeling that Mort Jones kept a gun on his premises and knew how to use it.

"What is it?" Avalon said.

"Just observing."

"You're such a liar."

"What?"

"You're imagining that one of the sofas there would have been a place where a dead woman might be displayed...in her twenties' splendor."

There was a little window slot on the door; when Fin knocked, it slid open.

A deep voice demanded, "Who's there?"

"Fin from the G-zone," he said.

The door opened. A large friendly-looking man with a white

mustache and beard opened the door; he appeared to be in his late fifties to early sixties, and was dressed in a suit that might have been worn in the 1920s or 1930s, complete with a fedora.

"Hello, and welcome. We don't open until five, so you've arrived perfectly to see the place while it's empty. You're Special Agent Finley Stirling? And Miss Morgan?"

"Thank you so much for agreeing to see us," Fin said.

"Come on down the steps. We're not heading to a real basement, just a slightly lower level. But going down steps to a speakeasy, well, according to rumor, you had to have a password and steps."

The little hallway with the steps was dark. They were led to a room where the walls were decorated with copies of well-known Art Nouveau and Art Deco pieces. The lighting was kept dim. The sofas were plush, and arranged in discreet, shadowy conversational areas.

The workers all looked as if they belonged a century in the past. Mort Jones had done a great job with the place; Fin could imagine police bursting in to break up the party.

"Prohibition ran from 1920 to 1933," Mort told them. "I guess it was a good thing and a bad thing that it all ended with the Depression. Meant some could sip away a few of their problems—and some could drink themselves right into the grave of depression. Anyway, I was always fascinated with the stories of passwords, secrets and the mob, the criminal empires…and the FBI, Bonnie and Clyde, Eliot Ness and *The Untouchables*. Right up your alley, I think."

"I believe it's changed a bit since those days."

"But the fight for right goes on," Mort said.

"Yep—and, time and time again, they get the bad guy through the IRS."

Mort smiled. "I don't believe that for a minute. Anyway, we were just devastated by what happened here. To think that it might have happened again, and again…" He shook his head.

"May I get you something? We have a full bar. Of course, you're working. We have anything you can imagine, lots of taps…oh! We brew our own root beer."

"I would love a glass of your root beer," Avalon said, causing the man to beam.

He had workers on, preparing for the night. But he walked behind the bar himself, pouring them two glasses of the house root beer.

"Come on over to a well-darkened corner—we'll talk," Mort said.

They followed him to a corner that was indeed dimly lit.

"This root beer is delicious," Avalon assured him.

He smiled. When he sat, he grew serious. "It looked as if that poor woman was coming here—from the picture they sent out. I mean, the papers carried the fact that she'd been… I guess gnawed on and decomposed and…well, anyway, I studied the sketch from the police artist over and over. I never saw her in here. We went through all our employees, and everyone who wandered in here during the next weeks. I think it's so heartbreaking that her picture went out there, and she…well, she just wound up being an unknown, though the community here got together and she's in the local cemetery, in one of the society tombs. Ashes to ashes, dust to dust… She was halfway there before she was interred, from what the police said to me. They never found out where her costume came from. They never figured out anything much, though, don't get me wrong, I'm not blaming the police. Someone killed that little girl and she wound up in our bayou."

"You'd never seen her here, and no one here claimed to have seen her before?"

"No," he said quietly. "I have a lot of customers from this region. And when they all say that they haven't seen a woman, I believe that they haven't seen a woman. You'd think that someone would speak up if they knew something. But the thing is, she was dressed up just like a young person on a Friday or Saturday night. Not so much during the workweek, but on Friday and Saturday nights, people like to playact."

"I heard you almost closed the place," Fin said.

Mort Jones nodded solemnly, shaking his head. "I got a daughter that age. She's up in NYC going to school—she likes it up there. She may come back, and she might not, and that will be her choice. Thing is, I love my girl no matter what her decisions might be. Somewhere out there, someone loved that poor girl, too. We can't find them—that doesn't mean that they don't exist. And I couldn't begin to imagine something like that happening to my daughter. Poor thing—made her call me every single night for ages after it happened. But she's a good girl. Lost her mom about a decade back and she makes sure that she comes back to bring me her love and make sure I'm not feeling like I'm alone."

"She sounds lovely," Avalon said.

"Absolutely," Fin agreed.

"Anyway, I got talked out of closing. The place had kind of been a dream of mine. And now it does well, I see my friends all the time, they encourage me…it's good."

"That's great," Fin told him. "I hear you have musical acts in here, too. We were just meeting with Paul McMasters. He was telling us how he played here when he was starting out."

"That's right," Jones said, nodding with approval. "They're not quite my type of music—I like the crooners, guys like Dean Martin, Tony Bennett and the Four Seasons. They were okay. But I like Paul McMasters, and I know he's a talented fellow. I want to entertain the customers here, not myself. Anyway, yeah, he played here—and he's going to do some kind of special event for me. People will come from miles and miles around and it will be ticketed and…well, it will probably pay the bills for a year." He looked at Avalon. "But you were in that video he did, weren't you? Miss Morgan, you gave that video something that far surpassed the music!"

"That's very sweet of you."

Fin pulled out his phone and showed the man a likeness of Julian Bennett. "This man comes around here, too, right?"

"Julian? Sure, he's from Baton Rouge. He's come down often enough. And I think he's friends with McMasters. Why?"

"Before or after the woman was found in the bayou?"

"I'm not so good with time." He shook his head. "Thinking about that poor woman. What is wrong with people?" he asked softly. "I think they believed, in the end, she had a date. And they were probably coming here, but something went wrong between them. A lovers' quarrel. And he killed her and tried to bury her on the embankment, and the water and earth encroached and…and well, she was found weeks after her death."

"We don't think that this was a lovers' quarrel," Fin said.

"You think that she was…oh! Dressed like a flapper. Maybe she was killed and…" He broke off, shaking his head again. "You think they meant for her to be found here? Like the woman on Christy Island? But something happened," he said.

"Do you know where she was found?"

"Down the bayou, southward," he said. "But in the time since she was killed and then found, the body could have shifted a lot. She might have been near here, and someone might have shown up."

"What time do you close the bar?" Fin asked him.

"Two o'clock is official. I'm around, and some of my bartenders, for a while after. Sometimes, people stay a bit later—they tend to be friends, and if they're not, they become friends." He gave them a weak smile. "This is supposed to be a great place in town to work. Good music, good food and my people get discounts on food and drink when they're off work." He sighed.

Fin noticed as someone else came down the steps to the Speakeasy. The man was tall and lean with dark hair with a curl over

his forehead. Like Mort, he was wearing trousers with suspenders and a fedora.

He nodded at Fin, coming toward him. "You're the law, right?
On that poor girl?"

"Yes."

"This is Special Agent Finley Stirling," Mort said as Fin rose
to shake hands with the newcomer. "And Miss Avalon Morgan. Sir, miss, please meet Casey Granger, my head bartender."

"You know, I didn't think a thing of it until now," Casey
said. "But it would have been right about a couple of weeks before that poor girl was found. Didn't occur to me then—they
thought that she'd been killed some distance from here. But..."

"But, what? Come on, Casey, spit it out!" Mort said.

"Well, I stayed late. I thought I heard something down by
the docks. We keep a shotgun out here—we're a distance from
the big-city lights, you know. I went out with the shotgun and
I thought I heard people scurrying away. Thought it was teenagers, or some idiot drunk up to no good. So I went all the way
down to the dock, but all that was there was Mort's little motorboat. I stayed a while, watching. Then Trina—she's a local
liquor salesperson—came in. I hadn't realized just how late it
was...or how early it was. She had an appointment with Mort
that morning and Mort showed up right after. But I checked
out that path and the boat dock with that shotgun. Whoever
had been there—and I know someone was there—skedaddled.
I don't think of myself as being threatening, but a shotgun can
do the trick."

He stared at them all in wonder, then winced and shook his
head. "It never occurred to me...and now it does," he added
softly. "I might have been there. I might have...stopped what
happened to that poor girl."

Fin stood. "No, you couldn't have stopped them. She was dead
before they came here. You might have prevented them from

going through with their full plan. You did what you could, and there was no reason you would have thought to go after them."

"Them. More than one," Mort said.

"We believe that the care necessary to display the victims requires more than one person," Fin said. "If you had come upon them and not known what you were up against…well, as I said. The way they work, we believe she would have been dead. But it's helpful that you heard what you did, and that we know you went out with that shotgun," Fin said. "Do you remember anyone unusual who was around in the time right before that night? Or who was around more than usual?"

Casey looked thoughtful, but shook his head.

"What about any members of that rock band—Pauly's Pariah?" Mort asked, scratching his head as he also tried to recall.

"I don't know…maybe. Paul comes around now and then," Casey said.

"Do you know Julian Bennett?"

"Ah, yeah. He comes down from Baton Rouge at least once a month. Sometimes alone, and sometimes with his latest fling." He shrugged. "None of his girlfriends seem to last long, but then, he flirts when he's out on a date."

"Julian has distant cousins," Fin said. "Cara Holstein, married to a Gary Holstein, and a man named Kenneth Richard."

"Yeah, he's come with another guy a few times, maybe the one you mean. Kind of…well, a little pudgy, thinning hair? I never did see him with another couple."

Fin pulled up a picture of Kenneth Richard on his phone. "Is this the guy?"

"Yeah. He's been here—not often, but he's been here. In fact, I think Julian told me once that he had a friend coming in from Texas."

"You've been incredibly helpful," Fin said.

"I never saw any of them do anything bad or…act weird,"

Casey said. "I mean, all I can say is that, yes, they've been around here."

"And have been for years," Mort said.

He glanced at his watch. The day was getting away from them; he wanted to get out to Christy Island with at least an hour of daylight left. They could return to the Speakeasy another time.

Fin stood, catching Avalon's hand and drawing her up with him.

"Thank you again," he said. He released Avalon's hand to give both men business cards.

"If you think of anything else—"

"We will call you!" Mort vowed, and at his side, Casey nodded grimly.

They headed back up the stairs and into the sunlight.

"Look at that," Avalon said. "Thick brush by the dock. They didn't come by a boat, but they didn't come up to the restaurant, either. Fin, this is horrible! Do you think that this man— or these people—have been doing this a long time?"

"Angela has been searching through cases across the country. If she finds anything else, she'll let us know. I'm hoping it goes no further back than this."

"But…"

He paused, turning to look at her. They might get to the island and have just an hour of daylight left; he wasn't sure it mattered. He didn't know what they could find that forensic teams hadn't already.

He still felt that they needed to go.

But now he also felt it only fair to tell her that a tech had pulled up a copy of the blog post that she had seen.

"Between Jodi and the people up at my headquarters, Avalon, they managed to get a copy of that post you read."

She stared at him, eyes wide, face a little pale.

"You've read it."

"I have. I haven't had time to go over it, but, yes, I've read it."

"It exists!"

"Tonight…later, I'll go through it. I'll get you home—"

"No, you won't. You'll do it with me."

"Avalon, I'm in law enforcement—this has been a life's decision for me. I don't need to drag you through all the worst parts."

She started to laugh and punched him in the arm. "Oh, yeah, great! You have me frightened of all my friends and you're dragging me around to murder sites. But you want to spare me a letter that I read first? Oh, no. I don't think so. And I might have more insight than you. I might…well, he isn't staring at men, he's staring at women. At a specific woman."

*And it scared the hell out of him that the killer's real fantasy might be Avalon, and that everything before was nothing but a dress rehearsal.*

He didn't say the words. He turned and started walking to the car.

"Fin!"

He stopped and turned back. "Yes, you have a point," he told her.

"So…"

"Maybe we'll stay here."

"What—here? On the grass in front of the restaurant? Or in the car?"

He shook his head. "In Houma. I'm not leaving you alone right now, and I don't feel like another night in a chair. Don't worry—we'll get two beds."

She didn't answer him. She pushed by, heading for the car. She tried to swing open the passenger-side door.

The car was locked.

She stared at him, angry.

"All right, sorry, maybe we could get connecting rooms… and I can keep the door open."

He clicked the car unlocked and came around to open the

door for her. No good. She swung it open and sat. He walked around and took the driver's seat.

"Look, Avalon, I am concerned for your safety. We will go through the letter together, but I don't want to do it at the house where everyone is staying."

She was staring at him. "For a rough, tough FBI guy, you are an idiot."

"Pardon?"

"Idiot."

"What does that mean?"

"I'm that unappealing?"

"What?"

"Chairs, couches, connecting rooms. Did it ever occur to you that I'd be safest next to you?"

He sat, surprised, and not terribly suave as he said, "But you barely like me."

"I'm not sure I do like you at all at this moment, but if we're staying out here..."

*She wanted to sleep with him?*

Or she just wanted him next to her. Maybe he was an idiot. In truth, he just wasn't sure!

"Okay."

"Okay, what?"

"I'll sleep with you."

"Don't go out of your way."

"Hey, anything in the line of duty."

He caught her hand before she could slap him; it would have hurt.

They stared at one another and he thought that it might turn into a brawl, he might have to take her home, he'd lose...

He didn't know what he'd lose. She wasn't an investigator... and yet she seemed all important on this case.

And if he was honest with himself, he'd been attracted to her from the beginning.

There had been so much static at first.

And still. He started to smile. She did, too. And they both laughed.

"I'm sorry," he said. "I didn't want to make any assumptions. I'd be honored to sleep with you. Ecstatic, in truth. Uh…in many ways."

She lowered her head. "I can't believe that I've just…"

"Been honest?" he asked.

"Hey! I'm still not sure how much I like you!"

"I'm a likable guy. You just decided you weren't going to like me."

"You're eternally suspicious."

"You're eternally optimistic…about those you choose to care about."

She turned away and said softly, "The sun is falling."

"Yeah."

He turned the key in the ignition and decided to drive down to the dock where he knew that a police cruiser was being held to get them out to Christy Island.

When they left the car behind and headed toward the dock and the boat, he saw that she hesitated, just briefly.

She just stared out at the island.

He'd been ahead of her. He walked back to her, taking her hand.

"This isn't fair of me. I can get an officer to take you to a hotel and stand guard. You don't have to go back to Christy Island."

She turned to look at him and squeezed his hand with a grim smile.

"Yes, I do," she told him.

"Avalon, seriously, you don't have to go back there because of me. I've really no right to ask you to do any of this."

"I'm not going back for you," she said. "I'm going back for myself. And for Cindy West and Ellen Frampton and Jane Doe.

I'm going back because I'll do anything that just may help in any small way to put the sick bastards doing this behind bars, or beneath the ground."

# CHAPTER TWELVE

Avalon watched as they approached Christy Island.

It was just like so many barrier islands, surrounded by shallow waters, created with a tangle of earth and vegetation.

Nothing too big could reach the island, in case rudders, propellers or other essential parts become entangled in the wildlife that grew near the shore.

Many such little islands existed as wildlife preserves. Others were privately owned.

None was quite like Christy Island.

And certainly not to her.

When she had come before, she had arrived with friends. They knew that they were free to explore the mansion—she'd just never had a real desire to do so. Boris had arranged for the cleaning of one room. The rest of the house...

No theme park could ever invent a horror house quite so... eerie. Spiderwebs ruled—she knew that much. There was a room, she'd heard, that had belonged to old Nolan Christy's wife, Sarah, who had departed life over fifty years ago.

He'd never moved anything in that room, never so much as touched it, after she died.

Most of the furniture was close to two hundred years old.

There were rats.

Years of dust.

Of course, none of that could be seen from the water.

Their approach was from the back of the mansion. There were docks in the front—those they had used when working on Boris's movie—and smaller docks to the rear.

It was ominous coming in this way. The cemetery had begun in the back. Tangled foliage crawled over many of the old graves, which were sprawled out over the south side of the island. The house itself had been built with the entry to the east and the rear to the west.

The police had been using the rear docks over the last few days.

But, in truth, there wasn't much of a presence left on the island, they learned from their escort. The forensic teams had finished, collecting all that they could. The work had begun but sorting prints from those belonging to cast and crew, caterers and more, had been daunting.

The area by the tomb where Cindy had lain had been gone over and over.

The house had been searched, but the teams had determined that Cindy's body had arrived by boat from the south, been carried through the tangle of the oldest section of the cemetery and brought out to the tomb where she had been placed—a good distance back from where the filming would take place.

They were on the island, walking the route the killer or killers had taken, when it occurred to Avalon that their placement had been strange.

"This isn't near where we were filming," she said to Fin.

He had her hand.

She was glad.

"If Kevin and I hadn't taken a walk that morning, it might have been another few days before she had been discovered.

Unless Boris had caterers or someone else coming out. That's something I didn't think to ask him."

"Did members of the cast or crew walk out in the cemetery often?" Fin asked her.

"Sometimes. I know that Lauren loves these old graveyards. And when she had nothing to do, she'd wander them—she said when she's in the north, she loves to go to the old graveyards and read all the inscriptions on them. She was okay going alone, but she's truly a people person, and she'd walk with people from the cast and crew. I guess, if you're fond of cemeteries, it's intriguing. It's so overgrown and…yeah, creepy. That's why Boris was so thrilled to be filming here."

They came upon the tomb where Cindy had lain.

There was nothing there. Not a bloodstain, nothing.

It might have been any of the other single-occupant tombs that littered the grounds, except that now, it appeared cleaner. It had been swabbed, tested, maybe wiped down.

Fin was quiet, standing there.

She knew that his mind was always working.

He looked around. He was also waiting.

For the dead—those who had remained here. Avalon closed her eyes, waiting, too. She opened them with a smile.

An attractive woman of fifty or so, lovely in an antebellum gown, stood beside a young man of maybe twenty or twenty-five.

"Hi," Avalon said.

"Told you!" the woman said to Fin.

She smiled at Avalon. "Forgive me, honey. I knew that you could see me when you smiled that day, and then turned quickly. You were letting me know that you saw me, and asking me not to make a scene."

"Yes," Avalon said softly.

"Avalon," Fin said, "may I present Vanessa Christy? And this young man is Henri Christy."

"A pleasure," Avalon said.

"Well, I'm so glad," Vanessa said. "Henri and I were quite reluctant to make an appearance when you first came to the island. Sometimes I have a sense about these things and we knew that you might see us, but we didn't want to disturb you. We could see that you were concentrating on your work."

"I understand the concentration needed for a role," Henri told her.

"Henri might have been a fine actor," Vanessa said proudly.

"Stage, of course," Henri said.

"The stage is wonderful," Avalon agreed. "I love working on the stage, and I am delighted to meet you."

"Have you seen or discovered anything new?" Fin asked.

"I beg your forgiveness, sir," Henri said. "We expected no evil—we weren't watching for it."

"No forgiveness needed," Fin said. "We were just hopeful."

"I'm quite impressed with the police and the forensic teams," Vanessa said. "They have been working very hard."

"Good to hear, and thank you," Fin said.

"I'm curious," Avalon said. "What was Nolan Christy like?"

"Mean," Henri said.

"Henri!" Vanessa protested. "Please, bear in mind, we wore the Christy name, too."

"Well, the lady asked," Henri said, defending himself. "And we've learned that the kindest people in the world are sometimes related to monsters. Sometimes hatred is taught—sometimes it's a lesson that won't be learned. So let me be truthful. Nolan. The man… Well, I'm sorry to claim him and ever so grateful that he didn't…remain. Here—as we are here. He was mean and strange—he was always here, except perhaps once a. month. Then he'd take off by himself in a little motorboat he kept at the south dock."

"Well, he didn't see us and didn't speak to us. That doesn't mean—" Vanessa began.

"He was mean to animals—to me, that marks a man," Henri

said. "He threw rocks at birds, at anything that ran or scampered across the island. We have nutria here. He loved throwing huge rocks at them. If he caught them, he tortured them. Many people don't like rodents, but they don't...torture them!"

Avalon turned to Fin. "I think we need to go to the mansion."

"All right." He looked up at the sky. The sun was going down. "Tomorrow morning," he said.

"You want to wait—"

"I do."

"Yes, wait until the morning. I daresay that the place has just about gone to rot and ruin. It's going to be much better if you can see what you're doing. Mr. Koslov went straight to his room when he came in at night—he didn't look right or left, just went to his room. And when the people had to wait in the mansion when the police were there...all were on edge! Please, even though there are a few policemen on the island, I will feel better if you wait for morning's light."

"All right. We'll wait for morning and be back. Will you be so kind as to accompany us?" Fin asked.

"We will accompany you, indeed, yes," Vanessa said gravely.

Fin looked at Avalon; he was ready to go.

She was not.

She was now convinced that Nolan Christy might not have been a sad old man, but rather a cruel one who might have somehow sown the seeds for murder.

But she knew they were right; the electricity at the mansion was sadly lacking.

"All right, thank you," she said to the ghosts.

Fin set an arm around her shoulder. She didn't protest; it felt good and it felt right.

*Which was good; she'd done something she'd never imagined that she'd do—she'd implied that the man should sleep with her. No, she hadn't implied...she'd been out and out obvious in every way.*

Darkness was just falling.

They headed back toward the south dock, Fin pausing to wave. He thanked the officer who was waiting. In about five minutes, a police cruiser came back for them.

She found out that night that the FBI had a standing reservation with a hotel chain. As they were heading to the reception desk, Fin turned to look at her.

"You can renege if you want," he told her.

"Why? Do you want me to?" she asked.

She liked his smile then. Really liked it.

"Hell, no," he said softly.

"Then, um, I think one room would be lovely."

She couldn't quite believe what she was saying, what she was doing. But no matter her feelings when she had started out with him, she'd discovered that there was something in his manner, in his look, maybe even in the way he spoke, that made her long to be close to him.

Intimate with him.

Maybe this was just for now; maybe it was what was happening around them, the intensity of trying—through the living and the dead—to discover the truth.

And maybe she just thought that she deserved a night of… something. Not with friends, though she loved her friends.

With someone who excited her, lit something up inside her, made her long to be held and touched, and touch in turn.

"I can ask for two rooms just for appearance's sake," he said.

"And waste taxpayer money? Never! Besides, I don't believe in appearances."

"You're an actress."

"But that's a known pretense."

He was smiling, laughing a little, and he made her smile.

"You're very hard to get, Special Agent Stirling."

"Well, I just like to make sure. And I don't…"

"Don't what?"

He laughed. "I'm certainly not easy!"

They'd reached the desk. He signed in, remembering that they hadn't intended to stay, and asked for toothbrushes and toothpaste.

"The young lady at the counter thinks that we decided on a rental room for a reason—a wild night of possibly illicit pleasure," Avalon said.

"I hope she's right," he said, and then paused. "Should you let someone know that you're staying here?"

"Yes. I'll text Lauren—she'll let the others know."

She sent the text. As they headed to the elevator, she noted that she had gotten a reply from her friend already.

A simple text, reading, Go for it!

Smiling, she shook her head as they went into the elevator. She wrote back with one word: Yep.

They reached their floor. Avalon followed Fin into the room. He closed the door behind her and then leaned her up against the door, smiling at her briefly before finding her lips. His kiss was long, wet, deliciously hot. His hands slid from her face to her shoulders, sliding beneath the collar and shoulders of her jacket to allow it to fall to the floor. His mouth still lingered on hers as he found the buttons on her blouse and began to slowly undo them, one by one. She hadn't realized just how much she'd wanted to touch him until her fingers brushed over his cheeks, before she entwined her arms around him.

"Can't," he said.

"Can't...what?" she asked, a brief touch of dismay coming to her.

"Can't reach the buttons this way," he told her.

She laughed as they broke apart.

"I mean, I can't just rip them off in a movie display of undying passion," he said, his fingers moving on the buttons again before his eyes met hers. "We didn't bring a change of clothing."

"I'll do my best not to rip your clothing off," she told him seriously, and then they were laughing again, struggling, pausing to kiss again…and for him to set his gun and holster on the nightstand. At last their clothing was cast aside and strewn around the room and they fell together, naked flesh touching, to the bed, where the laughter dissolved in another deep kiss. Their lips and hands moved then, as if neither of them could give up the conquest to discover more about one another.

He was an amazing, patient and giving lover. She felt as if she flew with emotion, torn between electric tremors deep within and the sweet sensation of writhing and arching in a sea of searing steam. His fingers brushed her flesh; his lips teased it. She whispered words against his body, sweet and evocative, and they were returned to her. She never wanted it to end, and yet she reached ever higher. She felt him inside her, the movement, the pulse, and somehow she felt as if she'd never been more intimate with anyone in her life as she was with this man.

Sensation peaked cataclysmically; so much so that there was nothing but sweet oblivion for long moments after. And even then, she was in his arms, feeling his flesh, the life within him, the wonder of being with him.

After a moment, cradling her close, he murmured, "I guess I like you."

She rose on an elbow and punched him in the arm.

"Well?" he teased.

"Now I may really dislike you!" she said.

He grinned and pulled her close again, and said softly, "I wonder when it was that I realized you were probably the most incredible person I've ever met, and that I did, desperately, want to be with you."

She smiled, loving the dark green of his eyes, the way his damp hair was plastered on his forehead.

"That was pretty good. Maybe you're palatable now."

"I hope so. Because… We did only get one room."

She leaned her head on his chest. "When we go back…"

He lifted her slightly, frowning as he studied her face. "Avalon, I didn't mean we had to be together. We could have taken two rooms."

"When we go back, I'd like you to just stay with me, in my room in the French Quarter. I mean, I'm not putting any pressure on you—I know that your life is, well, pressure. And that you travel, and that your home is in the DC area. But for now, while all this is going on…"

He nodded. "That will work. I'm afraid to let you out of my sight."

That caused her to frown. "Hey! I didn't want an intimate relationship as a protection detail!"

"Touchy! No, I'd have stayed on that damned sofa."

She smiled again.

"I assumed you wanted more," he said.

"What?"

"I mean, here we are…"

"Ah, you're that good!"

He grinned. "I'm that crazy about you," he whispered.

She leaned against him then, sliding her body against his, feeling the damp glistening of their bodies brush together again. She found his lips.

The kiss grew heated.

*He'd assumed right. She wanted more, and more.*

Sometime, they slept. She was startled to wake up and find that he had slipped into one of the room's terry robes and was seated at the desk, studying his phone.

"Fin?"

"Hey, sorry, I didn't want to wake you."

"What are you doing? Has anything happened? Something else?"

He shook his head. "No, no, I'm sorry. It's the—the post you saw that night, that Jodi and some folks in our tech department found long enough to download. I'm looking at the way it's written, remembering voice patterns, just reading the words and—" He paused, looking over at her. "I do think that it was written by the killer—one of the killers."

She crawled out of bed and headed for the closet, grabbing a robe to put on, too. Then she walked over and stood behind, reading off his phone.

"First, I'd stalk my prey. She'd be unknown, a goddess, but I would see her, and I would know. I would watch the way that she moved, the way that she breathed, the way that her eyes would light when she laughed. I would be close enough at times to smell the sweetness that emanated from her supple flesh. I might brush by her."

She looked at Fin and said, "He knows his victim or knows of her. Maybe he just sees her every day, or has seen her some-where, and knows how to get close to her."

"That's what it sounds like."

Avalon read again.

"Beauty knows no bounds. I have seen these goddesses in every ethnicity. Beauty covers the continents. True beau-ties are rare, but they come from every continent—they are Asian, African, Australian, South and North American, European…a little laugh here, okay, I've yet to encounter a goddess from Antarctica."

"Strange paragraph. A serial killer trying to prove that he's an equal opportunity killer, and trying to make a joke at the same time?" she asked.

"I do think that this man finds beauty everywhere, and you have to remember, he probably doesn't even consider himself to be bad or evil. He has an agenda, and he has desires and needs—and those desires and needs outweigh the wants or needs of anyone else. This killer is a psychopath. He feels no remorse, only pleasure in memories."

"But...we don't believe that it's just one man."

"No. A shared fantasy. But someone seems to have the need to put it out there—he's proud of himself, like a trophy-hunter in Africa stalking a lion. The lion means nothing. As much as he applauds the beauty of his victims, they mean nothing to him."

This time, Fin read.

"But I am good. I am a hunter, a stalker, and I know how to smile and laugh and charm. And I find my beauties... Fantasy. So... I find my goddess. I am a gentleman, a rugged, charming gentleman. We play and we tease, and we drink, and it's divine. That's just it—it's all divine. I did say goddess. I wait until we are so relaxed. She's at ease with me. I make it clear that I don't expect intercourse... yet. And when she is laughing, playing, enjoying me, looking at me with that divine sparkle in her eyes, I strike...

"It's so beautiful."

"Whoever Cindy met when she left that pizza shop, she knew," Avalon said. "And that seems to be...he's charming. And you don't have to be handsome to be charming, just nice, someone nice, capable of laughter and putting someone at ease."

"The most frightening kind of monster," Fin said. "The monster you don't see in the darkness of the closet, but, rather, the wolf in sheep's clothing."

She looked at the phone again and read aloud.

"Watching her. Because she cannot fight—she knows and knows that she cannot fight. And I hold her and assure her and watch the light slowly fade. She's in my arms— she's still warm. There's a perfect temperature and I wait for that...and then, I give her the divine ecstasy of my love.

There is no greater high. When we are done, I take her
so tenderly. I care for her. I lay her out in beauty. Eternal
beauty. And it's all as it should be, ashes to ashes, and dust
to dust, with all that is beautiful and divine in between…"

"Oh, God! This is so—so depraved!"

"I told you that you didn't need to do this."

"I thought that…well, here you go. You're wrong. I know
the people I work with. None of them wrote this, and none of
them is sick like this! But, yes, I know, especially after today,
you're going to be suspicious of Boris."

He shook his head, looking at her. "Avalon, I like Boris. I
want him to be everything it seems that he is. But we have to
look at all possibilities."

"Julian Bennett," she said.

"Why Julian?"

"He's…slimy. In my mind, he thinks that he's God's gift to
women. He goes from one to the next. He's charming—he could
probably persuade most women to go with him, especially if
he's being polite and respectful."

Fin nodded, studying her. "Possibly."

"Or—or Kenneth Richard."

"Hardly charming."

"But he could be the second. There are two. Maybe he's the
dreamer, the writer, and Julian just shares his sick fantasies, and
Julian has the ability to lure the women and both… They both
commit murder and then…"

"I'm going to get in touch with Ryder. I want to start bringing people in. For tomorrow, I want to know that he has his
eyes on them."

"But Boris?" she said.

"Avalon, that's for Lauren's safety, as well. As I told you, I
like Boris. He seems like the real deal—a talented man out to

help others in his field. But he's been in the places where things have occurred."

"He hasn't done any film work in Mississippi that I know about."

"And Mississippi is a short jump from here, and from Christy Island. Avalon, it might not be a bad idea to have the Christy heirs think that we're looking at Boris."

"You could ruin his reputation forever."

"Not if he's innocent—didn't someone say that no publicity was bad publicity?"

"They lied."

He was looking at the screen again.

"'My turn,'" he said.

"Pardon?"

"I think that the writer here is part of the duo—and his partner has made the choices so far or done the killing or even chosen the display or intended display. And he has a victim in mind—and now considers it his turn."

"Oh," she said. She shook her head. "I don't know the others as well as I know Kevin. He's like my brother. He's with Lauren. He won't let anything happen to her. Besides," she added quickly, "trust me, Boris is innocent."

He hit a button on his phone and the screen went blank.

"No more of this tonight," he said softly. "We'll wake up to it. I shouldn't have done this tonight."

"Time is of the essence, and you don't want anyone else falling prey to this monster," she said softly.

He nodded, stood up and swept her into his arms.

"You know what's beautiful?" he asked her.

She grinned. "Were you going to say me?" she asked.

"Sleep," he said gravely. "It's really beautiful stuff."

She grinned and nodded, and he carried her to the bed.

They didn't sleep right away, but when they did, he was right.

It was beautiful.

*Friday*

Avalon could have slept a lot later, but they were on their way back to Christy Island at just about nine thirty. Fin had set the alarm for eight thirty, claiming when it went off that he was glad that they weren't in a terrible rush and that it had been good to sleep late.

She realized that they had different conceptions of the idea of sleeping late, but she also understood his sense of responsibility.

The night had been good. Amazing.

*Except for trying to enter the mind of a killer.*

They were in the police cruiser and Avalon had just been appreciating the feel of the salt breeze in her hair, the cry of seabirds overhead in a crystal-blue sky, when she suddenly turned to Fin and told him, "Whoever wrote that blog post, Fin, he's getting anxious. I think the writer has been playing second fiddle. He's been doing the main body of the work, maybe even as an apprentice to the other man. But if everyone is being watched..."

"He has to wait," Fin said. "Which may cause him to grow reckless, which means that hopefully, he'll trip up before managing to kill again."

She nodded. "You're ready for the mansion?"

"I hate it with a passion, but yes."

"Take care up there," the boat captain warned as they arrived at the dock. "We have a few officers left on the island—one at each of the docks—but there's nothing else here, you haven't cleared it for any kind of work to begin again." He paused, shrugging. "We both know you can get here without using either of the docks."

"Right. We'll be careful," Fin promised.

They waved and went on through the cemetery.

Fin had Avalon's hand. They walked slowly, and she knew that he was waiting for Vanessa and Henri to see them and join them.

"Unusual, don't you think?" Avalon said.

"What's that? This whole situation?"

"Well, yes, but…they stay here. Vanessa and Henri. It's an island and for so many years, it was so isolated. In my experience…well, those who linger do so for a reason, and even when they're not sure what that reason is, they prefer life. Yes, sometimes they may return to a cemetery or a battlefield, but… well, I can see haunting Bourbon Street—there's so much life. Lafitte's maybe—pirates reliving their glory days. But for Vanessa and Henri…"

"They hop on boats and go into the city now and then. I believe that they were both enamored with your whole group."

"Yes. I guess I just found this place depressing—no matter how perfect it was for what Boris needed—even before Cindy was left here."

"I can only tell you that I don't begin to understand why some people do…linger. Or how time goes by for them, but I've always assumed a person who was decent in life is going to be decent in death, and face it, there are things we don't understand now about living, much less dying."

"Miss Avalon! Fin!"

It was Vanessa. She was weaving her way between a tomb and a giant winged angel.

Henri was behind her.

"I'm so glad you waited for morning," she said.

Avalon tried not to smile as she said, "So am I."

"You had a nice night?" Henri asked them.

"Yes, thank you so much," Fin said, a twisted smile on his lips.

"And now a bright day, blue overhead! Yes, much better to see the mansion. There is electricity and it's still on," Vanessa said. "But the shadows in that place! It's better by day. And Lord knows! You must be careful while digging into things. There are those awful spiders—"

"Brown recluses," Henri said.

"Yes—deep in the drawers. And they're very dangerous," Vanessa warned.

"More so than black widows," Henri said solemnly.

"We will be very careful, I promise," Fin assured them. "We will be careful—how sad it would be for an experienced law-man to be downed by a spider."

"Hey, that's not a joking matter," Avalon said.

"I wasn't joking."

They reached the front of the house. Avalon stared at it: a Victorian mansion, painted gray with white trim, the gray dark-ened and chipping through the years, the white turned to some-thing almost darker than the gray. The windows looked out at them like a multitude of eyes, gables over the attic seemed like hunched eyebrows and the whole of it was decaying and eerie.

Even below a bright blue sky.

She remembered sitting in the great room or grand parlor, waiting her turn to be questioned. Sitting with the others, know-ing that Cindy was dead... She felt her fingers curl into fists at her side. There was something in that mansion, she was certain.

She turned to Fin. "Let's do this!" she said, and she was de-termined. She wanted the truth; the truth required courage.

She was suddenly grateful to Fin for more than a fantastic night.

Somehow, he had also given her something she had lacked.

The courage she felt she needed.

The house was just a house. And she wanted the answers it might yield.

# CHAPTER THIRTEEN

Fin wondered how anyone had lived in the house, even if it was a "mansion."

The dust and grime were enough to have killed anyone living there.

"Boris's room," he said quietly.

"Of course," Avalon said dryly.

They headed up the wooden staircase. Fin wasn't sure which room, though he knew that the police and the forensic team had been through the house. He'd never thought that Cindy West had been killed on site, in the mansion—anyone creating such a display of her body would have been careful enough not to be easily traced through the house.

But he wanted to see where Boris had been living.

"This one has been cleaned and Boris had someone in to clean the one room," Avalon said, after opening one of the doors off the hallway.

"Gloves," Fin said, handing Avalon a pair.

She frowned, looking at the thin blue gloves he offered her, then nodded.

"Okay," she said.

"Not to worry, we don't leave prints," Vanessa said lightly.

They went in. Boris's things had been removed, brought to him by the police since they had determined not to let anyone back on the island until the forensic team had finished.

Now, they'd finished.

And they had nothing.

The room had a balcony that looked over the front and the sprawl of the cemetery. Fin went there first, wondering how Boris hadn't seen a thing.

But he would have had to have been standing on the balcony when Cindy's body was being set on the tomb, and even then, it would have been dark. And if he wasn't standing on the balcony, he would have been at such a distance that he wouldn't have heard anything.

From the balcony, he really couldn't see any of the root-and-brush-laden shore.

Seemed like Boris might have been telling the truth.

"There's nothing here," Avalon said.

"I think you're right," he said.

But he wasn't through. He opened the closet door and there was nothing. He kneeled and went all the way down to look under the bed.

"Once," Henri said, "this was my room." He was quiet. "I died here."

"I'm so sorry," Avalon said.

Vanessa sighed. "I was in the attic, until after the war. As head housekeeper, I commanded a room at the end of the hall."

"Where is the master bedroom?" Avalon asked. "I'm assuming that Nolan Christy would have had the master bedroom."

"Oh, he did. Down this way," Vanessa said.

She led them down the hall and opened a door. It led to a suite. An intricately carved headboard boxed in one end of the bed with a matching footboard. A trunk sat at the end of the bed.

A balcony looked out over the domain of the home. The

room offered a massive hearth, a seating arrangement of a day-bed and chairs, all upholstered in rich cranberry velvet that time had seasoned to something very dark, and doors to a dressing room and bath.

"Hmm. Bigger than an apartment I had in New York once," Fin said.

"Hey. It is a mansion on a private island," Avalon reminded him.

"When my grandfather was alive," Henri said, "this was a happy place. The trunk you see there was filled with toys. My grandfather loved to play with the kids. He was a good man."

"That's great!" Avalon told him.

Fin moved into the dressing room. Nothing had been touched since Nolan Christy had died; his medications remained on the dressing table. A brush and comb sat there, and in the bathroom, just beyond the dressing room, his electric toothbrush remained…now covered with dust, like everything else in the house. He walked back to the dressing room.

The closet, part of the dressing room, offered racks of clothing on each side, and to the back. He found himself looking through the man's clothing.

He was certainly prepared for the cold that could come sometimes to Louisiana; he had at least a dozen coats, short and long, some with hoods, one a cape.

He found himself thinking of the man who had met up with Cindy outside the pizza parlor.

*A vampire.*

Yes, in legend, a vampire might have worn such a coat.

Fin didn't have any large evidence bags with him, but he was intrigued by the coat. He pulled out his phone and called Ryder.

"Where are you?" the NOPD detective asked.

"On the island. I came back here because there must be something somewhere, and I believe, between Mississippi and Houma and Christy Island, we have a connection. I've found a coat in here that matches up with what we learned about the man Cindy West saw outside the pizza parlor. There could be dozens—even hundreds—of such capes in the area, what with Mardi Gras and other fests, not to mention the vampire rage at Halloween. But it is in Nolan Christy's closet. I don't have anything to bag it in with me."

"I'll get someone out. There are still two officers on duty out there, but they aren't prepared to collect evidence—the forensic team went over the place."

"I know, but they wouldn't have looked too closely at old man Christy's closet."

"Right. Okay. Maybe we will learn something from it."

"You've got an eye on everyone?" Fin asked.

"I do. The gang from the house headed out about thirty minutes ago. They seemed to be just wandering. Went to Fifi's—guess theatrical people love wigs. Then they crossed over and, as last reported, they're having coffee on Royal Street."

"Thanks, Ryder. What about the others—the Christy heirs?"

"Four different directions, giving us a bit of a run. Julian Bennett drove out in your direction. Your people are tailing him. Cara and Gary are at the movies. Kenneth is wandering around the aquarium."

"Thanks. Ryder, I think our killer has been busy. And we have to stop him now."

"Do you want us to bring anyone in?"

"Later today, maybe. I think we're going to bring several of the major players back in for questioning."

"I'll be waiting."

"Thanks, Ryder. Since we can't make a connection with solid evidence, we'll question them through the NOPD later today."

"Who do you want to question?"

"Julian Bennett…and Boris Koslov. I'll be back later with more."

He ended the call. As he did, he heard Avalon let out a cry of horror and disgust.

He practically entangled himself in his own legs and nearly tripped over himself in his haste to get back to the main area of the bedroom.

She was seated on the floor by the trunk. She'd opened it. She had what looked like a scrapbook open in her hands.

"A forensic team went through here, and they didn't think anything of this?" she demanded.

He hurried over to her and hunkered down.

The old man had kept an extensive porn collection, he quickly saw—unlike what anyone might have imagined.

Avalon was glaring at him. "He was...oh, Lord!"

The pictures in Nolan Christy's collection were beyond the usual. He had images of bondage, of beatings, of subjugation—beyond a doubt, some of the most offensive material Fin had ever seen.

He shook his head.

"This has to mean something, Fin!" Avalon said.

He understood her reaction. The images didn't seem like they were of consenting adults exploring kinks. They felt exploitative. He sighed. "Avalon, it means he was a dirty old man. There are no bodies in here and no suggestion that he killed anyone, or that anyone is dead."

But his eye caught on one exceptionally disturbing photo taken in what appeared to be an old hunter's shack. A woman, bound and gagged, lay on the ground while a man stood over her like a hunter with a trophy, a baseball bat in his hands.

"But...ugh, Fin!"

"I'll see that a team comes back—I already have someone coming. They can bring these in and test for prints and find out if the heirs were looking into these, or if..."

"Boris was looking at them," she said quietly.

"Avalon, when an investigation starts, every possibility is investigated."

She nodded. "Of course."

"I keep telling you—"

"I know. You like Boris, too."

"I do."

"Are you ever wrong about people?" she asked, meeting his gaze steadily.

"I wish I had more talent in that direction," he said.

He realized that Vanessa and Henri were at the door, uncomfortably staring at the two of them.

"Well, he was a mean bastard," Henri said.

"And…she's right. How…deplorable, how—"

"Disgusting," Avalon said.

"However deplorable, disgusting, perverted, whatever—it looks as if he preferred his women alive," Fin said. "And he couldn't have killed Cindy."

"He could have begun a line of killers," Avalon said softly.

"Yes, he could have done so. That is a possibility, and we will investigate," Fin promised.

Avalon nodded, biting her lip and staring at the trunk. She stood and stepped away from it, as if afraid dirt from the trunk might wrap around her.

That was a possibility in the most literal sense—everything in the room was covered not just with dust, but with a miasma created by time and the elements and the humid weather of Southern Louisiana.

Fin had his phone out to call his main Krewe offices—he wanted Ryder's people involved, but it had become an FBI case, and he knew that Angela would make sure that they all worked together…and that Nolan Christy's porn collection would be tested and analyzed.

Avalon waited, listening to his call.

Vanessa and Henri did the same.

When he had finished on the phone, Vanessa stepped forward and promised, "Henri and I will watch everything. We know that Nolan was a loner—here most of the time. But once a month or so, he did take off."

"You never...followed him?" Fin asked.

Henri let out a snort. "I couldn't stand the man. I wouldn't have followed him anywhere."

"Understandable," Avalon said.

"Okay...let's finish here and get back to New Orleans. I need some things to start moving there," Fin said.

They went room to room. But the other spaces yielded nothing but dust and memories of the years gone by.

Finally, Fin was satisfied. He thanked Vanessa and Henri, then he and Avalon headed for the dock.

Forensic crews were arriving just as they prepared to leave. He paused to speak with the head of the team—one from his own offices—and then a police cutter took them back to the mainland docks.

Avalon was silent as they returned to his car.

"What are you thinking?" he asked her.

"Foremost?" she asked. "I'm thinking that I desperately need a shower."

"Give me two minutes to grab a few of my things, then we'll both shower at your place."

She arched an eyebrow at him.

"I don't want to leave you alone anywhere," he said.

She smiled. "These guys are really cowards. They need to charm or seduce a woman and get her away from everyone else. You heard what they said at the Speakeasy. When a gun was in the picture, they chickened out and their plan didn't go through."

"But that was a while ago. They're learning. And if you have a shotgun, you didn't tell me about it!"

She smiled. "I don't have a shotgun. I have Lauren and Kevin."

"Still—"

"Fine. We'll get your things. Those…pictures—that porn collection… Man, he was the epitome of a dirty old man!"

Fin laughed softly. "That from a woman doing the website for a dominatrix."

"Hey, she doesn't do anything nearly as…depraved as what I saw. And she's in control in all her scenarios."

"True," he agreed. He smiled at her and reached for her hand as he drove.

He realized that he loved everything about her.

And they were headed back, possibly toward a serial killer.

He thought of the blog post.

He was afraid. There were at least two killers. And one wanted his turn.

The way that he described a woman, seeing her, touching her, sensing her…

He couldn't help but wonder if the killer didn't pine for Avalon.


When they got back to the rental house in the French Quarter, after swinging by Fin's hotel to grab his bag, Avalon could hear voices in the courtyard. She knew that her friends and co-workers had been out during most of the day, walking around and playing tourist. She arched an eyebrow at Fin and he indicated the courtyard gate.

She used her key and opened it, and the two of them went in.

They were all there—Boris, Brad, Terry, Leo, Lauren and Kevin.

But they weren't alone.

Gary and Cara Holstein were sitting at the large, tiled courtyard table with them, Cara pretty and tiny in a little sundress, Gary casual in a polo shirt and jeans.

They had a large tray of chips and guacamole in front of them, along with glasses filled with what looked like lemonade, but might have been something stronger.

"Hey there!" Kevin called, rising as they entered. He looked at Avalon with a mixture of worry and amusement, raising his eyebrows slightly and nodding his head toward Fin.

She simply smiled.

"Welcome back," Gary Holstein said, rising. "I hear you were in Houma, looking into an event that might be related to what happened on the island."

He seemed anxious.

"Were you back on the island?" Boris asked. He'd risen, too. They'd all risen.

"I'll get two more chairs," Kevin said quickly.

"Thanks, Kevin," Avalon said.

Fin answered Boris's question.

"Yes, we checked in on the Houma case, and yes, we went back out to the island. Didn't find anything new, I'm afraid. Except…oh, yeah, I forgot. We went out and had homemade root beer at a cool place—it's called the Speakeasy. Boris, I heard that friends of yours—people you worked with—spent time out there. Of course, Avalon knows the band, too. You worked with Pauly's Pariah. The lead singer, Paul McMasters, really appreciates everything you did for him," Fin said.

His manner was easy and friendly as he sat back talking to Boris.

Avalon knew that he was watching for Boris's reaction.

Boris was enthusiastic. He smiled, looking at Avalon. "Super! Avalon, I didn't know you were going to see Paul. That's great! That's great! I guess not so strange except that they're on tour a lot now, but he is from Houma. He's good—still himself?"

"He's good and it was nice to get to see him," Avalon said.

"I'm always so proud of that shoot," Terry said. "I mean, think about it. Boris, you, me, Lauren and Avalon! We were all in on the video that really helped put those guys on the map." He grinned. "Thank goodness Avalon's mom dragged her to Arthur Murray when she was young—she's a beautiful dancer.

She managed to get Paul doing a great waltz. It was so romantic! Oh, uh, well," he said, looking at Fin. "They were acting—Paul McMasters is married."

Fin laughed softly. "It's a great video."

Boris turned to Fin and said, "I am proud of that video. There are a couple of tempos going in the song. Like Terry said, we had that Viennese waltz, and then the upbeat rock for the crowd. And if I do say so myself, yes, it was a damned good video."

"McMasters credits you with his fame," Fin said.

"Thanks," Boris said. "I liked McMasters and his bandmates. We were friendly. And I liked the place he liked to hang out—where you had your root beer. The Speakeasy. Nothing wrong with Houma, but it was more unusual than most of the hangouts. And, hey! You're looking at two more of the people who worked so hard on that—Lauren did spectacular makeup and Terry…well, couldn't have gotten things to look right without Terry. We had to film in an old mansion and outside. That's not easy when you're trying to make a band look spectacular on a budget."

"You've been there, haven't you?" Fin asked, turning to Gary and Cara.

"The Speakeasy?" Cara asked, shrugging as she looked at her husband.

Gary shrugged in return. "Um, don't know. Don't remember."

"Your cousin, Julian, used to hang out there a lot, I understand. Small world. I thought you didn't know the heirs before the video, Boris," Fin said.

"I didn't know that I knew an heir. It never came up. And to tell you the truth, I hadn't really thought about it—there are islands everywhere, and you don't think of any place until you need that kind of a place. I'd met Julian at the bar—we talked, and he knew Paul McMasters. In fact, when he heard about the video, he'd asked Paul if he could be in it. Guy likes music. I never knew that Julian was one of the heirs to Christy Island until I read it in the paper. Then, yeah, I called him."

"You were never there with Julian?" Fin asked Cara. "He's your cousin—"

"Second or third cousin!" Cara said. "Seriously, I'm sure we've told you sometime in there—our parents hated Nolan Christy. I don't know what he did—it wasn't like any of them talked about it. But we didn't really see him, or each other. I mean, I have seen Julian—and Kenneth—now and then through the years, but…if I went there with Julian at any point, I don't remember."

"Oh, you'd remember it," Fin said. "The place is different."

"Very cool," Boris agreed. He was looking at Avalon. "You're all dusty. In fact, it looks as if the two of you have been rolling around in a playground…or fighting in a dirt pile."

"We were in the house—the mansion," Avalon said.

"Are we going to be allowed back soon?" Cara asked anxiously.

"I believe so. I'll have to check with my superiors and the New Orleans Police Department," Fin said.

"Was there anything there?" Cara queried. "Anything that might help at all?"

"Not that we found today, nothing that pointed at what happened to Cindy," Fin said. He stood up, staring at Avalon. "You do look like you were rolling around in the dirt."

"Me! You should see yourself."

She was surprised when he said, "I say we should shower."

"I agree!" Kevin said.

"And maybe you should go in and do that quickly," Brad suggested. "We were thinking about dinner. As in, we were about to leave just before you got here. I mean, if you'd like to join us."

"Sure. We'd love to join you. Dinner sounds good," Fin said. "If you don't mind."

"Of course not!" Boris said. He looked at Cara. "And maybe we should call Julian and Kenneth?"

Cara shrugged. "If you want—they might be nearby. But let's not wait forever, huh?" She looked at Fin apologetically. "Sorry. We were talking about dinner before you two came."

"That's okay," Fin said. "I get the hungry thing."

"We'll hurry," Avalon promised.

Lauren let out a bit of a strangled sound; she was laughing, Avalon noticed.

She was laughing…and she was happy for her. In the middle of all of this, she was happy for Avalon.

She approved of Fin Stirling.

"Okay, we're on this thing," Fin said. He stood and reached for Avalon's hand, clearly stating that they were together as he smiled at her.

"I think they *were* mud wrestling," Leo said.

Avalon grinned and laughed softly, hurrying behind Fin.

"You two! Shower, and that's it—we're all hungry," Kevin called. "I mean, seriously, you have a room, just remember that for later."

Inside, Fin looked at her in seriousness. "That was all right, I hope."

"It was all right with me," she assured him.

"You get to go first," he told her.

"I thought that—"

"No, they want us right out."

"We could still just share water—"

"Maybe you could. I couldn't." He grinned.

She had left her room locked; she unlocked the door and left him to follow behind her, then gathered fresh clothing and hurried into the shower.

It was hard not to linger, not to let the hot water wash away her memories of the mansion…and the porn stockpile of Nolan Christy.

She forced herself to bathe quickly, and thoroughly. She didn't want to take the time to wash her hair, but she couldn't leave it as it was. Air-drying would be just fine, but she had to wash it.

She was still quick and emerged in a halter dress, clean and fresh, in a matter of minutes.

With a nod, Fin approved of her speed.

He'd been on the phone; he was just ending his call when she emerged.

He took his turn. She smiled, watching him, and marveled at the way events and feelings could change. Maybe they hadn't changed, but rather they had grown. Nope. She was sure that she had disliked him at first!

When he emerged, he was dressed in a T-shirt and jeans and a jacket. She knew he wore the jacket to cover the gun in wore in a holster attached to his belt.

He looked her up and down and gave her a soft whistle. "Amazing," he said.

"Sweet."

He strode to her and took her in his arms. "Amazing...that you're with me."

"Oh, that's really sweet! And hard to believe that you could be amazed by anyone. Hulking FBI guy...life couldn't have been too bad!"

He smiled at that. "Ah, come on. Tell me that you haven't backed off sometimes because you knew that someone would never really know you, that you'd be living a lie, and that it would never work because the lying and pretending were just too hard?"

"Hmm. I see the dead. Is that why I'm so amazing?"

He shook his head. "You're amazing in your existence, in the way you breathe, care for others, and...let's see, your looks aren't bad, either. And you do want to be with me."

She grinned. "Okay, so I don't even just dislike you anymore. I think you're somewhat amazing, too. And your looks are kind of okay."

He kissed her lips, fingers threading through her still wet hair. There was a knock at the door, so he broke away.

It was Lauren. "I didn't mean to disturb you. That's a lie— I was sent to disturb you just in case you needed to be disturbed. I mean…it's real, isn't it? Avalon, you are an actress…"

"It's real," Fin said. "Are we ready to leave? Did anyone reach Kenneth or Julian?"

"Um, not sure," Lauren said. She smiled at the two of them. "All right then, let's go on down, huh?"

"Did we pick a place?" Fin asked.

"Yeah, the place that serves Italian, American, Creole, down on Decatur. Touristy, but they have long tables and we'll all be able to sit together."

They headed downstairs; the others were waiting in the courtyard and they went out through the gate in the courtyard.

Avalon had made certain to lock the door out to the courtyard.

Boris had nodded at her, and, last out, he'd locked the door from the courtyard to the street.

He fell into step with Avalon.

Fin was just ahead with Lauren.

"How was today?" Boris asked. He waved a hand in the air. "I'm not referring to the teasing the others are giving you. I mean… I am worried, Avalon. I'm worried about you and I'm worried about Lauren. And, I guess, the rest of the women in the reachable area—unless this was a total stranger who somehow wandered onto the island." He shook his head. "This whole thing… I've never believed in such things, but I'm wondering if that damned island isn't cursed."

"Boris! It's not the island. The island is just…earth. Surrounded by water. And I don't think it's going to be that much longer that the island is off-limits. I know finishing the movie is important to you."

"Screw the damned movie. I'm worried about people. I don't

know how much information is out there, but there was an anchorman on the news earlier who was drawing a lot of connections, and complaining that the police and FBI have done nothing to 'stop a serial killer.'"

"I don't think that the police or the FBI are even certain yet that there is a serial killer out there," Avalon said. "They're investigating."

"Someone has gotten wind of the investigation," he said. "I believe there's a press conference scheduled for tomorrow morning."

"Is there? I didn't know."

"Well, anyway," Boris said, and sighed. "In all honesty, I'm surprised I haven't been hauled in by someone. I was the only one staying on the island when Cindy—" He paused, wincing. "When Cindy's body was set out on that tomb. And, yes, we were all in Houma working on that video, and I was at the Speakeasy. And, yes, I did know Julian Bennet. We didn't make a big deal out of it because he had to present the idea to two distant cousins that he didn't know all that well."

Avalon took his hand and squeezed it. "Boris, we're going to get through all of this."

He grinned. "I'm glad you're with him, and that he's with us."

"Life is strange, isn't it?"

"If it was or wasn't, I'm glad to have the guy around now."

Avalon shrugged and then grinned at him. "Nice to have your approval, pops," she teased.

"That's right. Good friends will tell you when you're dating a jerk."

"Like that horrible—but extremely well-endowed—girl who was dating you that time, thinking that you were a producer and director and you could get her a role in a superhero movie?"

Boris winced. "Yes, yes, all of you warned me!" He shrugged. "We all learn, right?"

Lauren had stopped just ahead of them. "Kevin and Brad hurried ahead to get a table. We're trying to make a count. Cara and Gary are two, the group of us—you two, me, Terry, Brad and Leo—make another six, and Fin, so that's ten…and Cara talked to Kenneth and Julian, but she's not sure if they're coming. But if we have a table for ten, if one shows up, we're perfect, and if they both show up, we can squeeze a bit."

"Excellent directing!" Boris told her.

She made a face at him.

They continued down the street and cut toward the square on Chartres Street, passing the beautiful Old Ursuline Convent, shops and restaurants.

New Orleans was truly alive at this time of night.

Those in the lead took a left, maneuvering them toward Decatur.

Boris linked arms with Avalon. "They still haven't told us anything about this cousin who was coming to see about arrangements for Cindy. If nothing else…well, damn. We're going to see to it that she's cared for. I believe, maybe because I must believe to excuse my own existence, that there's more."

"Oh, I believe that, too," she told him. "And, yes, we may be sometimes broke and struggling actors and artists, but we will do right by Cindy."

Kevin headed back toward them as they turned onto Decatur Street.

"Guys, hurry! They have a table, a group our size just paid and left."

They hurried on. Fin had waited to take up the rear.

Avalon found herself wondering again who had called when she'd been in the shower…and wishing that they had talked about his call rather than being "amazing" for one another.

She walked in beauty. She moved in beauty, breathed in beauty. Her scent was a sweetest brush of heaven.

Her flesh, to touch her, to hear the melodic sound of her voice...

But most seductive of all...her eyes.

The beauty, the life, the passion, the vibrancy in those eyes!

The time would come...he wouldn't have to care with his every word, he wouldn't have to watch others.

He'd be rid of the man who...

He was annoyed when his fantasy reflection came to a crashing halt.

The man...

Special Agent Finley Stirling.

Fury awoke in him. He wanted the man before him, bound and chained. He wanted to rip the flesh from his face, burn his fingertips...

He forced a smile as he moved through the street. Patience, time.

There would be a way.

She would be his. Those eyes of hers...

He calmed himself with the dream.

The fantasy.

Because he knew, in time, that the fantasy would be real, sweet enough to linger with him through time.

He just needed to touch her.

To feel those eyes on his. Watch them. As they changed, as she became truly his...

Yes, his time would come.

He hurried on through the street, smiling all the while.

# CHAPTER FOURTEEN

At the restaurant there was a fair amount of confusion—good, polite confusion—as they all found seats at the table.

Fin maneuvered and wound up at one end of the table with Avalon to his left and Terry Jenson to his right. Kevin was to Avalon's left, and Cara Holstein was to Terry's right.

A waitress came and took their drink order. Fin asked for tea; down the table, Boris noted his choice.

"Always on duty, huh?" he called.

"Always on duty," Fin agreed.

"Well, I'm not!" Boris said. "I think I'm going with a double of something."

Cara was studying her phone. "Hmm," she said.

"Anything wrong?" Fin asked politely.

"Just Julian… He said that he was coming to join us, and now…"

"Is something wrong?" he persisted.

She looked up, staring around the table. "He says that he's been asked down to the police station."

"Under arrest?" Lauren asked, looking stunned.

"No, maybe— I don't know! His text just says, 'Sorry, not going to make it. Been asked to go to police station!'"

She stared at Fin. "I thought—I thought you were the head of this investigation."

"I am." He stood. "I'll find out what's going on. Forgive me—I guess I'm going to renege on dinner, too."

Kevin looked at him. "I'll be with Avalon and Lauren. I won't leave them for a second."

"Maybe I should go with Fin," Avalon said.

"For what? You're suddenly a cop?" Lauren asked. "Tell her she needs to stay here with us, Fin— we'll all stay together. Trust me—I'm a coward. We'll stick like glue."

Fin smiled at her. "You won't leave this restaurant. Not until I'm back." He turned to Cara. "What about your other cousin, Kenneth?"

"Third cousin, removed cousin, whatever! He texted me that he thought he'd make it, but he wasn't sure," Cara said.

"Well, I hope so. I'll find out what's going on with Julian," he promised. "They're probably just hoping he might have some insight into something."

Fin looked at Avalon. She was staring at him with a frown of reproach. He probably should have told her that he'd talked to Ryder…and he knew what was going on. He had orchestrated it. But as good an actress as she might be, they were playing for high stakes. These were her friends. It was best that she didn't know now.

He nodded to them all and headed out of the restaurant.

A patrol car was waiting for him about fifty feet down the block. A uniformed officer was leaning against the wall near the restaurant.

"If they leave—"

"Call it in immediately and follow them," the officer said solemnly.

Fin nodded. "Thanks."

He went on to the patrol car. Another officer was in the driver's seat, and he nodded when Fin got in thc car. "Straight to the station, right?"

"Straight to the station. Thanks."

Ryder was waiting for him when he arrived. "I've just had him in there, waiting. He's not under arrest—have no evidence, so we can't arrest him. I told him we're asking for help. We've been nice—got him coffee, promised we'd be quick—but I haven't talked to him. We've waited for you."

"Thanks."

"We're going to have to let him go, you know."

"Yeah, I figured."

"Just stirring the pot?" Ryder asked.

Fin nodded. "Someone has to react to something."

"You're convinced that one of them has been involved in all this?"

"Ryder, Christy Island and the murder in Houma are so close to each other. And Mississippi not all that far away, easy access for any of these people. All the travel could have been done by avoiding toll roads. They all have access to boats. That Jane Doe in Houma… Ryder, I'm sure she was intended to be part of a display at the Speakeasy. One of the employees was there late that night—the guy went out with a shotgun. I think the killers panicked, and if it wasn't going to be perfect, well, hell, what better place to get rid of your victim than the muck and mess of the ragged areas of the bayou?"

"It could still be…"

"It would have to be someone who knew about the place. Boris, Terry, Lauren and Avalon were involved with a video shoot in the area—that's where Boris and Julian Bennett met for the first time."

"So, you think it's Boris…and Julian working as a team?" Ryder didn't look convinced.

"Not really. I'm not sure, but I think one of them has something to say that could lead us to what's going on. Or maybe the most likely is the truth—they are involved. Anyway, let me get in there with him, and then I'll take him back with me. I'm working on being the nice guy in this thing, as I told you on the phone."

"Good cop, bad cop. I didn't think I'd ever be playing that game," Ryder said wearily.

Fin shrugged. "Hey, you're not the bad cop. You're just the cop who asked him to come in. And you're just a sweetie, Ryder. You got him coffee."

Ryder groaned and rolled his eyes, then he led Fin down the hall, pointing to one door.

Fin knew Ryder would go farther, to the second door; he'd head into another room to observe the exchange.

"Hey, Julian," Fin said, entering the room.

"Hey! They brought you in here. Thank God. I think. I mean, I swear to you—I have nothing to do with all this sick stuff going on. I heard that they're connecting this to an unsolved case from Houma. I heard about it, at the time. But they said that she was... so decomposed that they had little to go on. They thought she was a call girl because no one came forward to claim her. Even when Cindy West was...found, I didn't think... Oh, man. Yes, I know the Speakeasy—love the place... Oh, man. This is so... sick."

"Julian, is there anything at all that you can think of that might help? You were out there around the time the girl was killed."

Julian shrugged. "I like the place. The costumes, the girls, the way they dress—and I like the music. Great music."

"Right. And Boris... When you were an extra in the Pauly's Pariah video... Boris didn't know you were a Christy heir?"

Julian laughed. "I didn't know I was a Christy heir! I know that each one of us—Cara, Kenneth, me—has told you that our folks loathed the old man. Said he was weird...and scary." He hesitated a minute. "I think that my mom…well, I'm a Christy on my mom's side, you know… I think that when she was a kid, the old man…"

"Assaulted her? As a child?" Fin said gently.

"She used the term 'diddled around.' I'm not sure what happened. I think he scared her, and she was convinced that he was gross and creepy. We just stayed away. There was no reason for me to tell anyone that I was a Christy heir. I didn't expect that I would be one. And now, it's cost me rather than having given me anything. The movie—we didn't charge Boris a lot, we understood that he was working mainly on his own. But he was still paying us. And now…it does seem kind of sick to think of the place becoming a tourist attraction, doesn't it? But maybe someone will rip it to shreds, tear down the reminders of the past." He shook his head. "I don't know. I don't understand any of this."

Fin leaned in. "I have a question for you. Did you ever go to the Speakeasy with Cara and Gary, or Kenneth?"

He was thoughtful a minute. "We hardly ever saw each other… I'm not sure. Maybe I went with Cara once when Gary was on a business trip. I'm not sure. Usually, I met up with Kenneth when he came to Baton Rouge on business. Usually. Maybe five times in the last five years."

"Thanks. Okay, anytime that you were at the Speakeasy, did you see anyone act strangely, did you come across anyone who watched women in a fashion that might have made someone uncomfortable?"

"Like one of my cousins? You can't think that—"

"Anyone. Anyone at all."

Julian pondered for a moment. "I mean…people look at people all the time in bars. People go to bars to pick up people. That's hard to answer."

*He had answered*, Fin thought.

"I'm looking for help from any direction," Fin told him. He

stood. "I'm sorry for disrupting your evening. And thank you. Thing is, Julian, whoever is doing this…well, we asked you in because you are a charmer."

Julian looked at him, frowning. "I'm a charmer? Okay, I may be better-looking that Kenneth or Gary, but that's not much of a stretch!"

"Whoever is luring the women out is someone they trust."

Julian laughed. "I'm a trustworthy charmer? Maybe I like that." He looked at Fin earnestly. "I am trustworthy. I swear!"

"Good. Okay, come on. We may still make dinner."

"Huh?"

"Dinner—I told everyone I'd see what was going on. You've been great and I thank you for coming in. But let's go—the movie cast and crew and Cara and Gary are still at the restaurant on Decatur. We can maybe get a main course while they eat dessert. They were just ordering beverages when I left. Let's go."

"Just like that? That easy?"

"Sure. Let's go."

"Well, okay. Good. Great!"

Julian stood to join him. Ryder met them in the hallway. "Thanks so much for coming in, Mr. Bennett," he told Julian. "We're grateful for your help."

"I'm not sure I helped."

"Sometimes not seeing something is as useful as seeing something," Ryder said vaguely. "Anyway, thanks."

"There's a car to take us back?" Fin asked Ryder.

"Right outside, waiting for you."


Avalon wasn't sure she was glad about Kevin being at her side. He had too much fun teasing her about her relationship, then applauding it.

"Finally. A really decent guy."

"She's been too big on no guy for a long time," Lauren said.

"Oh! I guess you're dating the FBI guy now, huh?" Cara asked from down the table.

"I'm not sure we've been on an actual date," Avalon said.

"She's just sleeping with him right now," Kevin quipped. "I'm not sure why we call it 'sleeping,' though. I have no idea of just how much sleeping those two get in!"

They'd started by ordering drinks and then appetizers. Dinner could be one of those things that was expected to take hours in NOLA. Avalon found herself playing with the crawfish on her plate.

At one point, Kevin whispered to her, "Don't let them die in vain!"

She made a face at him, but then he whispered softly again, "So help me, Avalon, you've been my friend through thick and thin. I'm not a tough FBI guy, but I'd die before I let anything happen to you."

"Ah, Kev! Love you, too," she said. "I'm not scared, I'm just…"

"Anxious?"

Once again, she really wished that she knew who Fin had called. She was supposed to be the actress—when Fin had left, she hadn't been able to tell if he had known that Julian Bennett would be taken in, or if he was just as surprised as the rest of them.

The waitress had cleared away their dinner plates and was taking coffee and dessert orders when she looked up to see that Fin was returning…with Julian Bennett.

Cara rose to hug her cousin, anxiously demanding to know what had happened, why the police had wanted to see him and did they think he could be guilty of anything in any way?

Julian explained that they had just wanted to know anything that he knew about Houma and the Speakeasy.

"Oh!" Cara said. "Maybe it's that rock-band guy. What do you think?" she asked, looking around the table.

"Paul McMasters?" Terry asked. "God, no, he's a great guy. He has a wife. A family."

"Serial killers have had wives and families before," Gary noted gravely.

"McMasters wasn't in Mississippi when Ellen Frampton was found," Fin said. "We checked on that immediately."

"Well, Mississippi isn't much of a drive in the scheme of things from Houma," Gary said.

"Right. Except that Paul McMasters was playing in Seattle for the dates in question," Fin said. "I talked to Ryder—Detective Stapleton. They had my report from Houma, and they were just wondering if Julian might have seen something or someone acting suspiciously."

"Oh," Cara breathed. "Thank goodness. Julian, did you ever see anyone behave suspiciously there?"

"I told them all that I know. People try to pick up people in bars—how can you tell if that's suspicious or not?" Julian asked. "I'm ravenous. Think they'd still get me dinner?"

"Sure, we'll order dessert," Brad offered. "Bread pudding with vanilla sauce—yeah!"

"Key lime pie," Terry said.

"We're in New Orleans, not Florida. What's the matter with you?" Leo demanded.

There was laughter. Dessert was ordered. Avalon watched as Fin ordered the fish of the day, and sat back, easy again, just watching what was going on.

Eventually, it was time to head back. And while a few of the others were going to sit together in the courtyard, Cara and Gary and Julian begged out, saying they were heading back to their own place, and Avalon had no intention of sitting.

She wanted to know what had happened.

"I'm going up," she said, glancing at Fin.

He nodded.

"Um, no one will disturb you two now," Lauren assured them.

"Thank you—I really do need some sleep."

"We talked about that whole 'sleep' thing, you know," Kevin teased.

"With friends like you…" she teased.

"We're the best!" Lauren said.

And they were, she thought. She gave them a wave and turned to head up to her room.

Fin grinned and waved to the group, then hurried after her.

In her room, she closed and locked the door.

Then she turned on Fin. "What the hell happened? Did you know that they were going to bring Julian in? Why didn't you tell me what was going on?"

"I didn't really have a chance. But it was better that you didn't know. We could all be surprised and dismayed."

"Seriously?" she demanded. "And…do you think that Julian Bennett could be a killer?"

"No, actually, I don't."

"Did he say something to clear himself?"

Fin seemed to hesitate. "Nothing definitive. It was more in what he didn't say."

"That makes no sense."

"Avalon, trust me, it does. I was listening to a speech pattern."

"Speech pattern?" she said. "To—to go with the essay?"

"Something like that." He hesitated again. "They're going to bring Kenneth in, and Boris—just in the same way. Boris isn't going to be arrested."

"You don't want to bring Kevin in, too?" she asked, wincing as she realized she sounded defensive.

"Kevin was in New York when Jane Doe was killed," he said.

She let out a soft sigh. "But I must have been in Houma then. Or…maybe not. The mansion was in the Houma area, but a lot of the video was filmed by the Chalmette Battlefield. I guess it doesn't matter. You're only talking about an hour and a half in driving distance, maybe an hour with no traffic and two hours with traffic."

"Right," Fin said.

He set his gun and holster on the little table by the bed, then started disrobing.

Avalon sat at the foot of the bed.

Naked, Fin came up behind her across the bed on his knees. Fingers on her shoulders, lips near her ear, he whispered, "Think they're listening at the keyhole?"

"What? No!" she exclaimed.

She turned. He was looking at her thoughtfully. She searched his face. She didn't mean to kill the moment, but she needed to know. "I just... Are you going to be called out tonight for something else? Should I be... I mean, is this real?"

"God, yes," he whispered.

She twisted all the way around, meeting his kiss.

Then she pulled away.

"Fin?"

"We have the night," he promised. "Avalon, I'm all yours tonight."

He made good on his promise.

His fingers moved gently down her cheek and she slid into his arms as they both fell back on the bed.

She felt the brush of his lips against her flesh as he slid the halter dress up and over her head, and then as he continued to disrobe her.

She felt the heat begin to rise in her, the sweetness of touching and tasting, and dissolving into him. Forgetting the world in moments of fiery ecstasy.

And then simply lying beside him.

In his arms, she slept, and it was sweet sleep, deep and dreamless.

# CHAPTER FIFTEEN

*Saturday*

Morning found everyone downstairs in the kitchen, digging through the groceries they'd gotten.

"Cereal! The good stuff, the kid stuff, loaded with sugar," Brad said happily, holding up a box with cute little creatures on it.

"We have frozen waffles," Lauren said. "Did anyone remember to buy syrup?"

"Oh, yeah, I would never buy frozen waffles and forget the syrup," Terry assured her.

"Hi, diddly dee, an actor's egg for me!" Leo said.

Boris had one of the cabinets open. "Yes—grits! But, hey, dammit, can anyone here make some decent grits?" Boris wondered.

"Right—maybe you can whip up some great grits yourself," Lauren said, laughing.

"I say we take a walk to Café du Monde," Kevin suggested.

Then came the knock at the door. Boris looked at Fin, who shook his head.

"We won't know until we answer it," Terry said wisely.

Avalon came hurrying down the stairs. Fin felt her eyes on him. He hadn't had a chance to tell her that Ryder was coming by.

She'd been sleeping so peacefully when he'd awakened. He had sat up on an elbow, just watching her for a while.

Wishing he wasn't quite so...in love?

*You didn't fall in love in a week*, he told himself.

But it was something. He was happy to be there, just watching her. The fall of her lashes against her cheek, the way she slept with her lips just slightly parted, and ever so slightly curving, as if she even slept with a sweet smile. He'd lain awake most of the night, torn between watching her and going over, and over, every aspect of the case.

He had finally risen, showered and dressed.

And so, he had left her sleeping when he had slipped out and joined the others downstairs. As he and Boris headed to the door, Fin assured the director that he could prepare cheese grits that were damned good.

They opened the door for Ryder.

"Folks, I'm always sorry to bother you," Ryder said, looking past Fin and Boris to the others, who had lined up behind them. "We're just trying so hard to piece some information together."

"I thought you were lead investigator on this thing," Lauren said to Fin.

"We're a joint force," Fin said.

"We're just hoping that Mr. Koslov and Mr. Jenson won't mind coming in with us—they may know something that they don't even realize is helpful about Houma," Ryder told the group.

"I'll go anywhere and do anything," Boris said.

"And I'm happy to do anything if it means finding Cindy's killer," Terry vowed.

"I should have called you, Fin, and asked you about this, but sometimes, showing up in person is the best way to do things. We do work together, but sometimes..."

"It's all right, Ryder," Fin said. "I had figured we'd all keep talking here, see if something didn't occur to someone, or maybe take a trip back to see McMasters again and hope that something might pop between all of them."

"Pardon me, Fin, but I was thinking that our rooms are quiet and give people a chance to think—easier than in a group, where we tend to get distracted. I mean, you're the head of this investigation according to the powers that be, but this is my city, and that island fell to me, no matter who was drawing the jurisdiction lines."

"Yeah, look at the state lines. Sometimes you have to wonder who was drawing them," Leo said. "Like, seriously, Alabama wants the Florida panhandle in the worst way."

Boris sighed, looking at Fin. "I didn't do it, I swear it," he said wearily. "I know that I was the one staying on the island, and, yes, I've been to the Speakeasy, and yes, I've been in every state in the southeast. But I swear, I didn't do any of this."

Terry stared at Fin. "You can't really think that."

"Terry," Fin said, "I don't think that you're guilty and I don't think that Boris is guilty. Ryder is telling the truth. We're hoping that because you were in on that shoot, you might have seen something at the Speakeasy, or anywhere in the vicinity, or heard anyone who seemed strange. We're desperate for help."

Terry nodded slowly.

Fin looked at Ryder. "I have an idea. It's Saturday morning, no days of rest, but let's do the best we can here. We'll go ahead and get breakfast going, and we'll sit and talk. It won't be distracting; Lauren and Avalon were there, too, after all."

"Not at the Speakeasy, just at the shoot," Lauren said. "I love Pauly's Pariah. And the guys were great to work with. But I was also bone-tired." She glanced over at Avalon. "We were sharing rooms on that shoot—both in the Houma area, and out by the Chalmette Battlefield."

Fin started to say that was fine, that anything anyone thought of might help, but to his surprise, Avalon took charge of the situation.

"We'll have breakfast and we'll all sit out in the courtyard. For as long as you like, Detective Stapleton. We were Cindy's friends. And, yes, what's happening with the cousin? Is the medical examiner going to release the body?"

"Cindy's cousin's name is Myrna West and she'll be taking Cindy home next week," Ryder told them. "The funeral is going to be in Atlanta. Cindy will go into her family plot there. When arrangements are made, she'll let you all know."

There was silence for a minute. Avalon turned to head back to the kitchen. Fin followed her.

"Avalon—"

"Make your grits—I heard you claim you're good. I'm going to throw together some omelets. Is that the plan for today? Just sit here and talk it all to death again?" she asked.

"I don't know yet. I'm waiting."

"For?"

"I need to hear from Tom Drayton, or the police force out by Biloxi, and Captain Tremont in Houma."

"Because?"

"I'm looking for an old hunter's shack."

Boris came into the kitchen, followed by Lauren, and Fin fell silent.

"Cereal, too—I have an urge for crunchy stuff," Lauren said. "Leo did want eggs… I'll bring stuff out to the courtyard table, get it set. Fin—you're a chef, too?"

"Yep. I prepare just about three meals really well," Fin told her.

Lauren grinned and went into the cupboards for a supply of paper plates.

"Boris, want to grab some forks, knives, spoons and paper towels?"

"Will do," Boris said.

Fin found cheese, grits, salt and pepper.

Avalon worked with eggs and whatever else she could find to dice in the refrigerator.

She didn't speak to him.

Kevin conveniently came into the kitchen right when Fin felt the vibration of his phone. He handed Kevin the large wooden spoon he was working with and asked him to take over.

He walked out to the entry area to take the call.

It was Captain Tremont.

"Special Agent Stirling," Tremont said. "We've found your shack. We're not going to touch anything until you get out here. How soon can you make it?"

"You've been in?"

"Oh, yes."

"And?"

"It's a bloodbath."

Fin was leaving. He wasn't staying for breakfast; he was just leaving. And he wasn't taking her.

Ryder was at the house; she could only presume that he felt they were all safe with Detective Ryder Stapleton.

Fin went upstairs, and she tore after him.

"Fin?" she asked anxiously.

He took her by the shoulders and pulled her to him.

"Avalon, you helped me a lot with this—you were the one who went into Nolan Christy's trunk. There was a picture in there that made me wonder if Nolan Christy had been busy off the island, as well. One of the pictures was of a rotting wooden shack. He was in the picture, and a woman was in the picture and... Captain Tremont and his people have found the shack."

"I can go with you."

He shook his head. "Not for this. There's—there's no reason, Avalon. I don't think there's any reason at all that you need to see this."

"And you know that I'm okay because Ryder is here."

He nodded. "Avalon…"

"Right," she said.

"Help Ryder, if you can."

"But I was never at the Speakeasy. And I didn't even realize that Julian Bennett was in the video as an extra."

He paused. "What about Lauren?"

"What do you mean, 'what about Lauren'?"

"She did the makeup for the shoot."

"I doubt that they did makeup for extras in a concert scene."

"Right. Sorry. I don't know… I mean, just see what you all can think of, okay? Draw out Boris and Terry."

"Fine."

He took her by the shoulders, looking down into her eyes. "Avalon, this guy scares me. Scares the hell out of me. These guys, I should say. Yes, I desperately want this solved. And, I've told you—no, I don't think that Boris is really a maniacal killer. But any little thing—any little thing can help."

"You're afraid for me," she said softly.

She was surprised that she wasn't more afraid. But then, she was usually with him.

His eyes as he looked at her now were the deepest forest-green. She felt a trembling within her, just from the way he looked at her. And she was glad—there was so much passion in him, and determination. She slept so easily, so deeply next to him, entwined with him. She had never been with anyone like him.

She had never felt anything so intimate, in the most sensual of situations, or just when they lay curled together.

She didn't want it to end.

But right now, nothing could just be good, nothing could

just be real. Not while this murder case was like a darkness that encompassed everyone involved.

She nodded, gave him a quick kiss on the lips and told him, "Go. I will do my best to dig deeply into the minds of my crew!"

He smiled. "Avalon, I just want to keep you safe," he said.

"You know, I have had some martial-arts training, and I've even worked with a sword. Okay, a dulled sword, but we get that stuff as theater majors, if we choose, you know."

"Gotcha. I don't have a sword handy, so stick with Ryder."

She grinned. He kissed her lightly again, drawing away quickly as if he was afraid not to.

Then he headed out the door and she hurried downstairs to join the others out in the courtyard.

"Well, there's one absent chef," Kevin said, giving her a fierce frown. "First FBI guy runs out, and then you leave me a frying pan filled with half-done omelets."

"Oh, Kevin, I'm sorry—"

"Just remember, I was the final creator in all this," he said.

"Where did Wonder Boy go?" Leo asked.

"I don't know—maybe his office called," Avalon said.

"But," Lauren protested, "you just went up there after him."

"And that's what he said, something about the fact that he had to run out, he'd gotten a call." Avalon smiled sweetly. "Maybe Ryder knows."

"I'm NOPD," Ryder told them. "But he knows I'm here."

There was confusion for a few minutes as platters with eggs and toast and waffles were passed around, along with bowls of grits, boxes of cereal, milk, coffee and orange juice.

Ryder wanted to know about the video, from beginning to end.

Boris explained the concept, and then how they used the house for the dream sequence, and then brought in extras when they were headed out to the battlefield area.

"So how long were you in Houma, and how many times did you go out to the Speakeasy?" Ryder asked.

Boris didn't get a chance to answer; there was a knock at the courtyard gate.

"I'll get it," Avalon told them.

She hesitated at the gate, surprised that she was suddenly afraid to open it.

She was with Ryder and her entire group, and she had determined that she wasn't going to be a coward. It was stupid to be afraid to open a gate.

She was startled to see that it was Samara Stella.

"Hey!" she said.

"Hey," Samara said.

Avalon didn't realize that she was just standing there, staring at the woman, until Samara asked quietly, "Do you—do you mind if come in? I'm sorry. I don't mean to intrude. I guess I was hoping that you'd be here. I—I didn't want to be alone."

"Of course, come in. I'm sorry. You just took me by surprise."

"I've been nervous since that—that doll made to look like me was found knifed in my theater."

"Well, you're safe here. Detective Ryder Stapleton is here."

Ryder, like the others at the table, had grown silent as Avalon had gone to the gate. She turned quickly; they'd been talking about Houma. Maybe Ryder wouldn't be happy about the fact that Samara was here. But what could she do?

The woman was frightened and asking for help.

"Miss Stella," Ryder said, rising to welcome her.

"I'm so sorry. I didn't mean to interrupt your breakfast," Samara said.

Avalon had seen photos of the woman in all her splendor—leather, chains and more. But when she was out, it seemed, she had her hair up in a messy bun and wore jeans and knit shirts.

"Miss, please," Terry said, leaping up to give her his chair.

Avalon thought that her whole group hadn't yet met Samara, so she introduced them all quickly. Then she realized that she hadn't locked the gate. She turned and nearly screamed; there was a man standing there.

It was Kenneth Richard.

"Uh, hi," she said.

Ryder was suddenly standing behind her; he must have seen her initial reaction.

"Sorry, I guess I'm bored silly. I figured I'd come by and see if you all were just hanging around," Kenneth said. He looked around. "Oh, sorry. I'm disturbing you—"

He broke off. He was looking at Samara Stella.

"Samara?" he asked.

"It's me," she said.

"You two know each other?" Boris asked. "Small world."

"I've been to one of Samara's shows," Kenneth said, smiling. "The one in which Anne Boleyn knocks the shit out of Henry the Eighth. Oh, sorry... I mean, you know, the one in which the beheaded queen doesn't get beheaded but gets the guy instead."

"Well, thank you for being in the audience," Samara said.

"I'll—I'll get more plates," Boris offered.

"No, no, I'm sorry—" Kenneth began.

"No problem," Lauren said. "I mean, I don't think there's a problem," she said, looking at Ryder.

"The more the merrier," Ryder said.

But, as more plates were retrieved from the kitchen, chairs taken from inside to provide for their number and general chaos, Avalon noted that Ryder was texting.

She figured that he was writing Fin.

"You haven't seen my cousins, have you?" Kenneth asked.

"Not this morning," Leo said. "But—"

"I have a feeling they might come by, too," Ryder said. "Nothing like the gang all being here."

★ ★ ★

Fin was torn. It was important to see the shack.

But Ryder had texted him.

He'd barely been gone an hour when not just the entire Christy clan had shown up, but Samara Stella, too.

Captain Tremont's people had found the shack, and he had said that the place resembled a bloodbath.

Fin found himself thinking about the woman in the photo with the man with the baseball bat standing behind her. She'd had long dark hair.

That could be Avalon, yet.

Or Samara Stella. Had she possibly been involved with Nolan Christy at some time?

Nolan Christy had only been dead a few months.

But he had been alive when both Ellen Frampton and Jane Doe had been murdered.

However, he couldn't have killed Cindy West.

The drive seemed to take forever; however, he managed to arrive at the road leading down through a trail to the old shack in good time, not an hour and a half after he'd left the French Quarter.

Captain Tremont was waiting for him himself, leaning against a parish car, sipping coffee.

"How the hell did you know about this?" he asked Fin. "I've got a forensic crew ready to go in, and I haven't let anyone trample the place. Strange thing, the flies and smell led us to it—we're just so far off the beaten path. Anyway…well, you'll see."

Officers and members of the forensic team were at the shack, all nodding in grim acknowledgment as Fin arrived. He returned their nods, then walked up to the shack and opened the door. One officer brought a flashlight with a powerful beam to light up the place.

There was a cot with a rotting mattress against the far wall, which was splintering and all but caving in. There was also a large, claw-foot porcelain tub in the room and the floor was pooled with dried blood. Stains covered the ripped and torn mattress.

The walls, too, looked as if they had been sprayed with blood, or as if an errant child had used blood for a frenzy of finger-painting.

"I'm assuming this is where our Jane Doe met her demise," Tremont said.

Fin explained to him about finding Nolan Christy's stash of pornographic pictures, featuring just about every sexual deviation there was.

"I sent you the picture," Fin reminded him.

Tremont shook his head. "Drugs, domestics, greed, jealousy… I've seen bad stuff. We're not big-city, but we're not illiterate innocents out here, either, and I did a stint in NOLA myself before I came out here," he said. "But this…"

"None of us is accustomed to anything like this," Fin assured him.

He stepped back.

"But how—?" Tremont began.

"The victims were all bled out, Captain," Fin said. "I figured that the people doing it had to have a place to kill…and a place to clean and dress their victims. We're close enough to the water—seawater and fresh water—for them to have gotten a supply for that bathtub. As to the weapons used and everything else… Well, they're in the muck and the dirt, sunk in the water, or…the killers took them with them. For this, they'd have been covered in blood themselves, but we passed what looked like a fresh-water stream coming down here, so they cleaned up themselves after they finished creating their doll…or dolls."

"You think the woman in the photo was a victim?"

"We need a lot of analysis. Maybe, just maybe, the killers nicked themselves, or left something behind," Fin said. "In fact,

I'd say there had to have been something, but this old place has now seen so much time go by."

"Everything is going to be degraded," a member of the forensic team, standing nearby, noted. "But we'll do our best."

"I'd bet there is at least one more of these shacks somewhere," Fin said, looking around, listening to the buzz of the insects that had found good homes in the decay. "This wasn't used recently. There's nothing on Christy Island. It's been gone over, and over. Cindy West was killed, bled out, bathed and dressed somewhere before she was brought out to Christy Island. I believe that the Biloxi people will find something similar, and there will be one more."

"We've got people on it," Captain Tremont assured Fin.

He nodded.

"We'll try. God knows, there could be something in here, the way the blood dried. We'll do our best to find prints," Tremont said, nodding toward his team.

"Thank you for getting right on this," Fin said.

"You bet. Hey...we found Jane Doe," Tremont said. "It would be damned good to find justice for that girl. Sex worker, runaway, whatever she might have been—poor girl can't be helped in life, but we'd sure like to see justice for her in death."

Fin thanked him again and asked to be informed if they found anything, no matter how minute.

Captain Tremont solemnly promised.

Fin walked slowly back to the road, trying to feel the air around him, hoping...

But whoever had been murdered in the shack was gone. Long gone. And he was grateful; no soul should have to linger where something so horrible had taken place.

He walked slowly, then moved on, leaving the overgrown trail behind, and reached his car.

There, he texted Ryder, not wanting him to have to speak

in front of others, but anxious to know that everything was going well.

*That he was still with Avalon.*

He was.

Fin drove back, wanting to be part of the conversation going on at the house.

Because the gang was all there.

He only rued the fact that he now smelled revoltingly of blood and decay himself; he would have to shower again before joining anyone.

Or would he?

Maybe his best appearance would be for him to join all the others…

Just as he was.

Smelling of rot, and decomposition, and blood.

They had talked all afternoon.

They had talked about the video several of them had worked on for Pauly's Pariah.

Boris and Julian had talked about the fact that they'd known one another, but until Boris had seen the article on Nolan Christy's death and read that Julian Bennett was one of the heirs, neither of them had ever thought to bring up Christy Island.

Cara Holstein was disappointed that they weren't finishing the movie—she'd hoped to be an extra in one of the scenes that was now being scrapped.

Kevin had talked about Broadway; Brad had talked about filmmaking, and he and Samara seemed to hit it off, though Terry seemed to enjoy talking to her just as much.

Every now and then, Avalon glanced over at Ryder. He would just give her a nod, and she assumed it was to assure her that everything was okay.

Breakfast was cleared up by lunchtime. It wasn't until late in the afternoon before Leo mentioned that they hadn't eaten in a long time.

Cara yawned and said, "Maybe we should just head home tonight, or our home away from home, guys," she said to her cousins.

Julian asked her, "Why?"

"Because we're imposing on these people."

"You're not imposing. We're all sitting here…waiting."

"They will clear the island for use again. Probably tomorrow," Ryder assured them.

"So you could film again?" Cara said hopefully.

Boris shrugged. "We're broken down. We've figured out a way to edit the movie together without shooting the remaining scenes. And I thought you wanted to go ahead and sell the island."

"A sale will take time," Gary said, glancing at the others and lifting his hands. "Hey, I'm just Cara's husband, not an heir. But I'm just saying."

"I don't know," Boris said. "Maybe my heart's not in it."

"Well, I'm hungry. Should we order something, or go out?" Lauren asked.

She didn't get an answer. There was a knock at the gate.

"It's going to be Fin," Ryder told them.

"I'll get it," Boris said, walking over to unlock the gate.

Fin walked in.

"Hey, everyone is still here," he said. "Thanks, Boris. I'm beat. It's good to be back."

He walked over to the table. He hadn't come very close before Avalon noted the smell.

It was awful.

Apparently, he didn't know. He saw an empty chair and pulled it back, falling into it as Boris returned to the table.

Fin leaned back, closing his eyes, then opened them to look

around. He offered the group a weak smile. "Hey, anyone else hungry? I'm starving."

A little sound escaped Lauren. "I *was* hungry," she said.

Fin frowned. They were all still looking at him. "Oh… I'm sorry. Am I offensive? I should have realized that I'd be…" He looked at Ryder and shook his head and then told them all, "The Terrebonne Parish police found a shack. They were hoping that it could give us some clues to Cindy, but…well, it was last used a long time ago. Probably when their Jane Doe was murdered."

"Oh, God!" Lauren said. She stood and walked away from the table.

"I wish so badly I could remember something that would help," Julian said.

"We all do," Boris said. "We've been trying to remember if we saw anything strange at the Speakeasy. But when you're out for a fun night, you're not paying attention to that kind of thing."

"I never saw anyone being…obnoxious there," Julian said. "It was a fun place to go. Sure, women flirted, men tried some bad pick-up lines…"

"I wish I could help," Cara said. "I—"

"You were there, with me once," Julian told her.

"You tell me that, but I don't remember. I'm married. You're the one who goes to bars," she said lightly. "Well, alone. Gary and I both love music." She laughed. "I'm sorry, Julian, I just don't remember. I'm not sure why I would want to be at a place like that with you, where men were picking up women and women were watching men, trying to find the studliest or whatever!"

"I know of the place," Gary said.

"The thing of it is," Kenneth said, "no killer is going to walk into the place with a sign on that says, 'Hey! I'm a charming, good-looking dude, but I'm also a serial killer!'"

Cara went on, "And how the hell would you know if someone was acting strangely, watching a woman in a bar? Stalking her. Correct me if I'm wrong—I know people go out in groups. But women—just like me—like to take a good gander at a member of the opposite sex without looking like they're taking a long gander at the opposite sex. Men look at women. Women look at men."

"That's probably true," Fin said.

"Was it any help?" Ryder asked Fin. "Finding the cabin—was it any help for the Christy Island case?"

"In a way."

"How's that?" Avalon said.

"Well, I found the shack through one of the pictures you found in Nolan Christy's trunk…or, rather, the police in Terrebonne Parish found it."

"My great grandfather is dead," Cara said. "He couldn't have—"

"No, but we could be wrong. He might have killed others when he was alive, and someone who knew about it could be killing now. Or Nolan Christy might have just liked really sick stuff."

"There was a reason our parents hated him," Cara said.

"We know that the cabin was once the scene of a horrible crime. A forensic crew is going to be tearing it apart. And you know what? Sometimes, even with a site as degraded as that shack is going to be, something can be found. Like a fingerprint time does a number, yes, but…there was a lot of blood in there, and someone had used it to paint on the wall."

"Oh, my God!" Samara Stella rose and walked away.

Ryder looked at Fin. "I think it's you. No offense, buddy, but you smell to high hell."

"Oh, my apologies," Fin said. "I'll shower now." He stood, glancing at Avalon. She wasn't sure how, but she knew that he had sat down on purpose first—she knew, too, that he didn't want her following him.

He had to be alone to steam and scrub away all that he had encountered that day.

"We'll grab some food when you're down," Ryder said.

"That's a plan," Fin agreed.

"Hey, this is like an investigation. We'll put the bill on your tab."

"We'll give it to Adam Harrison," Fin agreed, hurrying toward the house, then pausing.

"That door is open," Boris called to him.

Fin headed in.

"Damn," Lauren said, coming back to the table. "How in hell could such a good-looking man smell so…"

"Disgusting," Cara said. "Blood, I guess."

"Old blood," her husband said.

"Are we ordering food, or heading out?" Samara asked. "I mean, I guess we should keep it down, if we're really not paying the tab."

Leo laughed. "Wait—when someone else is paying the tab, you don't worry as much about it."

They talked casually, and as they did, Avalon kept smiling, and yet something had disturbed her.

She wasn't sure what.

"Hey, aren't you supposed to do your shows at night?" Brad asked Samara.

"I've taken a few days off—I'll get back to it next week," Samara said. She glanced over at Avalon, and Avalon wondered if she wasn't very afraid that the killer was after her.

Fin returned, his usually bronze flesh reddened, as if he had taken a scouring pad to himself.

Maybe he had; his hair was wet, a dark honey color against his head.

He smelled good.

They opted to call out for food, and have it delivered. Italian seemed to fit the bill again; a large lasagna, baked ziti and several other shareable dishes arrived.

Avalon watched Fin as he talked to others, and she realized that he did a lot more listening than he did speaking.

She watched as he excused himself, digging into a pocket for his phone.

He looked at it; he'd received a text message.

Fin looked up. "Ryder, we're in New Orleans. This should be yours. Will you please arrest Mr. Kenneth Richard?"

"What?" Kenneth demanded. "On what charge? What the hell—"

"Murder, Mr. Richard. You're going to be arrested for the murder of Jane Doe, and while you're being held, they'll be gathering evidence to charge you with the murders of Ellen Frampton and Cindy West."

"What?"

"Fingerprints, Mr. Richard. You really should never finger-paint in blood!"

# CHAPTER SIXTEEN

"No!" Cara screamed. "No, that's impossible! Yes, our great-grandfather was a monster, but…no, no, no! Kenneth is not a monster."

She was on her feet, screaming at Fin. "You're a liar. You're a horrible, lousy liar! You said that the house was degraded, that…you can't get anything back that fast. I know—I watch TV. You're full of it—you bastard, you can't solve a crime, so you're going to throw it at anyone!"

Ryder was already standing, asking Kenneth to do the same. He read the man his rights. Kenneth was dead silent. Then he said, "But… I didn't."

"Kenneth, shut up, not a word!" Cara snapped.

"This has to be wrong," Julian said, trying to reassure Kenneth.

"We'll have our lawyers out as soon as possible. Just keep your mouth shut, Kenneth, don't say anything at all to these bastards," Gary warned.

"Kenneth, you will have to come with me," Ryder said quietly.

Cara kept protesting, torn between tears of disbelief and ranting fury.

Gary kept telling Kenneth not to say a word—that they'd twist and use anything against him.

Julian repeated that they'd get an attorney, and that Kenneth shouldn't worry. His family knew that he wasn't a monster.

Fin took the brunt of Cara's rants, but he didn't say a word. Cara, Gary and Julian followed Ryder and Kenneth as they left the courtyard.

Then they were gone and there was dead silence, the others in the courtyard staring at Fin.

"I'm sorry," he said. "That wasn't…a great way to end the day."

"Is it   is it real?" Lauren whispered. "I mean…is that it? They really found something? Kenneth murdered Cindy?"

"Oh!" Samara had been standing; she sank into a chair.

"Can it really be over?" Boris asked.

"I'll talk to him in the morning," Fin said. "We won't interrogate him until then. Ryder will keep him in a cell overnight without saying anything more."

"Julian was insisting on their attorney—they aren't going to let him talk," Kevin warned.

"We'll see," Fin said. He knew that Avalon was looking at him, and she seemed doubtful of everything that had just occurred.

"Okay…" Avalon said. "Cleanup time, let's get this into recycling and trash bins and… I'm going to bed. Wait, Samara, we'll give you a ride—"

"I'll get her home," Brad offered.

Samara had evidently decided that she liked Brad. She said, "That would be great. And then I'm okay, really." She looked at Avalon. "It's great, living in a house with a cop. I mean, staying at the house—he's married. I'm in the guest room. Honestly, I'm a performer, not a home-wrecker."

Soft laughter arose from many in the group, and it was good

to break the tension—they were all still reeling from the sudden end to the night.

"Not to worry," Brad assured her.

"Thank you—all of you," Samara said. She headed for the gate, followed by Brad.

"A budding romance," Lauren said. "A man arrested, a murderer…taken. All right, I'll help clean up and then I'm going to bed. I love you guys. But I need to be alone. I need to process this… I…wow. Kenneth. He watched us day in and day out. I used to talk to him all the time when you were setting up shots. Oh, God. Wow."

She picked up the dishes to clear. Avalon joined her, as did Terry, Boris and Leo. Fin pitched in, too. Lauren left the kitchen for her room.

Avalon finished washing the last one of the serving spoons they had used, put it away, glanced at Fin, still wide-eyed and silent, and then headed up the stairs.

He followed her into her room, closing the door behind him.

"Are you okay?" he asked her.

"I'm in shock. I mean, I want to believe that it's true, and so it's over, but can it really be Kenneth? Was it him? Is it over? You think he did it all with help."

"Hopefully, he'll tell us who."

"But can it be? Did they really get a print? And if they did, could they have identified it so quickly?"

"We have prints from the heirs and from all of you—for comparison," he told her. "When you have nothing to compare a print with, it's not very helpful. But…"

"But what?"

"It was a partial print. That's not a solid case. Not yet. It may prove to be. The shack was really degraded badly."

"I know. I smelled you."

He nodded. "Yeah, well…"

"You did that on purpose, too."

"I did."

"And you think that Nolan Christy murdered the girls before Cindy?"

"I'm not sure. But we're on the right track. And sometimes,
you need to push a few buttons to get to the truth. We'll learn
more tomorrow."

"Not if Cara Holstein has her way."

"We'll see."

She nodded.

Fin was exhausted. It wasn't even late, but he'd barely slept
the night before.

He laid his gun and holster on the bedside table, then removed
his shirt. Avalon was still just standing in the center of the room.
He paused, turning back to her. "Are you all right with me here
tonight? I swear, I practically scrubbed skin off, but—"

"No, no, you're fine."

He stripped down to his briefs and crawled into the bed.
She gave herself a little shake, then sat down on the edge of the
mattress.

"I'm sorry. I'm thrown," she said. "You were so matter-of-fact,
and it feels like... I didn't really suspect Kenneth. Julian is the one
who seemed connected to everything."

"We believe that Kenneth is involved," Fin said. "Again, they
have a partial print. It won't stand up in court."

"Then why arrest him now?"

"We're watching the reaction," he said.

"Is that...legal?"

"Yes."

She nodded. Slowly, she took off her shoes, and then stripped
out of her jeans and shirt. She lay stiffly next to him on the bed.

"I'm just rattled," she said.

"That's okay, I understand," he said softly.

She was silent. He didn't want to push her in any way; he

wanted her to have her space. And to stay away from him, if she chose.

"Avalon, we will discover the truth," he said softly.

"Yeah," she said.

Time passed. He closed his eyes. He was tired. He was glad that she was near.

"There's just something," she said quietly.

He forced himself a bit more awake. "What's that?"

"I keep feeling that there's something I should have caught today when we were talking…something was right there, and I missed it."

"Let it go," he said softly, "and it may just come back."

After a while, Fin thought that Avalon had fallen asleep.

Then she curled against him, her whisper touching his ear with soft breath and warm heat. "I'm not *that* rattled." He felt her lips move to his throat, her body ease against his with an evocative rub of flesh. She brushed over his chest as she moved against him, kisses searing his skin.

He eased his arms around her, drew her to him and found her mouth, kissing her long and deep on her lips, and then her throat and breasts and beyond, feeling the caress of her fingers against him, the hot, wet movement of her lips against him. Touching, writhing, arching, moving against each other… It was unique, it was necessary, it was beautiful.

He wasn't as tired as he had thought.

But in time, he slept.

*Sunday*

Men watched women.

Women watched men.

He watched her.

It had been so thrilling to be near her, to breathe her in. So exceptionally thrilling to just be near, breathing her in, watching the fluidity of her movements, see her smile, hear the crystal melody of her voice.

He couldn't see her, not at that second.

But that didn't matter. Because he would see her soon, and the wonder of it was sweet. Because they were all so blind, they didn't understand. It would be today...

He didn't need to follow her, stalk her, watch her as he had, because now, her scent lingered in his memory, he could close his eyes and see her...

And imagine. Because it was now or never, because the idiots couldn't see or touch the truth, but they were stumbling close.

And it had to be today. He didn't say so, he didn't dare...

But if he just held her, watched the sky-blue of her eyes as the light within them changed and died, if he just held her and touched her and loved her...

He would die with her. Because life, and death, would then be complete. Life and death, the fantasy, the reality.

Close, so close...yes, he could still breathe in her scent in his memory...

And know that fantasy would be reality.


Avalon opened her eyes. Fin was awake, showered and just sliding his jacket on over a tailored cotton shirt; he was all business this morning.

She smiled at him.

"What?" he asked.

"I'm waiting for the day that I wake up, and you're still in bed!"

He smiled, paused by the bed and leaned down to kiss her.

"I'm going in to talk to Kenneth Richard," he said.

"Of course. Fin, do you think this will be the end?"

"I think we've stirred the pot. And that could trip someone up. Anyway, we do know that there is more than one person involved in all this, and if Kenneth is one of them, I'm hoping he'll give up the other before…"

"Before anyone else dies. But, Fin, these killers…they went months and months between victims. If you can't find evidence against Kenneth, he—or whoever is doing this—could go underground for ages again, and then strike."

"We know of three victims," he said quietly. "There could have been more. And if life is going to go on for any of the innocent here, it all must be stopped now. I'm going to talk to Kevin and Boris—make sure that this group stays here until I get back."

"You trust Boris now?"

"As much as I trust anyone. With Kevin, Boris, Leo, Terry, Brad and Lauren all here, you're a group—and there's safety in numbers."

She nodded, leaping up. "I'll shower later—wait for me!"

She grabbed jeans and a shirt from a drawer and plunged quickly into the bathroom, almost tripping in her urgency.

He was waiting at her door when she came out, and they went downstairs together.

Kevin was in the kitchen at the coffeepot when they came down, smelling the coffee and smiling as he greeted them. "I can see you're off somewhere," he told Fin. "What are you up to today, Avalon?"

"Kevin, will you all stay here, together, please, until I get back?"

"Happy to. Except that Terry and Brad already went out—one of them is on a beignet kick. But just beignets—we have good coffee here. He's getting bags of the things. I don't think he was walking down to Decatur and Café du Monde—there's a place about a block or so from here. He'll be back shortly. Boris and Brad are up, but they're in Boris's room working on dailies. Lauren isn't up…and I'm here." He gave Fin a thumbs-up.

"Kevin, you're great. Thanks," Fin said. "Lock me out!" he told Avalon.

"No—you're great. I'm still trying to wrap my mind around this. It was Kenneth. Wow." Kevin shook his head. Avalon walked with Fin to the front door and when he had exited, she keyed in the alarm and locked it. Heading back to the kitchen, she found that Lauren had come down for coffee. "Why am I so tired?" she asked. "I haven't even been working!"

"I'm sleepy, too," Avalon said.

Kevin nudged Lauren. "But she's busy nights," he said, teasing.

Avalon groaned. "You guys—we're not in high school anymore!"

"We still thrive on ribbing one another. Seriously, I'm happy for you. Someone both decent and cool in your life."

"Thanks. I guess I may go back to sleep," Avalon said. On her way out of the kitchen, she turned back to look at the two of them, grinning. "I need to keep my energy up."

She heard them laughing as she headed back up the stairs. She smiled. Good friends weren't always easy to come by, she knew. She was lucky.

But under her happiness, she still had a ridiculous sense of having missed something. Maybe it was Fin's fault—he'd talked about patterns of speech. Something someone had said the night before had bothered her.

She shook her head and closed the door to her room, then pulled out her phone. She now had a copy of the chilling blog post she'd discovered when first looking up info on Samara Stella.

She started reading, chewing her lip in thought. But before she could get very far, there was a pounding at her door.

"Avalon!"

It was Kevin. She hurried to the door and opened it. "I'm getting both you and Lauren to the police station...now. This is getting worse and worse. Kenneth didn't do it. I want you two back where there are a ton of cops. And guns! Come on, please, let's—"

"Kevin, what happened?"

"Samara Stella. They found her—it's on the news. They found her in her theater. Not a doll this time—they found Samara! She was on her Anne Boleyn daybed for real, with a knife through her chest."

"No," Avalon whispered. Her legs felt weak.

Then she frowned. Kevin had been looking at her, anxious, but determined.

Suddenly, something about him changed. His eyes widened and looked glassy.

Then he crashed to the floor.

Kenneth Richard had an attorney at his side, but, apparently, Cara hadn't been very good at getting a well-paid and expert attorney to him.

The lawyer at his side, Carl Hewett, Esquire, was barely a kid out of law school.

That could be an advantage for Fin.

"Mr. Richard is seeing you here only in the spirit of cooperation. He doesn't know what you think you might have found. But he'll talk to you, because he's innocent," the young attorney told Fin and Ryder.

"Kenneth, I'm sorry—you seem like an all-right guy," Fin said. "But evidence leads to you. And pictures we have from your great-grandfather's stash…well, they implicate you, too."

Kenneth shook his head. "Look, my great-grandfather was a horrible human being. We knew that because our parents hated him. They never explained exactly why, but I think we all believed that he was a pedophile. We saw him so rarely. I don't think that anyone in the generation ahead of us could prove anything against him, they just kept us away from him when we were kids. I don't know what he might have done. I only know what I haven't done!"

"Then who is it?" Fin asked. "Kenneth, we're going to be able to prove that you've been involved."

"If anything was done, the old man did it."

"Not by himself," Ryder said.

"Kenneth, you know what's going on. I know that you do," Fin said.

"State charges, federal charges...and the death penalty in the state of Louisiana. Wait—Mississippi has the death penalty, too, but you can only use lethal injection on someone once."

To Fin's surprise, Kenneth suddenly began to laugh and cry, at the same time. He stared from Ryder to Fin. "Lethal injection!" he said. "Now there's a piece of cake next to...oh, Lord. Next to so very much."

Fin leaned forward. "Dammit, Kenneth, tell us who was working with you, killing with you, and we'll lock them up and then they can't get to you, don't you see? And if you cooperate, we can ask that the attorneys not seek the death penalty. Kenneth—" There was a tap at the door. Fin sat back. Ryder went to the door, but before Fin could say anything else to Kenneth, Ryder called Fin over.

"Be right back," he promised Kenneth.

He rose and went to the door of the interrogation room, where Ryder was standing with an officer.

"They've found Samara Stella at her place, knife in her chest."

Fin gritted his teeth, damning himself. They'd had officers watching her.

Patrols could only go so far.

Taking in Fin's grim expression, Ryder continued. "Believe it or not, she's hanging on. She's at the trauma center—there's a slim chance. But, Fin—"

Ryder broke off as they both heard a choking sound from the interrogation room.

"Help! Sweet Jesus, help!" the young attorney screamed.

Fin swung back into the room.

Carl Hewett was standing, looking at the floor behind the chair where Kenneth Richard had been sitting.

Fin rushed around. Kenneth was on the floor; his mouth was filled with foaming saliva and he was choking and seizing.

"Medic!" Fin shouted, trying to swing the man around and stop him from biting off his tongue.

Whatever—whoever—the man had been afraid of, that fear had been stronger than the will to live, the will to take a chance that the police could help him.

Paramedics rushed in.

"Smell it—cyanide!" one exclaimed.

Fin moved out of the way. Help moved in. Fin knew that it was too late.

He leaped to his feet and rushed out the door.

"Fin!" Ryder called after him.

"The house—I have to get to the house." Fin shouted over his shoulder. "Get a cruiser out there, the closest cops. They're going to go after Avalon, so we've got to move!"

He still wasn't sure how it had all worked. But he had a growing fear that there was one suspect that they hadn't looked at seriously enough.

And he felt raw terror...

Because others wouldn't have begun to suspect that one person, either.

At first, the situation was so bizarre that it didn't register in Avalon's mind.

Kevin on the floor...

And a *woman* behind him, smiling at her.

*Cara Holstein.*

Next to her, her husband—with a knife against Lauren's throat.

Then it all registered too quickly.

Kenneth might well be a killer, but he hadn't been working alone…as they had surmised. But none of them had thought it was Cara, tiny Cara Holstein, still holding the gun she'd used to clock Kevin, smiling and obviously enjoying the fact that Avalon was in pure shock.

"Don't scream. Gary's knife is razor-sharp. We have to go, and we have to go quickly."

Avalon feared she'd fall to pieces; scream and collapse, despite all that she'd promised herself about being brave.

But, to her amazement, she didn't.

"Cara, you helped your husband write that essay. Fantasy murder! That's what I've been missing, Cara—well, I just missed it last night. The way you were talking, something along the lines of 'men watch women, women watch men.' It's *your* pattern of speech! You even used the word *stalking*. Wow. Well, I guess you should be proud of yourself. None of us… I mean, we knew one of you was involved."

"Kenneth is a murdering bastard," Cara said. Then she glanced at her watch. "I should say *was* a murdering bastard, that sniveling little coward…well, I'm sure he took care of matters himself. Let's go. Now. Or she dies."

Avalon could see Lauren's eyes were filled with terror.

They would both die, she thought. Where were Brad, Leo, Boris and Terry?

Terry and Brad had gone out, but the other men should be somewhere nearby. "Now!" Cara demanded.

"Fine!" she snapped. Kevin was on the floor.

She didn't know how badly injured he was.

No. She wouldn't think that way. She'd keep Lauren alive, and she knew that Fin and Ryder would be there, that someone would come.

"Where?" she demanded, hands on her hips as she stared at Cara.

"Step out of the room and follow Gary, and don't make one tricky move. My hubby will slit her throat and I'll shoot you dead here and now. Got it, you snooty bitch actress? You know, you're not my type in the least, but Gary has been pining after you for the longest time, and I am a good wife. So move your skinny perfect little actress ass and do not make a false move!"

She walked out into the hall. She heard a thundering noise from down the hall. It was coming from behind another door, where Boris and Leo were apparently locked in a room.

One of them would have a cell phone. Surely, they'd be calling for help.

She moved, but as slowly as she dared, as she tried to figure out a way to stall.

"If the cops show, they'll shoot us, but I'll make sure sweet little Lauren dies first!"

"Where am I going?" Avalon asked.

"Out to the navy SUV—right into the back seat. And fast."

Avalon walked, wishing the police would arrive—worried what would happen when they did.

*How could she help Lauren if this went any further, if there was less chance of help?*

"Avalon," Lauren whispered. It was barely a breath.

Gary, his expression as bland as a pastry, until she looked that way.

Then he smiled. It was the most frightening smile Avalon had ever seen; rich in evil and amusement, so twisted and sick…

She walked.

Heading straight to the door.

There, she found out what had happened to Brad and Terry.

The alarm was blaring, and two patrol cars were parked in front of the house when Fin and Ryder arrived.

The door was just being broken down.

Running to it, Fin saw one officer down on the sidewalk by

the steps; he saw that Brad and Terry were there. Brad's eyes were open, and he was staring ahead, dazed, a trickle of blood running down his forehead.

"EMTs are on the way!" one of the officers shouted to Fin.

Terry was propped up against the wall, his head falling to the side.

"Both breathing! Barely!" the officer said.

Fin nodded and ran into the house. He could hear the pounding upstairs and he tore in that direction. The lock was stuck or broken. Using his full weight against it, he broke in.

Boris was there with Leo; Leo was trying to calm him, Boris was hysterical. "They... I think they got Brad and Terry. They had keys, they turned off the alarm... Where are they? Avalon and Lauren, oh, God...we don't even know who...oh, God." He began to shriek Avalon's and Lauren's names, rushing out to the hall.

Fin had never moved so fast in his life. He raced through the house like wildfire, aware that others were searching, too.

But the women were gone.

He cursed himself for a fool.

He burst out onto the street. He was stunned to see a familiar face, that of a woman in a feathered high hat and elegant gown, anxious as she looked at him.

She wasn't living; it was the ghost of Kathryn Anne McNeil.

She came right up to Fin and spoke urgently. "Just minutes ago, they forced both women into a car. The man shouted something to the woman about getting out of the French Quarter as quickly as possible. He was screaming that it was his turn, and his fantasy and screw the rest of it, he was going to make it perfect, all that he had dreamed. They have Avalon! And the other young woman. Go!"

He didn't wait.

He jumped into his car and started driving, but he didn't know where he was going.

And then he did…

The killer wanted it perfect.

They were going back to the beginning.

Avalon's head was killing her.

She woke confused, in pain. Then she remembered that Gary had struck her when she was getting in the car, and that explained the pain.

She was lying on something hard. And she was wearing something…smooth and soft. Silk, but she was lying on something hard, so hard…

*They'd dressed her! They'd knocked her out and taken her clothes and dressed her up!* She was a theater person, not particularly hung up about nudity, but the violation…it made her skin crawl. It was so horrible, so, so horrible…

She was worried about clothing, when she didn't know where she was, where they were, what was happening…

And then she knew.

She was lying on a tomb.

The tomb she had lain on during the last day of filming.

She heard a soft groan and tried to crack her eyes open a shade, not giving away the fact that she was conscious.

She could see Lauren. Her friend was still alive. She was slumped up against the wall of a nearby family mausoleum.

Then Avalon heard talking. The killers talking.

Cara Holstein was giggling. "I wonder if they'll still think that my stupid prick peacock cousin, Julian, was involved. Such an idiot. All of them. Such idiots. Looking at a handsome guy, too full of themselves to realize that a sweet little woman can cajole just about anyone anywhere!"

"I'm the one who got Cindy West to come with me!" Gary argued.

"And Kenneth got Ellen Frampton—and you both fucked up with that flapper girl in Houma!"

"We weren't caught, right? We lived to kill another day!" Gary said, bursting into laughter at his own joke. "Gramps taught you well, baby. But now, it's time for you to get the hell out of here. This is it! My dream, my fantasy—Avalon Morgan!"

"You do know, my darling, that most wives really wouldn't tolerate such deviant behavior!" she said primly.

"Hey, you taught me how to enjoy killing. And your great-grandfather...well. Hey, I'm not cheating on you, not really—not when they're dead, right?"

"How are you going to do it?" Avalon felt sick at how eager Cara sounded.

"The knife."

"You'll get blood all over her! There won't be a display! The displays are my part of this, and you already made a mess out of that dominatrix chick. That was sloppy!"

"Kenneth could be giving us up—"

"Kenneth is dead. Trust me, Kenneth was far more afraid of what he knew I could do to him than of anything else in this world. He knew what to do."

"So get out of here," Gary said. "It's time. Dammit, I'm not sure that cop is dead, there's another cop on the island somewhere, and I don't have much time! Get the hell out of here, Cara!"

"I do all of this for you—"

"You do all of this because you're a sick bitch who gets off on it!" Gary screamed at her. "This is it. This is my fantasy—go!"

Fear seared through Avalon's heart. He was going to kill her.

She struggled to move, certain that she was tied down. But... she could move!

But Cara had a gun; she had to wait for the woman to leave. She felt Gary's hands on her face...

Then she heard a voice, a woman's voice, familiar and urgent, "Stay low, low... I'll tell you as soon as she's walked out of the picture. You need to be careful—she's trigger-happy. They didn't kill the cop they ran into—their boat is pulled up in the weeds in the shallows. Don't open your eyes... I'll be distracting, I'll try to be distracting... Hold on, I know you can make it, honey!"

Gary paused suddenly, shivering as if he had felt a cold breeze, then pulled his hands away. Avalon dared open her eyes. Gary was looking around.

Avalon smiled. Vanessa was there, Henri was just behind her, trying to force a rock against a headstone to make a distracting noise.

Avalon didn't scream. Vanessa was running her hands over Gary's face, around his shoulders, and the man was shivering, as if he knew...

But then Gary straightened and raised his knife high.

"Look at me!" he screamed. "Your eyes, I must see your eyes!"


Fin hadn't waited; he'd jumped into one of the police speedboats, certain that the yelling officers would be close behind him, but that was good.

Reaching the island, he didn't want to make his presence known, so he cut the power and let the current take him close.

Then he just jumped in the water and raced through tangling seagrass and shrubs.

He didn't question himself.

He headed to the cemetery. To the tomb where Avalon had lain...

And she was there.

Gary Holstein had a knife raised high above her.

Fin had his gun, but Avalon was rising, as if she would fight off the blade with bare flesh.

If he fired, he could hit her...

He ran as he'd never run before, and somehow, didn't trip over broken stones, and sailed over and around broken-winged angels and reproachful cherubs.

He vaulted over the tomb and head-butted Gary Holstein right where his ribs met his abdomen, hearing the man scream along with the sound of a cracking bone. He fought desperately to remember that he was an officer of the law, that he couldn't pummel the man to death.

Fin stood and then straddled him, wrenching his arms behind his back, and cuffed his wrists with a sturdy zip tie. Then he looked up and saw a flash of white fury go by him.

Avalon.

She tackled Cara Holstein, bringing her down, just as he had brought down the husband.

Avalon wasn't an officer of the law.

She socked the woman with a right to her jaw that was stunning.

Then she looked up at Fin.

"She had a gun!" she announced. "She was going to shoot you!"

He dropped down by her. Cara was viciously spewing hateful words. He rolled her over and cuffed her. Then he staggered up, bringing Avalon along with him.

By then, the officers had nearly caught up with them.

The cemetery was spilling over with police.

"Medic!" he shouted.

They were racing toward him, and he stopped them, pointing to Lauren.

Then he looked at Avalon and she smiled…and kicked Cara, who was twisting in the grass.

"Damn, you have good timing."

"Damn, you put up a good fight!"

She smiled. "I had a little help!" she said, as he folded her into his arms.

He saw Vanessa and Henri. And he lifted a hand and mouthed the words, *Thank you.*

Then, he just held Avalon, and felt her shaking in his arms.

# EPILOGUE

It was a dream, and it was wonderful.

Avalon woke up to see that Fin was lying beside her, blond hair all disheveled on the pillow, eyes closed, body still so close to hers, one arm against her naked ribcage and breast.

She had awakened…with him still beside her.

He smiled, and then opened his eyes.

He didn't move. Then he reached for her, pulling her closer.

"So much to do today…" he said.

"You're getting up?"

The smile he gave her wasn't sleepy at all.

"Not yet."

"You're still half-asleep!"

"Oh, no, no, no. I have intentions…"

She laughed. He showed her his intentions.

The most miraculous thing about the finale of the Christy family killers was that on that last day, no one died. Kevin, Terry and Brad suffered head injuries and had to be hospitalized for observation, along with the two officers Cara had taken down on the island.

They had missed Samara Stella's heart, though they'd punctured a lung, and she would heal, given a lot of time and care.

Lauren hadn't had to go to the hospital; she hadn't been hit so hard. She would have been finished off once Gary had finished with Avalon.

There were so many reports to give.

And then somehow, they were back in the house.

They showered. Long. And together.

And it was with water dripping around them, steam in the air, that they talked. They'd only known one another a week, but they both knew they couldn't part. Avalon was confident that she could find work, whether it was acting or web design, anywhere. She'd follow Fin to DC, or anywhere else.

It was a long time before they rose that morning.

But in the afternoon, they took a drive. In Mississippi they went out to the Grimsby house.

They visited briefly with Robert Fryer, and then they went out to walk the grounds.

And they found General Grimsby, his son-in-law and Grimsby's beautiful daughter.

They told them that they had been instrumental in solving the crime. If they hadn't known about the trail, if the forensic team hadn't found the medallion, they'd have never gotten to Houma and talked to the band... It was thanks to them they'd finally caught the killers.

For Avalon, it was a first. She watched the three loving family members hug and celebrate... And then, with the sun filtering through the trees, there was a flash of light...

And then nothing lingered except the feel of their love.

When they were gone, Fin turned to Avalon. "Beautiful."

"It was."

"And you, too, of course."

"Ah, flattery!"

He took her into his arms. "I was just thinking of the feeling. I love you...that deeply. That fiercely."

And she smiled and assured him, "Into eternity."

They lingered a moment for a truly tender kiss.

Then they turned. They had to get back to New Orleans. There were things to do. Friends to check on in the hospital.

And more planning, of course.

Because life was beautiful, and they knew to be thankful for the lives that stretched out before them.

★ ★ ★ ★ ★